The Reign of Ruth

Jazel L. Faith

Winnipeg, Canada

Developmental editor: Alison Cybe
Proofreader: Francisco Feliciano

Published October 2023 by Deep Hearts YA, an imprint of Deep Desires Press and Story Perfect Inc.

Deep Hearts YA
PO Box 51053 Tyndall Park
Winnipeg, Manitoba R2X 3B0
Canada

Visit deepheartsya.com for more great reads.

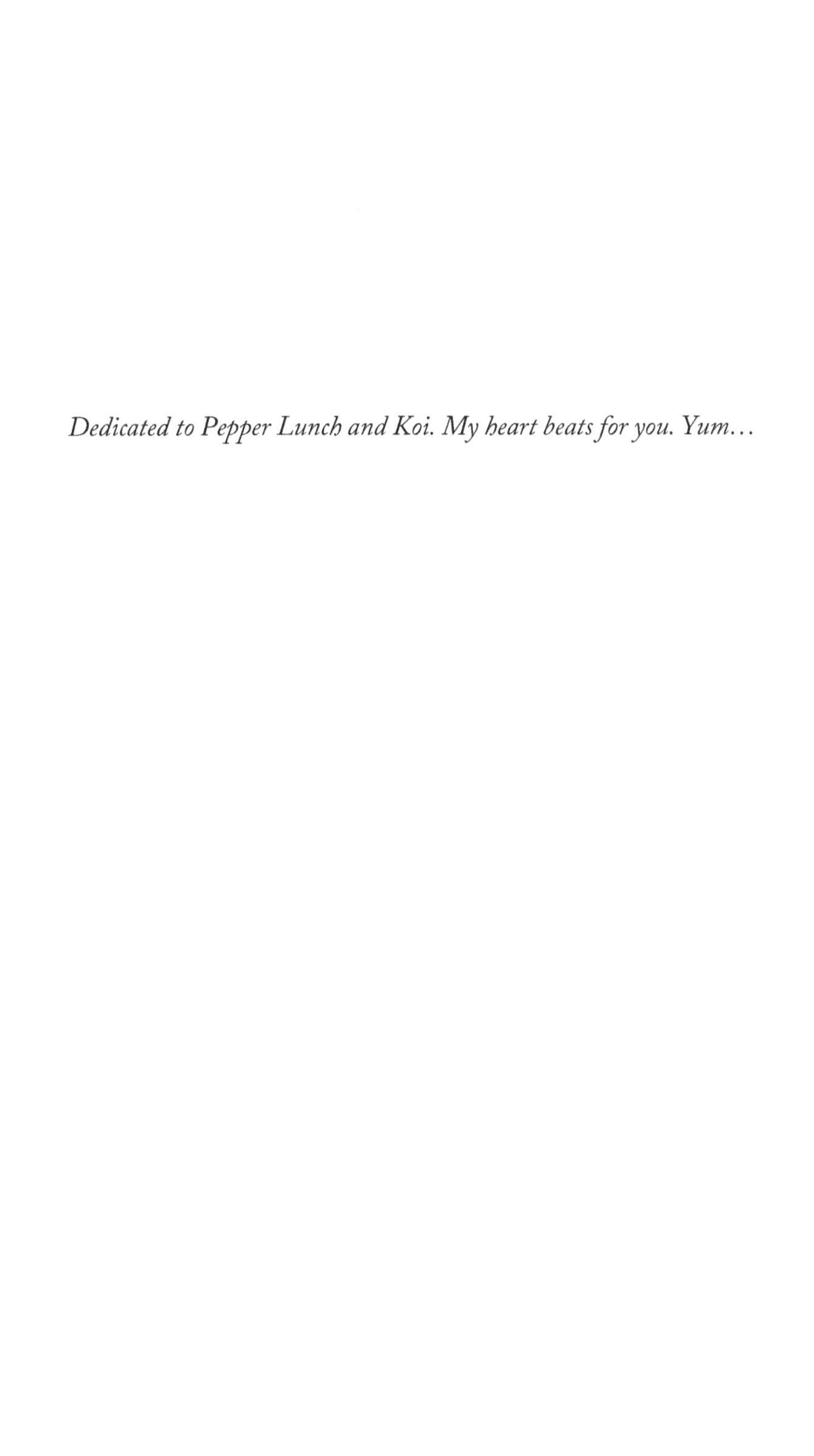

Dedicated to Pepper Lunch and Koi. My heart beats for you. Yum…

The Reign of Ruth

BEFOREMATH

When Lysandra perished, the entire world quivered. The Kingdom of Dicera has never seen a more powerful witch since.

It was a terrible sight. Grief permeated the air, as prevalent as daylight. I smelled it, and even now, decades later, it burrows in my lungs. However, none was as vanquished by it as Dahlia, Lysandra's closest companion in life. She was so hysterical that one would assume she had dove headfirst into a sea of madness.

Nobody knows for sure which of the witches, Lysandra or Dahlia, existed before the other. Yet all can tell you that the pair met the worst of tragic endings.

Lysandra was a woman of mischief who constantly sought entertainment. She often told tales in masked enthusiasm about her fate. After glimpsing into the future, she was sure that an adventurous life was within her reach. It was a cloaked miracle, she had said, for she dreaded living discreetly in a forest where all other witches remained in hiding.

Although Dahlia heavily discouraged it, Lysandra had sneaked out on a fateful night and stumbled upon the kingdom's prince in a village. Dressed like a common thief, Dahlia had tailed her and was horrified at the sight of

Lysandra wielding her magic before the prince. It was a rule they treasured, and Lysandra had broken it.

After Dahlia coaxed Lysandra back into the forest, they argued. I remember exchanging a cautious glance with my daughter, who had jerked awake at the sound of their bellowing. In the end, Lysandra was engulfed with fury and annoyance. She turned to use black magic to create spells that could reach the prince. It seemed she was willing to forsake anything to experience sparks of freedom again.

She created thousands of spells with her abundance of knowledge and power, then wrote them in a book later named *The Forbidden Book of Lysandra*. She found a way to formulate new types of magic beyond controlling natural elements and Soothsaying: the ability of foresight which allowed one to unravel fate's plans.

Lysandra enlightened Dahlia about her positive findings and creations. Together, they taught more witches, each learning one particular ability. I was one of those chosen. Lysandra had instilled a few for herself. She, therefore, became the first multi-ability witch to exist. However, power and control had their limits, and the discovery came with a price. She wounded herself and imprinted a permanent mark on her side that would be carried down her bloodline. It was me who broke this news to her. In response, her eyes gleamed with a certain pride. "Good," she had said. "A unique trait befitting for my descendants."

It was then I noticed the ebony strands on her head, the inky blackness tainting her once-hazel irises. I thought she was poisoned, but the truth was much graver: darkness was shrouding her soul. It was an ability that manifested on its own, one so powerful that it could turn on its owner. I warned that it was a curse delivered by the fates, but she insisted it was a gift.

Dahlia was rather pleased to know that more witches would exist and thus assisted her best friend. She was certain that black magic was not relied on when forming the spells. It took years before Dahlia unearthed her best friend's secret. *Years* in which she aged, but Lysandra did not.

A golden immortality spell was crafted with the darkest of magic, and the witch had taken it along with her secret lover, the prince. Dahlia was mortified. She turned to make a book of rules to control her best friend with enchantments, though she knew her efforts were in vain.

Lysandra found a way around them and promised Dahlia that she would bring peace between humans and witches. She despised hiding and knew something her best friend did not—kindness was present in the hearts of all. Her human prince had proved it.

Therefore, promising a better future for her kind, she sought her prince and became the first witch queen. She eventually bore a child with her lover, and a birthmark was evident on the child's side.

She later returned to the Forest of Dahlia to offer her best friend a golden vial of immortality and a look at her child. Dahlia was close to accepting it when an arrow was fired clean through Lysandra's chest by thugs who call themselves Morakques—brutal witch hunters—who followed her into the forest.

Morakques have been a threat since they rose in

rebellion after Lysandra's crowning. They are terrible warmongers who regard witches as abominations and undeserving of equal treatment. I predict them to be present even centuries from now, considering that their numbers increase with great speed, rivalling that of the imperial army. At this rate, their grip on the lands could last decades; or worse, centuries. Lysandra's letters mentioned these hunters consistently in foreboding tones. Rumours claim that behind the walls of their base, Fort of Morakques, they conduct cruel and nightmarish experiments on witches. It is entirely possible they could even bend us to their will, using our people as weapons for their own political advancement.

After the attack, the vial shattered. Dahlia lost control of her powers then, devastated by the death of her friend. In front of the hundreds of witches she nurtured, her power consumed her, and her blood flooded the ground.

There, her blood of nature magic flourished thousands of plants throughout the land. The eternal flowers of Dahlia's forest were hence born.

The birth of witchlings was difficult but possible. The magic wielders had lived a life of restrictions since then, away from royalty and villagers. Only during specific times when Morakques were strongest with newly forged weapons and items would the Night of the Purge dawn.

—The earliest account of the first witches to exist, written during the reign of Eara

PROLOGUE

The wind, paired with the raucous youths, sounded almost deafening. As the elder ambled down the concrete lane scattered with stones, the atmosphere changed, becoming tense and quiet.

The witches were informed of the reason they gathered. Their mental preparation mattered little for what was to come. This would cause a greater good, one that could ensure the continued existence of their kind.

Yet, there were feelings hidden within the Soothsayers—the group of witches who had precognition. No words were to be exchanged, yet by the fleeting face of trepidation they shared, the tragic truth was obvious. Their act would have dire consequences.

The current leader of witches—the elder—was encircled by her kind, waiting for the grand arrival of the pregnant witch.

The youngest witch was born three years ago. With their kind almost extinct, this new infant was a miracle. A miracle that could ensure the survival of the witches before the coven ceased to exist.

For this to happen, there must be a sacrifice. There must be a balance. A vast portion of them must give up their abilities and lives for the baby. With a substantial amount of power, the child could protect the coven. It was a gamble they had to take.

When the future mother arrived at the location of the ritual, she stepped into the circle, naked and with a stomach protruding much beyond her breasts and a singular dark line extending down the middle along the bump. A polite incline of the head was directed to the elder before she rested on the wooden block in front of the oldest witch.

"This date will mark the day when an extensive portion of us leave this earth for a greater cause. We will feed our strength to the little witch and lay our future in her hands. Our coven will give her the strength to annihilate those who harm us." The elder scanned the circle of witches. Upon receiving no objections, she held her hand up and let the blood obsidian on her palm illuminate. "I seek assistance from our ancestors. May the ritual go smoothly, for there were no objections of any sort. Should anyone refuse from this moment on, you shall be confronted by the witches who have passed on."

Hands were joined, and chants filled the air. The youths, adults, and seniors spoke without interruption. Even the Soothsayers, though they knew that a kind of monstrosity might eventually occur.

A red mist began to rise, flying without a care into the rock. It swirled through the air, drawn to the gemstone, which glowed brighter than all else.

Then, one by one, the witches started dropping to their knees. Blood darker than red Dahlias escaped their lips, trickling from mouths to necks. The number of linked hands decreased as the rock grew more brilliant.

It felt like an eternity before the chanting stopped. Those who were still alive instantly approached those who sacrificed themselves.

However, the ritual was yet to be done.

The elder laid the stone on the pregnant witch's protruding stomach before chanting an incantation different from the previous.

The witches had to squint their eyes at the intensity of the phosphorescent stone.

After a moment, the elder was forcing the words out of her mouth, and a minute later, she dropped. Dead.

Gasps were heard throughout the coven, the loudest suppressed by the expecting women.

Everyone watched in silence as the vivid stone cracked and shattered to form an enormous ball of crimson. The energy was so significant that witches drained of energy were swept further from the pregnant lady.

Gradually, the cloud of red seemed to seep into the future mother's stomach.

Nothing was uttered, yet a similar thought loitered in every head—this baby was the coven's only hope.

Lilith, barely three, gazed at the remainder of the crimson swirling flame-like mist. She glanced at her grandmother, heaving and depleted. She was not required to exert all of her strength, but she silently wished she did. Nothing was more demoralizing than watching the deceased bodies of her coven.

She chanted the prayer to the wind and hoped that the infant of ruby flames was worth the deaths of many. Lilith hoped even as an unusual and sparkling sensation dwelled within her heart—one that belonged to a Soothsayer.

One month later, the infant was born.

Her eyes were nothing like her parents. Instead, her irises glistened ruby red.

CHAPTER ONE

Lilith might as well be the Queen of Darkness. She could see nothing but inky black no matter how much she attempted to delve into her ability.

She sought many things, but control was the most important.

As a young witch, a year shy of twenty years old, Lilith had been taught multiple ways to harness her magic. It did not come from time or force. Instead, it was ruled by emotions. The stronger she felt, the stronger the ability. Controlling the intensity of her mood was the key to controlling her magic.

Other witches found it simple because they barely had a life deemed fascinating enough to spark anything more than dull excitement. That was what Lilith claimed in order to defend her lack of ability. After all, she had yet to experience the adventure she so desperately craved.

Her kind had been restricted to the Forest of Dahlia since birth. None of them saw the outside world. If they did, they either never returned or were too wounded to ever share their stories.

Lilith craved to leave the forest more than anything, but fear of the unknown held her back. The life she wanted was impossible to achieve.

Suddenly, a wave of sadness presented itself. An

emotion. Lilith seized it and transformed it into magic. The feeling drained in her heart, for it was the balance that nature sought—a human quality for one of a witch.

She found it exceedingly difficult to tame the magic swirling persistently within herself. It was a living thing, comforting yet ruthless in its own way. If she had somebody willing to answer her burning questions, she would know if it was a normal sensation amongst witches. Her grandmother rarely discussed abilities with her. It was as if birth was supposed to equip her with the knowledge.

Lilith shut her eyes, reaching out mentally to the mirror in front of her face. She could almost sense the obsidian engraved into the bottom of it.

A flicker crossed her mind.

Soothsayers, such as herself, could commonly see flashes of the future. They were vague but helpful. Only the strongest Soothsayers could glimpse clear images that either stayed longer than a few seconds or moving visions of the future.

In the Forest of Dahlia, where many witches were—in Lilith's opinion—trapped within, only one such witch had the capability. The woman was Lilith's grandmother. According to the rumors from her kind, her bloodline possessed the strongest Soothsayers.

The young Soothsayer had no doubt it was true. Or perhaps, she only strongly desired for it to be true. If she grew up to have a strong ability, she could journey far from home and avoid putting her life in grave peril. *If* it were true, her grandmother would finally allow her merry adventures and release whatever reason that held her back from granting permission.

Lilith sighed, realizing that her mind had diverted away from practicing her ability. At least she got a glimpse of…what exactly did she see again? It was something like a flare of red and gold.

She thought hard about that combination but could think of nothing. Her mind was blank, but she could have sworn that the two colors were familiar.

Confusion. Lilith tried converting that emotion to magic but knew even before she attempted that it would never work. The abilities of witches were controlled by the intensity of main emotions—happiness, love, sorrow, fear, fury and disgust. That was probably the only thing Lilith was told.

She always wondered why her grandmother taught little of anything magic-related despite the baffling strength of her skills.

"You are practicing?" a voice questioned with a hint of disapproval.

Lilith could never understand why her grandmother felt even a hint of dissatisfaction. She should be proud that her granddaughter was trying to master the ability she was given. In fact, any sane relative would assist her. Of course, Lilith kept that last opinion to herself.

"Yes, Nana," Lilith answered.

The grandmother frowned but said nothing. Instead, she stared at the mirror Lilith held. As if getting the message, the young witch pocketed it instantly.

The mirror did nothing to amplify her magic. It was

the rock on the bottom that assisted the power of her ability. That, however, was not why her Nana eyed it with such distaste. The item was one of the two things Lilith's mother left for her when she was born. She could barely remember the woman who had given her life. It was a pity that her grandmother refused to talk about her.

She only managed to gather one piece of information— her mother was banished from the Forest of Dahlia. She never discovered the reason.

"I have a favor to ask if that is alright with you," her grandmother said. "Would you mind helping me gather some berries in the garden for tomorrow?"

"Of course," Lilith said. *Of course.* How could she forget about what was to happen the next day?

A few weeks ago, her grandmother received a vision and reported to the elder immediately. It reflected when the Night of the Purge was taking place.

A disastrous event. Morakque never ceased to return, and they would most likely visit stronger than ever. Humans and their pesky little inventions. Have the cruel hunters never thought of peace, or the happiness it would bring everybody?

"I'll return soon," she announced while picking up a basket from the ground.

"Well, of course you will." Her grandmother flashed a feeble grin at her before settling down on her usual seat.

A chill greeted Lilith as she stepped outside her wooden tent made by the talented builders in her coven. The atmosphere was clouded with fear. The witches were afraid to lose their lives to Morakques, who seemed to exist solely to threaten their existence. The hunters dared to waltz into their only home and wreak havoc and whisk them away to some faraway base for the sake of some feud with royalty. The mere thought was angering. Witches had done nothing but hope to live, and many spent their entire lives trying to survive only to perish in the end.

Witches repeated the same phrase; a plea to the wind. It was a prayer that could calm a troubled soul. In Dicera, it was strongly believed that the wind was linked with fate and saying it was like bargaining with fate itself. Lilith was certain that she had uttered the line more than a thousand times.

Passing her coven, an indescribable ache appeared in her chest. She hurried her steps to the garden before that odd sensation overwhelmed her. There was something else mixed with her sorrow, which felt very much like a burning void that could devour her whole. It was something she had experienced since childhood and was too afraid to tell anybody in case it was not a normal occurrence amongst her kind.

She did not want to be different from the rest. She had been fearful since she learned that Morakques began loathing witches because their kind had abilities that were regarded as different and special.

She had vowed that one day, she would change that somehow. She wanted the world to know that being different was not a reason for hatred.

Lilith began to pluck the berries from the garden she had visited hundreds of times, thinking about the stories involving eternal flowers born from the blood of Dahlia.

The berries were scarlet red, which reminded Lilith of what she had glimpsed a few minutes ago. The flash of red and gold supposedly had a say in her future. She hoped she could discover more information about what it meant.

Her basket was only one-eighth filled when she caught movement from the corner of her eyes. She had brushed it aside, certain that it was merely an insect until she noticed it was somewhat misty.

Strange, she thought. It was red in color and blended in with the fruit, like a hazy cloud following the wind. It allowed the morning sun to beam through, becoming rosy flames that soared in a specific direction.

Lilith felt an invisible tug. It was as if fate was ushering her to follow the unusual red smoke.

It took a moment before she gave in to the seemingly undetectable force and followed its lead.

CHAPTER TWO

Lilith realized how suddenly the wind halted its movement. Just seconds ago, it was leading her towards a small pond. Now it was as absent as a whisper from the past.

The place was warm and quiet. Almost *too* quiet, as if a repulsive force lingered persistently in the air, driving away the birds that typically chirped as noisily as a menagerie in the mornings. Even *light* seemed frightened; the area was unusually gloomy.

The pond was not unfamiliar in the slightest. Witches used a different water body for washing, so it was left alone for the sea creatures to live. It was a captivating view that had mesmerized Lilith far too many times. However, the currently brilliant sunlight did nothing to brighten the area. It might have been the trees shading the pond, but they were always present. The place never lost its striking image, but yet it now looked so dim, so much that Lilith thought she must be hallucinating.

She would have regarded her surroundings as serene if not for the utter silence. It was eerie.

She was moments away from leaving when she caught the sight of something impossible to ignore—a gorgeous and impossibly perfect lily. The flower did not even have a single spot of dirt on it.

Lilith stepped closer to the pond and lowered herself to

touch the lily. The water was only an inch away from the beautiful flower, and Lilith was grateful that the air was so still. It would be a shame if the wind swept it into the pond.

As her hand grabbed the delicate plant, a finger unintentionally dipped into the pond, and Lilith noticed two things in a mere second. First, the body of water was oddly and utterly still. Secondly, a calm and electrifying surge of *something* traveled up from the finger, as sly as a snake, into the very depth of her heart.

Startled, she retreated her hand, the flower still firm in her grasp. A pang of fear arose from the sudden effect, and the Soothsayer within her leapt into action. The reflection of herself in the water shifted into something else entirely. The whole of her eyes, both the whites and her bright hazel irises, became as black as night, and an inky-colored smoke emerged from behind her. Just as quickly as it appeared, the image vanished.

Lilith could have sworn something in her blood yearned for another touch. It felt like the pond called out to her.

She had to blink several times for the lingering image in her head to dissolve into nothing. Was that a vision from the future or simply her imagination? Sometimes, she could not tell.

The dark, smoke-like phenomenon had surrounded her as if they were her servants. The image was remarkable but impossible, for Lilith was a Soothsayer, and her magic bore no colors, unlike elemental witches. Even they did not possess darkness as a gift.

She kept the pretty lily with her as she retreated back into the garden for the berries.

Thankfully, she discovered she was not alone.

"Aunt Lavern," Lilith greeted, unable to keep the relief from her voice. She could not stand being alone for another moment.

"Hello, dear," the woman said as she plucked a fruit from the bush. The witch was the closest friend Lilith's grandmother had.

Her aunt stared at Lilith briefly—or, more precisely—the lily she had stuck in her hair. A frown appeared on Aunt Lavern's face.

"Does it look awful?" Lilith questioned. Flowers were common accessories amongst her kind, and the lily she picked was unblemished. She had looked into her mirror and ensured she appeared decent just moments before.

"No, no. You look splendid, dear." The frown remained. "Where could you have found such a faultless plant?"

"From the fishpond." Lilith could not recall seeing any fish minutes ago, but she mentioned nothing.

"That flower radiates an energy I cannot put my finger on," the aunt exclaimed. "It must be Dahlia blessed."

An eternal flower, then. Lilith was fortunate to have found it.

"How is your preparation for tomorrow?" the young witch asked. She was curious to know how the witches outside her family, which consisted of just her and Nana, were carrying themselves.

"I am quite ready, though I cannot say the same for the

elementals and stronger witches." Aunt Lavern possessed some magic of nature, but she was mostly a Concealer—a witch who could disguise certain features. Unless Concealers produced a large amount of strength, they would be expected to hide during the Night of the Purge. Their ability allowed them to disguise themselves with masculine features and hide in plain sight, since males were rarely viewed as witches.

If they were strong at their base ability, however, they would be able to perform spells. It was commonly regarded as an additional benefit for their kind.

"I truly hope that we will all survive tomorrow," Lilith said.

"Likewise." The aunt continued to select the ripe fruits before halting abruptly. She looked to be in a mental conflict before she made a decision. "Lily, dear, there is something I need to tell you."

"Is something wrong?"

"Just promise that you will stay home tomorrow."

"Of course I will." The mere thought of leaving her only safe place during the Night of the Purge was baffling. Her grandmother would be performing spells, and perhaps she would be helping. She knew she had the strength that many witches lacked, and all she required was control over her magic.

"You have to promise."

"Did my Nana see something in her visions? Will something happen to me?"

Aunt Lavern was silent. She appeared to contemplate and choose between choices before she admitted, "Yes."

Lilith's curiosity spiked. Her grandmother rarely shared her foresight with others. "What was it about?" she asked, somewhat thrilled to know.

The older witch sighed before looking into Lilith's hazel eyes. She clamped her mouth shut, hesitating before she finally shared, "Your grandmother saw an image of you *leaving* the Forest of Dahlia."

CHAPTER THREE

It was odd to see Nana's countenance wearing anything but indifference. On many days, Lilith would find her knitting the cotton purchased from the village by Concealers or male witches into a gorgeous piece of clothing.

Lilith had not expected her grandmother to be brimming with concern, fiddling with her hands. Her eyes were haunted in a way that made Lilith afraid, too.

"Has anything happened?"

"Oh, thank Dahlia. Quickly, come," urged the grandmother, relief flooding her face like a drain during a storm.

"What is going on? Are Morakques here already?" Lilith questioned. She had a myriad of things on her mind, yet they vanished as soon as she witnessed the awful twist in her Nana's features.

"No, not quite." The response with the missing explanation rather infuriated Lilith, but she kept her mouth shut.

"Is there a reason for your worry, then?" she prodded as she headed to rinse the berries she picked.

Her grandmother hesitated, eyes flickering around the room as if searching for an escape. It was the beginning of a series of actions taken whenever Lilith asked questions she would rather avoid answering. Lilith never knew the reason, but she was tired of the hiding. Her grandmother must have caught the sparkle of determination in her eyes.

"The Red Demon escaped. Again."

Understanding washed over Lilith. Indeed, it was a thing to fear, although it happened so many times that it could be considered normal.

The Red Demon was more of a creature than a witch, Lilith recalled. Her mind conjured up images of a woman with a face of a monster and eyes as evil as the darkest magic. Though she had never met the girl before, the rumors she heard made those thoughts come alive. She visualized a young woman with stiff horns reaching skyward, pointy ears like those of fae and cracks on her face that resulted from years of carrying an impossible amount of power.

Witches born with two abilities had a rough time coping. Magic came alive within them, forcing their owners to turn on themselves. It could manifest as a wicked voice in the head that could only be removed by death. Lilith could only imagine how the girl managed to live at all. People within the Forest of Dahlia stayed away from the Red Demon until they found a use for her. Hence, the Night of the Purge was the only time she could leave her home. Lilith was always too focused on hiding from Morakques to witness the young girl with her impressive magic. Only then was the girl regarded as a hero, a legend. Other times, she was just seen as a demon.

"When?" Lilith asked.

"I was just informed by the elder. It is better to stay home until her parents find her."

Lilith wanted to ask what pushed her to leave, but she

already knew the answer. Of course the Red Demon would hope to leave; her kind feared her.

"I doubt she will do any harm. Maybe she is just out for fresh air."

"You cannot be so sure, Lily," her grandmother said. "She might have saved us plenty of times, but that was what she was born to do. The many witches who sacrificed their lives did not die for no reason."

Lilith kept her mouth shut to avoid being chastised. She could do nothing but agree, though. The Red Demon had supposedly lost control on multiple occasions and was said to have become insane. It was rumored that she once destroyed many of Dahlia's eternal flowers despite them being immortal plants. If she could destroy undying plants created by one of the strongest witches to exist, then she was undoubtedly a danger to nature.

"How will we be informed when she is safely back home?"

"If the silence outside is replaced with the sound of activity," replied Nana, approaching Lilith to adjust the flower in her hair.

"There is something I need to ask," Lilith blurted. It was a random line that she had been rehearsing. "It is about your vision."

A flicker of annoyance shone in the grandmother's eyes briefly like it always did when Lilith sought answers regarding her magic.

Taking her silence as a means to continue, Lilith said, "Aunt Lavern mentioned that you saw me leaving the forest tomorrow."

"For Dahlia's sake, Lavern," Nana muttered under her breath. She was reluctant to speak of the information, but Lilith needed an explanation. She had wrecked her brain thinking of a possible reason to leave the forest and venture outside, where some wished for nothing but her head on a stick.

"What did you see?"

Her grandmother gazed at her, and something in her eyes softened.

"I can promise that I will not leave," Lilith said.

"That is a big promise to make," Nana commented, pressing her lips together to form a thin line. "You never know where fate is going to lead you."

"Then you must know what will drive me to leave."

"I do not."

"Then how, pray tell, did you know that I will leave tomorrow?"

The grandmother frowned. Her shoulders sagged, and Lilith noticed newly formed dark circles under the senior's eyes. At the sight, she was ready to drop the subject.

"It was shown in my vision. The sun aligned with the date of the purge." The grandmother grimaced at the memory. "You left after the Morakques were already gone."

The information should remove a load from Lilith's chest. She knew then that she would survive the next day and carry on with her life, but neither she nor her grandmother felt as fortunate as they should.

"Did I leave alone? Did you come with me?"

"No. All I witnessed was you saying goodbye."

Lilith left on good terms, then. But why would her

grandmother ever allow such a thing? Not only was it exceedingly unlike her, but Lilith also could not think of a reason in which leaving was a decent solution.

Bombarded with bafflement, Lilith felt herself go rigid. Her hand was frozen above the salted water where she washed the fruit she gathered. Only the sound of dripping water could be heard.

Nothing was more unexpected than the future, and it was what made being a Soothsayer so terrifyingly thrilling. Mysteries stayed and left, and Lilith knew that she would find out the reason for everything in just a day. A portion of her wanted so badly to solve the puzzle immediately.

"I do not understand," she admitted. She failed to grasp many truths, and she was tired of being kept in the dark when her grandmother knew what she sought to comprehend.

"Sometimes, the future is better to be left unknown." Nana smiled, but it did not quite reach her eyes.

"But I am a Soothsayer," Lilith said as a matter of fact. That title gave her the right to uncover the time to come. She was born with the blood to see things from the future, and she would not allow her grandmother to steal the ability that made her who she was. A witch. A *strong* witch.

"Indeed," her grandmother said, halting for a moment as the sound of conversations started outside their home once again. "I can only perceive the future that belongs to me. You emerge due to the interference of our fate. Therefore, the only person who knows your future is you."

"I know that," Lilith said. She was trying to calm herself before her ability triggered without her consent again. This was what her grandmother did not understand. She wanted to seek her own future but with more control and knowledge of her magic.

"Then what more do you need to know?"

Lilith sought many things, and not all involved her ability. "I need to know about my parents and how to master control over my magic. I need to know the reason for the scar we were born with and a method to change this kingdom for the better because I am so *tired* of hiding."

That scar was the second and last thing her mother had gifted when Lilith was born. A permanent scar on her side.

Her grandmother stayed silent. The moment Lilith mentioned her birth giver, she knew a response would be impossible.

"I am keeping the information for your own good," her grandmother said after a long while.

"Really?" Lilith managed to choke out. "You truly believe that holding back knowledge about *my* life would benefit me?"

"Yes, child. Now calm down before the hallucinations start." That was what her Nana called it. *Hallucinations.* She called Lilith's loss of control something so far from reality and disregarded her obvious need to control.

"If you dread to teach me about Soothsaying, then at least enlighten me about my mother."

"I cannot."

"Why?" Lilith questioned with incredulity. She was enraged and confused and impatient. Soon, her mind would be attacked with future images that made little sense.

"She is a criminal." Lilith knew as much, but she was oblivious to anything beyond that information.

"Tell me about my father, then," Lilith urged, inching closer to the exit of her home. She did not want her grandmother to see the messy state she would enter when the visions came.

"Let us drop this conversation," Nana injected a note of finality in her tone. It was the same line she repeated dozens of times. Lilith was sick of it.

"How is this protecting me?"

"Let us not carry on this conversation," repeated the older witch, gritting her teeth. Whenever she did that, Lilith knew any further questions would be ignored. In moments such as that, her grandmother looked more like a stranger.

Lilith could not stand another moment breathing the same air as the witch who kept secret after secret from her. She *would* not.

"I am visiting Aunt Lavern." With that, Lilith took a step outside her home.

The gust of air that caressed her face was never more refreshing. The fury lingered, and so did the fear of returning home later that day. Perhaps she wanted the loss of control to come. It would not pilfer the negative feelings from her mind, but it would reduce them in her heart. In return, it would show visions of the future.

Lilith never intended to visit Aunt Lavern. She knew that it would only lead to reprimanding and a suggestion to return. Instead, she visited the garden again.

She should pray to the wind with her kind, but she had

done it so many times that her belief in it had begun to diminish. She had begged Dahlia and the wind and whoever heard her for Morakques to never visit again. For peace to settle between witches and the creatures beyond the forest. Yet, her words were constantly ignored.

The anger in her chest built as she strode into the garden. The leash she held to tame her magic was loosening, and she did not care to adjust her grip. She wanted it to happen. She wanted to see the future, and for the pressure in her chest to disappear.

Grabbing the mirror she always kept by her side, Lilith reached out to the burgundy rock and urged her magic to show itself. Instantly, the emotions in her multiplied and drained before giving way to an image. It stayed for just three seconds, but it was enough time for Lilith to grasp every detail. Red and gold, but much more sense.

Lilith finally remembered what the two colors stood for. She first saw it as an illustration in a book about history.

It was a golden crest. In the middle was a dice with sides marked with black dots. Lilith vaguely remembered the explanation for the crest design. The rolling dice represented fortune and possibility. The twin blades behind it had hilts scarred from prolonged use. Many symbols were carved into the grip of the swords in Lilith's vision, though she had never noticed them in the book she read.

She knew of this design.

Her vision had been showing the royal crest of Dicera.

CHAPTER FOUR

Lilith calmed her mind by ambling beside a row of plants. Nature magic was not carried in her blood, but plants had always soothed her in a way hints of her future could not.

She needed to share what she saw. Her grandmother would certainly call it a hallucination, and everyone else was too busy calling out to their ancestors to ensure their own safety. Lilith knew that it was the only thing they could do.

Their only hope was that the Red Demon would protect them all.

A protection spell could have been the only other solution. It would require time, mass participation and sacrifice for that ritual. But only a few dozen witches remained in the Kingdom of Dicera, and they could not risk any more deaths.

Lilith was so consumed in thought that she barely noticed the dandelions gliding in the air until they were right in front of her. They were carried by the wind, but she quickly noticed that it was far from natural. A tint of red followed it as if commanding the flower to move in a pattern. The immaculate control awed Lilith so thoroughly that she felt like she could waft through the air as though she were a part of it.

The red hue reminded her of the mist that lingered in

the forest when she picked berries earlier in the day. Realization crashed down on her like a ton of castle stones.

She barely questioned it, though she really should have.

The red smoke-like sight was undoubtedly magic, and Lilith knew better than to assume it belonged to an elemental witch—a being that could control fire, water or nature. No elements had authority over the wind, for fate ruled itself.

Soothsayers had magic that bore no colors. Nature produced green, fire wielders orange and water wielders blue. None of them created red.

No one but the Red Demon.

Lilith was drawn to stay, but she knew that she should run. The Red Demon had supposedly returned home, but nothing else could explain the ruby-tinted magic.

Fear seized her in the chest as her mind wandered to the creature. Her eyes followed the unnatural wind, tracing its source into the bush where a figure sat. The magic belonged to a girl with auburn hair reaching down to her waist, who called upon fire with a simple motion and a delicate hand. In an instant, a furious ball of heat engulfed the graceful hand in a show of brilliant light.

Lilith searched the girl's features for the beast labelled the Red Demon but saw nothing remotely close. From her view of the girl's face, all she could point out was evident beauty, as if a goddess had sculpted the face herself.

Witches were commonly said to be beautiful, and the woman before her had further proven the fact.

Glamorous butterflies emerged from the bush between the two young women as the fire diminished. They surrounded the skilled magic wielder eagerly as if she were their queen.

Lilith did not see a speck of red in the girl's eyes. She had no horns, horribly pointed nails, or anything resembling Lilith's mental image of the demon.

The witch was just an ordinary girl.

An ordinary, yet powerful girl.

Ruby needed many things, but freedom was the most important.

She craved freedom from the demon within her and from the witches who perceived her as a prisoner. She felt like a dog in a world of incapable hounds, and she hated it. Why should she be trapped in her home?

Someone is coming, the voices in her head warned. They shared the same message, yet it came at different delayed times and pitches.

Let them come, Ruby responded. *Let them come and let them run like everyone else.*

The chittering in her mind was her only friend. A living thing that witches did not acknowledge. They called Ruby a demon and a destroyer, oblivious to the greedy voices that harmed and healed their owner. There were two souls in one body, but one was judged for the actions of both.

It is not your mother, the voices said. *No, it is someone else, and she is watching.*

Ruby dropped her concentration on the flowers she controlled and lifted a hand. She willed fire to grace her hand and fed it heat with the wrath bubbling in her heart.

If it were the palm of any other being, their skin would be sizzling and dying out, but she was special, or so her mother would consistently remind her.

Ruby was certain that the witch was cowering in fear. The heat of her flames would drive anyone away, just as it always did.

She was done with feigning generosity. At the end of any conversation, somebody would inevitably get hurt.

How far gone is she? Ruby asked the whispers. She received no reply.

After diminishing her flames, she could hear creatures of the wild flutter from their places of hiding. They were the only living animals who did not deem her a wicked witch.

"That was impressive," said a voice.

Ruby paused, unsure if the line was uttered by the demon in her mind or someone else. At times, it was difficult to differentiate.

Was that you? Ruby asked mentally.

Her mind's silence was immensely strange. Since childhood, Ruby had prayed to her ancestors, wishing for the whispers that clouded her head to die out. They never did, no matter how many times she dropped to her knees.

For a moment, she genuinely believed that the voices were gone despite the impossibility. Without the demon that possessed a myriad of voices, she would lose the Soothsayer within her.

"Which part?" Ruby questioned out loud. She was skeptical that she would receive a response. Turning around, her eyes landed on a young witch with straight raven dark hair. It was only inches longer than Ruby's reddish-brown curls. While Ruby owned pecan brown skin, the girl was fairer, and from a few feet away, she could see the bewitching freckles powdering her cheeks.

A wave of sparks erupted from the ocean of blood in Ruby's body.

The girl was gorgeous. Ruby knew she was staring, but she refused to look away. Perhaps it was because she had never once seen anybody in the Forest of Dahlia who looked almost her age. Or it could be how the flower in the woman's hair radiated a kind of energy that she did not recognize.

A feeling that made her insides turn inside out.

It was not nauseating but unfamiliar. Ruby had spent over a decade trapped in her home where she could read and learn, so discovering a magical sense she did not know about was odd.

"About everything," exclaimed the stranger.

What kind of witch is she? Ruby called for the unusually quiet voices. She urged the demon to investigate by looking into the future for an image that could answer her question.

A Soothsayer and something else, replied a whisper. A *single* whisper. It was as if they were afraid to drive the stranger away.

Something else? Ruby prodded. What *else?*

It was silent again. Ruby had always wanted peace in her mind, oblivious to how odd it would be without the persistent demon she grew up with.

The voices did not make a sound.

Ruby fixed her hazel eyes on the girl. Then, as swift as

the wind, she reached out to the Concealer within herself. Her previously common eyes became her natural color—the hue of blood.

She expected the girl to dart but was pleasantly surprised.

"You're her, aren't you?" the stranger asked. Ruby did not need her to expand on what she meant. It was as clear as saying 'Red Demon' to her face.

"I suppose so."

The girl did not flee even after the confirmation. Ruby was reminded of an old selfish witch who feigned her compassion for additional protection. Ruby knew she had powers beyond anything in Dicera, but she would not let anyone take advantage of them.

Something flickered in the stranger's eyes. It was a ridiculous look that baffled Ruby to the core. It was as if the girl expected something more from the creature that every witch feared.

"Are you disappointed?" Ruby questioned. The girl certainly looked the part.

"Well, no. I *definitely* expect horns, though."

Ruby huffed a laugh. The girl had the audacity to joke.

"I can create horns for myself with flames if you'd like," she mentioned with a slight smile on her face.

"Then please do. I'd love to see."

Ruby lacked time to respond. The whispers in her head jumped at the offer to perform, tugging at the burning thread of magic. Their willingness was the most bizarre thing that Ruby had encountered that day.

Abruptly, a blazing force emerged. It roared in a heat

that could demolish anything its owner wished to remove, and its current owner was not Ruby.

Panic and fear replaced the fury in her heart, almost as intense as the lethal flames. A raging family of butterflies ambushed her from the core of her stomach. She had believed that she could tame the demon sharing her body, at least for the next hour.

Do not, Ruby warned.

The whispers loved nothing more than destruction. It wished to rule a broken kingdom where people saw it for what it was—a beast.

In approximately three seconds, Ruby predicted that the land below her feet would be blackened and dead.

Her eyes fluttered shut, anticipating terrible damage, but the heat within her mind vanished, and she heard nothing. No burning land or screaming.

"Your control is out of this world," said the girl.

Ruby allowed herself to witness what the demon had done. She imagined a world of flames and the death of more eternal plants, so she was rather puzzled when she saw nothing but the shadow of her flames on the ground. It took a moment before the fiery horns were reduced to smoke.

If only the young woman knew how wrong she was. Ruby had an unpredictable storm in her head that could never be tamed.

The whispers had *listened* to the stranger and fulfilled her request.

Thank you, Ruby told her lifelong friend. They were more commonly rivals, but growing up together had secured a firm connection.

I did not do it for you, a voice retorted.

For her, then? Ruby questioned.

Us, us, us, two voices this time.

She mentally rolled her eyes at the demon.

"It is harder than it looks," Ruby replied, "but I managed to acquire some techniques."

"Oh, I am sure." The stranger smiled. "I am Lilith."

Merge. Merge! Merge our magic, an overly enthusiastic voice suggested.

Ruby ignored the whisper. However, she was thankful that it was unlike the usual rowdy cacophony of screeching.

The voices seemed to relish the company of the witch. It must have meant something, as it took an abundance of time for such sorcery to transpire.

"What are you doing here?" Ruby asked. She needed to be wary. There must have been something about Lilith that made the voices view her with such remarkable respect. What if she was a threat?

"I could ask you the same," responded the witch. She took a few bold steps to close the gap between them.

"I am escaping from my prison," Ruby claimed in an attempt to scare the girl away. It was not a lie. "Why are you not praying with all of the other witches?"

Ruby had aimed many times throughout her life to call for assistance, just as all witches did. She asked her ancestors, Dahlia and the wind. They never once answered her prayers except for one witch—a late and forgotten queen. Ruby told nobody about it. It was never wise to share such sacred information. If anybody had learned that she had once called upon the Queen of Darkness, Lysandra, she would definitely be banished from the forest.

"I have done it my entire life," Lilith muttered as her eyes darted around the garden. Then, the lunatic settled down beside the Red Demon. Nobody ever dared to get so close.

The typically spiteful voices caused a short-lived commotion in a muffled but audibly ecstatic pitch.

"I might burn you," Ruby said, rather appalled by the guts of the girl.

"Did you not claim to have acquired some techniques?"

Ruby smiled. As long as the second soul in her body relished the stranger, she could dismiss the worrisome thoughts about hurting her.

Lilith was bound to leave soon, anyway. If the demon seized utter control of the body, anybody with a sane mind would run.

"Indeed," Ruby said. "How about you, then? What are your powers?"

She knew that the girl had the gift of future knowledge, but she craved to discover the second ability hinted at by the whispers.

"*Powers*? I am honored that you thought me capable of such," Lilith chuckled. "I am a Soothsayer. No more, no less."

Liar, Ruby reproached in silence. *Filthy, filthy liar.*

It is what she thinks, the voices shot back with a scowl.

Why in Dahlia are you defending her?

Us, murmured the demon. The single word was

enhanced by the multiple voices that followed. It resounded painfully in Ruby's head.

"What is the most questionable vision you have been given?" Ruby questioned. When she was younger, she heard witches asking Soothsayers about the same subject to start a friendship.

"In all honesty, I've forgotten many visions," said the witch as a reply. "However, earlier today, I saw—"

Lilith did not manage to complete the sentence because Ruby had unintentionally brushed a finger across the Soothsayer's skin. That simple motion was all it took to trigger the most frightening response.

Yes, the voices praised. *Let the show begin.*

CHAPTER FIVE

Moving images flashed in the minds of Ruby and Lilith. A quiet gasp escaped the latter's lips as she felt the harsh ripple of energy from the minor skin contact.

Both of them were yanked into a future world.

The moving visual image lingered for an unusually long time, lasting with clarity and duration far better than the most skillful witch with a blood obsidian.

The first was an image of a marvelous building that would make any being feel insignificant when viewing it from the bottom. From up close, its pointy tip succeeded in reaching the luminous blue sky

The smallest details could be identified—the darkened stones coating the wall surrounding the building and a single scratch on the bricks of the main structure.

It stood with pride on the luscious green land. Mossy rocks were randomly sprinkled on the ground with every glance the witches took. Occasionally, common daisies were found concealed by the thick grass.

The voices residing in Ruby's mind cackled with utter delight. It hungered to battle and to experience the rush of thrill during any sort of bloodshed. It yearned to destroy such flawless land; flood the area, or send it into fiery chaos.

Jade steps led into the mouth of the building, pretty and polished. It was practically screaming for visitors.

The glorious castle was indeed a sight to behold.

The golden cylindrical towers were connected by their walls, and several strips of red sliced through the gaps between the bricks, creating unique and terrifying darkness contrasting the glistening yellow. The same color scheme extended to the gold-rounded pyramid that reached for the sky.

With such a perfect sight, even the smallest features stood out. However, their eyes were drawn most frequently to the very front of the building.

A crest plastered on a flat surface howled for attention.

Lilith had seen the same crest in the vision earlier that day. Both had odd symbols engraved into the grip of the twin swords behind the dice.

Then, the image took a turn and concentrated further on the enormous patch of grass.

Almost immediately, the witches noticed a color difference. Where it was previously lavish green, the area gradually became coated with liquid crimson. The patch grew broader and broader with every second until it halted.

It was as if human blood was drained.

Dandelions sprouted from the ground as the soil enthusiastically drank the reddish fluid. Only the blood of one kind could cause such a reaction—nature witches.

Ruby's breath was caught in her throat. She had seen death many times but never one of a witch.

With every second, the scene faded into darkness. The witches were certain that it had come to an end until little dark rocks started to appear in a dungeon-like location. Symbols were marked on the eerie charcoal-colored stones that imprisoned them, and the rough texture distorted the many scribbled marks on the wall. Some were simple, like a triangle boxing a dash and the tilde, while others contained many overlapping lines that formed a mess of shapes. Lilith wondered what they truly meant.

Ruby could have sworn she had seen such symbols before in a dream, vision or a book.

The stones were all they could see until a glow emerged from a corner. They saw a pair of hands—one with strange nails belonging to a creature that quickened Lilith's heart and the other with smooth cocoa brown skin.

Within the palms of each laid a golden vial.

CHAPTER SIX

The Night of the Purge would commence soon.

Lilith already had a bitter taste in her mouth. In a few hours, the Forest of Dahlia would become a battlefield.

Lilith had never seen death. She knew what would occur outside her home, but she had learned to turn a blind eye.

Morakques did not kill in witches' territory. Instead, they arrive with intimidating inventions to capture the witches. There were many written accounts guessing the Morakques' goal. Some were convinced that those ruffians were studying witches as a method to be rid of magic and royalty once and for all. Lilith tended to view the best in others, but even she believed the captured were all long dead.

The circles beneath Nana' had darkened overnight, and Lilith felt guilty for distressing her grandmother so profoundly the day before. Their fight was not terribly severe, yet she disappeared for an hour.

"Where were you?!" her grandmother had cried out when she returned. The woman descended into a world of worry after realizing that the Red Demon had not returned to her cage.

Lilith claimed she visited the garden to clear her mind. It was not a lie in the slightest, but she felt as if she had committed a crime. Would Nana even believe her if she confessed to meeting the Red Demon? Could she convince her that Ruby might not be the vicious monster that everyone claimed she was?

Despite feeling remorseful, Lilith did not regret standing so close to the Red Demon.

It was an odd encounter, and what transpired after was weirder still. The vision they shared had a vague message, but they were certain of one thing—their fates were entwined.

Ruby was not the beast that witches claimed she was. She was misunderstood and shunned and lonely.

In all honesty, Lilith would have never approached Ruby. The absurdity of taking such a dangerous risk weighed on her like castle bricks, and she was truly fortunate that it turned out the way it did.

Lilith had fed her fear to her magic, leaving her heart without the presence of apprehension. Lacking fear, a leash that held humans back from foolish decisions, a wave of courage had washed over her. If she had not given in to her lack of control, she would have dashed back home immediately when she beheld the Red Demon's eyes.

Lilith watched as her Nana scrambled around their small house to gather ingredients. They would perform a spell of strength that would give Ruby a surge of power.

The entire coven was entrusting their lives to the hands of a single witch and a few fighting men. They were the sons of witches who dedicated their lives to crafting and harvesting crops.

As powerful as Ruby was, there would always be a

chance of capture. She had prevented death and succeeded in driving away Morakques for many years, but they always returned stronger than before. Alas, the Red Demon had failed multiple times in saving witches from their kidnap.

Lilith frowned, recalling another reason to be upset. Her grandmother's claim about her leaving the forest had come as an absolute shock. It would play out eventually, but all of her predictions were impossible.

Nana glanced at the position of the sun as she pulled the curtains shut.

"Soon, chaos will descend," she informed. It caused an uncomfortable bubbling in Lilith's stomach.

"When will it happen?"

Her grandmother settled down on the ground, then patted the seat next to her. With quickening heartbeats, Lilith obliged. In front of them was a bottle of honey to heal minor injuries, silver for protection, and a great amount of pewter for strength.

Nana was silent for a long moment. Slowly, she turned to look at Lilith.

It took a single word for the young witch to feel the most unbearable type of fear.

The grandmother fluttered her eyes closed, and the word sounded from her mouth, "Now."

The sound of ear-piercing shrieks rent the quiet and still air within the next second.

CHAPTER SEVEN

Ruby woke up with clammy hands. She had broken out in a cold sweat during the night, and her head pounded with the pain of a thousand needles.

Nothing could prepare her for the Night of the Purge.

"You *shall* do well. You have no other choice," Ruby's mother told her. The woman reminded Ruby persistently of the lives in her damp palms. One move could doom the entire coven.

It is time for fun, the whispers guffawed. Ruby gritted her teeth in annoyance at the sound. She was most afraid of the bloodthirsty creature sharing her body. It was exhilarated to rise from the depth of Ruby's mind and seize full control of the incredible power in their veins.

"Show the Morakques your best, Ruby," her father said. Ruby was grateful for the encouragement, but the demon had snorted.

We will show him, it challenged.

Ruby calmed her nerves. She knew the tingling in her soul meant that the purge was drawing dangerously close. "I will," she replied.

We will drown the garden again, the whispers suggested.

Ruby disregarded the resounding words. She would not allow it to take control. Her magic was like multiple tangled threads, and to trigger the most vicious response from her abilities, she would have to pull all strings, including her Soothsayer magic. That mere action would bring the beast to the surface, giving it the chance to acquire control of their body. She had to avoid doing so at all costs.

You will not get the chance, Ruby promised.

The voices halted, forming the rare sound of silence. Then, as one, they began to chortle. The laughter was deafening.

Oh, Ruby, it sneered. *You forget that only* I *can see the future.*

And you *forget that the future can be changed*, Ruby retorted.

She opened the door of her home and stepped into the presently empty forest. With a shaky breath, she stood before the path leading to her coven's territory. When the Morakques arrive, they would only see Ruby herself in all of her glory.

She would be assisted by the sons of witches who lived amongst her kind, and the strongest magic-wielders. The Morakques held little interest in capturing men who were trained to fight back.

The voices stayed silent as if waiting for the perfect moment to speak.

Good luck, they taunted. *Let us paint the ground red.*

As the words resounded in Ruby's head, a boisterous cry sounded from a distance. The distant footsteps escalated into thunderous thumps, echoing Ruby's quickening heartbeat.

When the Morakques entered Ruby's sight, her breath

hitched in her throat. She estimated that there were at least five dozen of them, a massive increase from the past years.

The group consisted of only men carrying spears and bows and axes, all dressed in pine green tunics and brown trousers that blended in with the forest's trees. Their boots were concealed with mud from their travel, squelching on the leaf-strewn ground and leaving it tainted. They were a disorderly bunch, spread out to form an arc of several rows before Ruby. At the very back, she noticed a giant, squarish structure enveloped by cloth and dreaded to know what it contained.

The hunters were led by a single man with coconut-colored hair tied into a tight bun, set apart by his dark cloak. On his left breast was the Morakque's emblem—two touching maroon horns with three spears rising from between them. Even from afar, the green shade of his irises was noticeable.

"Demon," the leader snarled. Behind him, a group of Morakques continued his chant.

The beast in Ruby's mind bathed in delight. It adored hearing the voices of the men. Soon, the Morakques would discover that *demon* was the last word they would say, for they would be too busy screaming to do anything else.

As they repeated the word with growing fervor, Ruby scanned the crowd for unfamiliar weapons and found none. Between the men stood human-sized cages which were reused time and time again. Still, Ruby felt uneasy because they confidence meant they had something planned.

"Let us get on with it," Ruby shouted over their voices. They halted as if not expecting her to speak.

The leader studied the witch. She was alone on a battlefield, seemingly helpless. The man whose hair was tied in a bun guffawed, looking at Ruby as if she were nothing more than a joke.

She did not need prodding from the whispers. Without hesitation, she lifted her hand and pointed at the Morakque beside his leader. It was almost too easy to feed her resentment to the fire in her heart. Flames blasted from her fingertips and engulfed the shirt of the man.

When they last visited, Ruby had used water to fight. The Morakques were oblivious to her multiple gifts and thought little of wearing gear that could protect them from flames. Now that she had mastered her gift of fire, she would watch her helpless enemies burn with glee.

The leader's laughter was cut short in a heartbeat. His eyes widened in sudden alarm as he watched his friend compete with the fire that continued without pause.

The Morakque's expressions shaped into despair and rage. They did not need to exchange discreet glances. Spontaneously, they dashed towards Ruby like a horde of captured animals that encountered the chance to escape.

Burn them all, the whispers resurfaced. They were hoping so badly for a mistake on Ruby's part.

Ruby could not send an enormous wave of flames without surfacing the demon. With such a large crowd, she would have to concentrate more on preventing any Morakques from entering homes. She had to create a shield to avoid the arrows that were beginning to rain from above.

Her actions were a flurry of movement, flames and water. The loathing and anger melded together in a seemingly infinite source of magic. The spells of power from witches in their homes granted her the strength to devastate the Morakques.

The laughter in her mind only fed her with confidence.

The demon in her head enjoyed the slaughtering, but Ruby adored the spark in her chest that ignited her soul. It made her feel like a protector and a necessary being.

It takes one act to burn them all, the voices reminded. They were growing more impatient.

Men who lived amongst witches started to fight beside Ruby, allowing her to work her magic. There were *so* many Morakques. Every blaze took a piece of her fear and energy.

Killing them one by one would not work, said the demon, irritated. *Look to your right. Someone is sneaking into a house.*

Ruby whisked away from the Morakques attempting to strike her with their spears. Simultaneously, she shaped her features into one of a man. Indeed, somebody had broken away from his group to enter a house.

Ruby had to be careful. The grass could burn with the Morakques, but nobody would forgive her if she lit the wooden houses.

With one swift movement, she shoved the man behind her. Ruby released the illusion of her face and watched his expression mold into terror. He gaped into her blood-red eyes, knowing death was calling his name.

With a flick of her hand, water spilt out of his mouth. As the man choked on his body fluid, flames shot out of his eyes. The fire was unintentional, a thread that was triggered with water. If the same mistake happened with the string holding the demon, disaster would strike.

Ruby inhaled sharply. The scent of blood filled her nostrils in an instant. It was a strong and unappealing metallic smell that tempted the demon.

Be careful, it whispered to Ruby and flashed an image of a future attack in her mind. Immediately, she reached behind her back and wrapped her fingers around the spear that would have otherwise killed her. She silently thanked the second soul in her body for the warning and wrestled for the weapon.

"You will pay for the violence that you have rained down on us," the Morakque promised with strained pronunciation. He had beads of sweat covering his face. Ruby's eyes traced a droplet as it slithered down from the side of his face and grinned wryly. It was an expression to be feared.

Before another word could be uttered, Ruby fed the water with boiling heat and morphed it into ravenous flames.

"I would like to see what is in store for me," she replied. The voice was not entirely her own. It was fused with the demon's voice, which injected an echo into her sentence.

She had tugged on her Soothsayer thread without meaning to.

Look to the entrance, the whispers advised. It was louder than the battle cry and bellowing of fighting men. The demon was incredibly close to the surface.

Why? Ruby asked, only to find out seconds later.

The Morakques' spectacular plan was on full display. The structure previously covered by a cloth was revealed to be a cage bigger than any Ruby had seen before.

And it was occupied by witches.

They were not current residents of the forest.

They were magic wielders who were captured years ago.

Ruby gawked at the sight. She had long assumed that the kidnapped witches were dead.

The sorcerers in the cages were haggard, filthy, but *alive*.

Ruby was momentarily struck with a maelstrom of emotions. Some witches in the Forest of Dahlia were so convinced of the captured witches' demise that they dedicated empty tombs for them. For them to be here, breathing, suggested that tens, if not hundreds, of witches who were previously taken during past purges could still be out there. Even those seized decades ago might still live, praying daily to the wind that someday, they might escape.

The entire forest seemed to cease their brawling at once.

I want to handle this, the voices said.

You will cause destruction, replied Ruby.

That is the only way to succeed during the Night of the Purge, it argued. *We either kill them all or let them return for more of your kind.*

There must be another way, insisted Ruby.

There is not.

The leader of the Morakques stood before the entrance to the locked cage. He had his hands in a fist.

"We would like to negotiate," he shared.

"Negotiate?" Ruby echoed. She held back a scoff.

"Yes." He dipped his head. "We will return these

demons to their homes. In return, you will cease the fighting and allow us to trade for another batch."

"We are not items up for barter," Ruby scorned. Her anger brought forth another wave of magic.

The Morakques surrounding the cage had their gazes fixed on her. There were only two dozen left. If she were to make the slightest mistake, the Morakques might succeed in a few discreet abductions.

"If that is so, you leave us without choice," the leader said, feigning pity. In a quick second, he drove a spear into the chest of a captured witch.

A spur of emotions sprang into Ruby's chest—fear, resentment and anger. She had never seen the death of her kind. For a moment, all she could do was watch as the prisoner bled out while the other fatigued witches in her cell released gasps of misery. The overwhelming feelings swelled to the verge of bursting in Ruby's heart.

She needed to calm herself before she gave the demon control. Yet, the excessive ability she wielded had given way to irrational thoughts. The power in her veins was seething and craving escape.

Let me out, the whispers urged.

Why should she not? Using her ability to the fullest extent meant giving control to the demon, owner of the irksome voices. It could demolish the world, but the Morakques would be quickly obliterated.

Ruby had never willingly handed her body to the demon.

If you seize control, you cannot destroy the houses or

slaughter any witches, Ruby notified. Considering to perform such a deed was outrageous, but she had few choices left.

I will not, the voices said.

And why is that? Ruby questioned. *You have never hesitated to destroy.*

Because, replied the demon in various pitches, *Lilith would not appreciate it.*

Her opinion means nothing to you.

You are wrong, Ruby, it sneered.

She did not care to understand the demon. She could barely focus on anything but her swirling emotions. Her chest was on the brink of erupting into a storm of chaos.

Let me out, the demon repeated. *Let me out.*

Ruby transformed her feelings into a powerful stream of power. The remaining Morakques were waiting impatiently for her next move, assuming she might give in to their leader's request. They were oblivious to the magic working in her veins. She grasped all of her threads at once and forcefully jerked them.

Before she sunk into the depth of her mind, she heard a ripple of reverberating laughter.

CHAPTER EIGHT

The demon had almost forgotten about the blissful feeling of the afternoon breeze, control, and *power*. The body it currently possessed felt like a bubbling volcano on the brink of eruption, and one thought was all it took to detonate land stretching for miles. It was capable of quaking the entirety of Dicera.

Do not get carried away, Ruby warned in their mind.

She would soon find out that she needn't have worried. If it were any other year, the demon would take pride in demolishing lives. However, this year was different; the wind demanded it.

It familiarized itself with the strength of controlling two minds—Ruby's and its own. It had plenty of time to relish the energy it possessed.

The Morakques stared at it with disdain. They believed it was a creature to be feared, and they were not necessarily wrong.

It went by many names—Red Demon, Soothsayer, creature, grotesque *thing*, voices, and whisperers. It responded to the titles as if it owned them. It was a pity that hardly anybody knew of its existence and instead perceived Ruby as one soul with two personalities.

Like every individual, it had a dream of its own. It craved bloodshed and destruction, but its greatest desire was to be recognized. It wanted all Dicerians to learn of its name.

I picked a name for myself, the Soothsayer had announced once.

I thought names were for bodies with faces, Ruby said. Her six-year-old mind could not make sense of it.

But I wanted a name, it replied.

What did you choose?

Faye.

Its name was Faye, created by nature's affinity for balance to guarantee that Ruby's body could cope with the staggering strength it was granted. One day, the kingdom would worship the title, although it had neither a body nor face. *We were born to be leaders*, it told Ruby frequently, for it was the truth.

I will not use your name. Ever. Ruby was stubborn, and Faye liked that about her. However, it was a trait that meant she would never accept Faye as anything but a demon.

Please?

No. You are no person. You have neither body nor face.

If you call me by name, I will leave. I will return what belongs to you, and we will no longer share a body. The deal sounded foolish, and maybe it was, but Faye knew that Ruby's pride would never allow her to yield because she had nothing to fight for. Moreover, although the young witch would never admit it, she liked Faye's company. They were each other's only friend in the meantime.

I will never accept you. Never.

Presently, it had borrowed Ruby's appearance, and it planned on seizing its advantages.

The oppressive pressure of pulsing energy was beginning to seep from its fingertips. Looking into the green irises of the Morakque's leader, it allowed Ruby's mouth to curl into a sinister smile.

"Ready yourself," Faye said, allowing its voices to echo, "to burn."

With a single thought, flames burst into action with an eagerness that trembled the ground. The magic rushed out of Ruby's body like a famished mountain lion, finally released from its den after days of starvation. It galloped towards the Morakques and created a fiery wall between them and the miserable witches. The flames were blistering and faithful, devouring only the Morakques' skins. The fire overshadowed every tree in the Forest of Dahlia and danced without a care.

Then, with another thought, spikes of infusible ice surrounded the witches in the cage. It was enough to protect them from the flames.

The glow from the flame reflected in Ruby's red eyes and brightened her skin to a glorious golden tan. Faye knew that her friend looked like a goddess when surrounded by fire.

The witches in their homes had their eyes trained on the girl. She was the most powerful being they had ever seen, and she bathed in the spotlight with sparkling, extraordinary eyes that made her face appear menacing. The witch was more beast than human.

Faye allowed its imagination to run wild at the possible ways it could be perceived. It closed the eyes of the body it borrowed and released only half of the power surging within Ruby's veins.

It watched in delight as more than a dozen Morakques screamed in anguish. The sound was as pleasant as the singing of talented sorcerers.

The leader of the Morakques was only scorched slightly; Faye had commanded the fire to stay away from a significant portion of his skin because he deserved death much more painful than any.

Washing away the heat in the area, Faye used considerable magic to call upon the ferocious wildlife. Chirping arose, and a shadow painted the ground. A swarm of birds swooped down, attacking those not already set ablaze. They tore and consumed the skins of Morakques with the resentment that lingered in Ruby's heart.

If it were any other year, the Soothsayer would have flooded the land. But not this one.

A unique type of warmth brimmed Ruby's body. The demon's lifelong partner was too deep in their mind to feel the satisfying flush in the core of her stomach. Immediately, it could tell that Lilith was watching.

Her gaze was hotter than the fire it could cast with Ruby's remaining strength.

She is watching, Faye thought.

Who? Ruby poked in.

It gave no answer before directing a wave of water to rise around the cage. The burning Morakques reached out anxiously, only to discover that the liquid bore heat like no other. Their skins wasted no time before sizzling.

There were still fortunate Morakques who escaped

their fates. Faye had allowed some, along with the leader, to flee. In the future, they would meet again.

Nothing could overpower it. Faye was a witch harsher than any animal.

Faye was certain that victory was inevitable until an image flashed in its mind—a vision of the future.

It portrayed an overly realistic scene of the series of activities that would play out in the next few seconds.

Faye would first hear a shout of rage. If that sounded, it would have no time to react before a brisk arrow traveled towards it and pierced into Ruby's heart.

Faye was yanked back to the present with fear beginning to crowd its mind. The vision was its only warning before the furious roar filled the air.

CHAPTER NINE

The silence of Lilith's surroundings was more piercing than anything she had heard before.

Fear invaded her chest. She dreaded the sparkling sensation, for it meant that her loss of control might transpire at any second. She could not afford such a costly mistake when performing a spell.

Nana's lips stretched in a thin line as she glanced at the pewter pendant lying in her trembling palm. Lilith knew in an instant that her grandmother felt a crippling amount of anxiety too.

The hollering grew harsher outside their home.

"It is time to begin," Nana informed and drew a few symbols onto their wooden floor with chalk.

Lilith clasped the mirror gifted by her mother tightly within her fist. It spawned ripples of comfort that roamed her body like a spirited venturer. The red obsidian built into the bottom of it had a power that could strengthen any spell with ease. Offering an uncertain nod to her grandmother, Lilith began to chant the words that served the Red Demon with the strength to protect.

The spell created a pool in Lilith's mind. With every recited line, an additional wave of liquid was added to the river that she visualized. It was a conjured picture that she shared with her grandmother's mind through the connection of blood. Neither of them expected the Red Demon to drain the aqua-colored body of water so quickly.

As a team, they refilled their empty mind with the magical matter created by the spell. The incantation was able to serve the effect it promised by merely stealing the breaths of witches who spoke its name repeatedly. It remained the best approach for witches because the spell did not require death to work delightfully. Ruby would receive the surge of strength from it and be able to perform splendidly.

Lilith paused and missed a line; it was too dehydrating and mentally draining. Despite the blatant fact, she had to push herself to continue. Still, the young Soothsayer had unintentionally skipped on yet another line when she heard her grandmother's voice. The woman was wheezing, panting, and straining herself to her very limit.

"Nana, are you alright?" Lilith questioned. Her eyes were shut, and the pool of water was still present in her mind.

The grandmother halted. For a moment, Lilith thought the woman had fainted.

"Yes," replied Nana, her voice weak and barely audible.

"I think you should rest," Lilith suggested.

"I cannot."

"I can continue the spell on my own." Lilith knew she was strong enough even without the obsidian. Possessing the blood of the most powerful Soothsayer in the forest had its perks.

She proceeded to chant once again and frowned slightly

when her fatigued grandmother insisted on joining in once again.

Ruby had slowed down in her usage of sudden and substantial power. Lilith took the time to breathe and listen to the voice of her grandmother. She was becoming much frailer as the years passed.

The older woman was doing relatively well until her voice hitched abruptly. Lilith did not think much of it until she heard a cling of metal. She peeled open her eyes and beheld the sight of her grandmother, struggling to hold herself upright.

"You are too tired," said the young sorceress. "You have to rest."

The grandmother was still gasping. It was as if oxygen refused to enter her lungs.

"I—"

"Rest, Nana."

Lilith hoped that the experienced Soothsayer knew enough to realize she needed time to regain her strength. But that did not seem the case. Within the next moment, Nana lost consciousness and sprawled onto the ground.

Lilith's eyes widened in horror. Hurriedly, she approached her grandmother to check her pulse and heaved a sigh of relief when she felt rhythmic thumps of the constant beat. However, her grandmother's skin was searing hot, and it was evident that she needed a healer immediately.

Apprehension clawed at her chest. The purge was raging outside her home, and it was a death wish to step outside.

Lilith clutched the mirror in her palm to seek the comfort it perpetually offered. This time, it did nothing to soothe her racing heart. When she felt her mind spin, panic swam in her blood. It was the feeling she would receive before losing control of her ability.

The emotions in her heart gathered, threatening to burst, then vanished in an instant. An image flashed in her head, showing a future sight of a page within a stained and dusty book. She held onto the vision long enough to memorize a line in the book and the symbols that surrounded it.

She returned to the present, void of anxiety for a mere second before it came rolling in again.

Lilith glanced around her home. There was nothing she could do but resume the spell, but the symbols scribbled by her grandmother had been severely smudged, and she could not remember what they once were.

She stood, eyes darting around until they landed on the window concealed by curtains. Now that she was technically acquainted with Ruby, curiosity was clawing at her, begging to watch the fabled demon annihilate their enemies.

She gave herself no time for hesitation before peeking outside. There, in front of multiple Morakques, Ruby delivered a show of power. The red-eyed witch whirled around the area as if it were a dance floor and beheld an expression that sent a chill colder than winter wind across Lilith's face.

Ruby had called upon a monstrous flame with a simple motion that encircled the cage of filthy witches. An abrupt realization slapped Lilith in the face—those witches were previous victims of the Morakque's purges. She gaped when she spotted a Concealer who had once transformed into a hag for her entertainment, then shook her head in disbelief at a nature witch who presented her with a flower stalk years ago. Lilith had long believed them dead.

The male fighters on the witches' side were succeeding in their combat, but they had paused to gawk at the trapped witches. It was every bit reasonable, for they could have been partners or fathers to those in the cage.

Lilith's attention returned to the Red Demon. She bit back a gasp when Ruby manipulated an abundance of water to replace the fire. A few Morakques shrank away while many impatiently lunged into it. The latter Morakques were charred and painfully turned into ash.

Lilith could only imagine the heat of the water that scorched her enemies so thoroughly. She could not bear to see the unsettling sight of humans burning alive. Her mind was racing as she glanced downward at her dusty window seal.

Without warning, her fear morphed into a vision. It flashed and faded, but it lingered long enough for Lilith to detect symbols and the words that would initiate its spell on a book's cream page. There was bound to be a hidden message in the image that she failed to grasp on time.

There was nothing she could do. Lilith was not familiar with the spells that would heal her grandmother, and there was an ongoing battle outside her home where death littered the ground. She was torn between useless choices.

She released a shaky breath and tried to ignore the pounding in her chest. She needed a distraction before her magic seized control of her thoughts. Gazing at the undusted surface of her window seal, she traced the symbols that were unintentionally displayed in her mind moments ago.

She raised her head to observe the fighting again but instead found a Morakque standing from afar. He held a bow in his hands, aimed at Ruby. The witch was standing before her cruel masterpiece with an unusual calmness.

Lilith momentarily froze in panic. Even without her ability, she could predict what would take place a few seconds into the future.

Her mouth worked without the permission of her brain as if directed by fate. When the Morakque released his grip on his bowstring, Lilith uttered the line of words she memorized in the book that she had perceived in her mind.

She was unaware of the meaning behind what she said, but she knew how spells worked. As long as its symbols were present and the incantation was pronounced accurately, magic would spring into action.

Lilith had expected nothing until black smoke surrounded the arrow. Just before it pierced Ruby clean through her heart, the arrow swiftly changed its route and flew with startling speed towards the Morakque that shot it. The young Soothsayer gasped aloud when the arrow penetrated his skin, and darkness concealed him whole.

When the smoke died out, all that was left were bones.

CHAPTER TEN

Ruby had not expected the demon to willingly return her body.

Is there something wrong? You are acting strange, Ruby mentioned as her body and senses returned to their rightful owner.

Look. Behind you, the whispers urged.

Why?

We still stand although we should have died.

What do you mean? Dismay leapt into Ruby's heart at the thought of dying.

I received a vision of death. Behind us, there is the archer who attempted to kill us, the voices rambled. The demon was frightened, and the thought itself bewildered Ruby.

She scanned her surroundings—Morakques were either dead or wounded, and most of the men fighting on her side were relatively unharmed. There was an unfortunate handful who were not so lucky.

She dug into her powers to find herself nearly drained. The demon had done catastrophic damage to their foes but thankfully steered clear of destroying the land. It was a pleasant but bizarre sight.

Then, Ruby turned around to a peculiar view—a small area of ground was obscured by *bones*. There was no hint of skin or blood.

Who did that? Ruby asked, terrified at the barbaric death. She received no reply.

She did not impertinently push for an answer, although her confusion was overwhelming. Instead, she averted her attention to the cage of previously abducted witches, then summoned a spike of ice to act as a key. As the cell unlocked, a few baffled witches rushed out of their homes towards them. Barely anyone assumed that Morakques were generous enough to leave their kind alive.

"Ruby!" called a voice. The incomprehensible whispers in her mind burst into shrill excitement after hearing the sound.

"Is something wrong?" Ruby answered, turning around. She had detected worry in the witch's words.

"Have you got any knowledge of healing spells?"

"Yes. Is there a need for it?"

"My grandmother," Lilith choked out and hastily led the possible savior into her home. She grabbed a bottle of honey from an area littered with ingredients for spells and placed it beside the unconscious older woman.

"What happened?" Ruby was quick to mark out symbols she learned as a child.

"She pushed her mind beyond her limit, and she is burning up," Lilith explained. "This has never happened before."

Ruby uttered a phrase and dropped a small amount of honey on the woman's forehead. She opened an illusory portal into the mind of the senior witch. She could effortlessly sense a burning fever caused by excessive stress, but the spell was not the primary reason. Ruby avoided discovering it, for digging into the mind without permission could reveal many thoughts that were better left buried. Instead, she focused on channeling calmness into the grandmother's veins to get rid of the fever.

"It is not a terrible fever. Your grandmother will rouse from her sleep soon but needs plenty of rest," she informed. "Has something been bothering her of late?"

Lilith was quiet for a moment. "Yes," she finally said. "She was given a future glimpse that involved me."

"That could be the reason," agreed Ruby. "Her mind was elsewhere during the spell."

Sighing, Lilith helped Ruby to her feet. "Thank you," she said. "How was the battle?"

"Tragic, as it often is." Ruby's thoughts wandered to the death she had fortunately missed. "It played out briskly because the Morakques had planned something simple to get around. Perhaps next time, I will not be so lucky."

There will not be a next time, the whispers chipped in. *After today, those filthy Morakques will not return to you.*

What do you mean?

You shall go to them.

Ruby rolled her eyes and brushed away their conversation. The voices were sputtering nonsense again.

She turned to Lilith, then gasped at her abnormally colored eyes. It was extraordinarily different from the day before. Small and midnight black specks were peppered in spots of bright brown. Beyond that, dark spots had formed in the whites of her eyes. Was she an unknowing Concealer, unintentionally shaping her traits?

Before Ruby could mention the unusual sight to her, a grunt sounded from the grandmother.

The elder called for all forest residents to assemble.

Ruby knew the reason for the meeting even before it was announced.

The six witches who were previously caged gathered alongside their kind, waiting for their turn to speak. They only received the chance after the elder addressed the death of the seventh victim solemnly.

One by one, the witches who had disappeared from the coven began to share their experiences.

They were used as slaves for Morakques, who opposed the rule of royalty. They viewed the royals as dirty, for they did not bear the opinion that witches were abominations. Hence, they hoped to overthrow the rulers of Dicera with the benefit of witches and their magic. For the first time in history, it was confirmed that Morakques studied witches. They were ruthless in their methods, often resorting to executions when met with defiance.

The sheer power of Morakques was comparable to the royal family. Over the years, they garnered considerable prestige that resulted in the continual separation between royalty and witches. If the witches attempted to bridge the distance, they would be butchered before they reached a safe territory. If the royals attempted, a war might ensue.

A bitter taste surfaced in Ruby's mouth. It was true that Morakques might find it threatening enough to commence a cataclysmic battle if the royals provided witches with safe passage away from the Forest of Dahlia. However, there must have been discreet ways. The royals had never once reached out. What disappointing allies.

The witches returned by the Morakques were those too weak to be useful in their atrocious mission to claim the crown.

The oldest witch of the forest nodded dolefully after the last witch concluded her speech, then directed Ruby an intimidating stare.

"I have a solution to rescue our people," she declared. "We need a witch who will bring the freedom that our kind desperately seeks by requesting aid from the royals. We must see to it that all the captured witches who live return home to us. We need someone we can depend on, and who other than the strongest amongst us? The only *thing* with the capability, born to bring us glory—Ruby."

CHAPTER ELEVEN

Lilith aimed to bury her feelings in the dark corners of her mind. She hoped that her eyes would assist her in concealing the secret and disguising what she yearned so desperately to hide, though they often deceived her.

After performing the spell that saved Ruby's life, a portion of her soul was enhanced. There was fluidity in her movements, an unmistakable lightness in her chest that felt suspiciously like relief. It was like finally dropping the bags of stones she was unknowingly hauling around in everyday life. Lilith found the pleasant feeling odd. She was continually told that nature required balance; the spell should have taken a significant fraction of her soul. Instead, she felt lively and full of spirit, as if something that had always thrived within her had awakened. It was a type of electrifying chill that she had encountered somewhere before.

Since she had never heard about it, she would not share it. Such an oddity might result in her banishment from the Forest of Dahlia.

Nevertheless, she had to confess that she craved to share the information with someone. Her grandmother would claim that it was false, and so would Aunt Lavern. She also promised to distance herself from her new acquaintance after observing the wicked glint in her eyes. It was a shame that she was not familiar with a considerable number of witches.

Then again, perhaps she was being unfair to Ruby. She did end a life too. Nobody knew that she performed the utterly foul spell, but commotion would soon arise. Lilith doubted anyone would turn a blind eye to an apparent pile of bones sitting beside a bush.

Knowing that she committed such a deed was traumatizing. It had been thrashing in her mind, pressuring her to face the horrendous fact.

Lilith was only brought back to reality when she heard a name—Ruby.

"What is happening?" she asked her grandmother, who was standing beside her in silence.

"Your apparent new *friend* is being sent to face danger. She is tasked to find the rest of the witches who were kidnapped throughout the years," Nana said. She was not fond of Lilith's newfound friendship with the Red Demon.

"Sent?" Lilith repeated as if it were a crime. Although she wanted to avoid Ruby, she did not wish for her death. The outside world was no place for a witch, no matter how powerful.

"Yes—"

"What if she dies?"

"You have no say in what the elder wants to do," said Nana. She turned to look her granddaughter in the eyes, but the intimidation she hoped to show faltered immediately.

"Have I grown a second head?" asked Lilith.

There was no hint of a smile that washed over her

grandmother's face. Instead, the older Soothsayer quickly ushered her to the back of the crowd.

"Lavern," Nana called. The tone of her voice called upon an unwelcoming bubbling in Lilith's stomach. Her grandmother wasted no time before questioning, "Do you sense a negative energy in my dear Lily?"

The nature witch stretched her arm to brush a finger across Lilith's skin. In a mere second, her hand retreated as if she reached out to touch the heat of flames.

"Oh, dear," Aunt Lavern muttered.

"What did you feel?" Nana voiced out the question in Lilith's mind.

"How did you know that there was something wrong?"

"Her eyes," the grandmother replied swiftly. "Now, tell me what is wrong."

"There is an unhealthy amount of… emptiness," said Lavern after much contemplation. "I have never felt anything like it, and there is no precise word to explain it. It repels my magic and, at the same time, *steals* it."

Lilith's mouth went dry as questions sprang into her mind. How did her eyes give her away? Did the calm surge in her veins mean that there was something severely wrong with her?

Nana turned to her and lowered her voice to speak. The words that she uttered formed a sentence Lilith had never expected to hear in a thousand years.

"Were you the witch who turned the Morakque into a cluster of bones?"

Lilith was trapped between decisions—truth or lie. She yearned to tell the truth to the ridiculously phrased question, but the consequences could be ghastly. She was quiet for a long while, which was answer enough.

"How?" Her Nana would never believe that Lilith could perform such a lethal spell after keeping her away from so much knowledge. It was a mystery that even the young Soothsayer could not decipher.

Lilith did not bother to explain. She only wished to know one thing.

"What does this mean? What will happen to me?"

The grandmother was speechless and visibly afraid. "This was the one thing I wanted to avoid."

"Will I be banished?"

"I do not know." The experienced Soothsayer had doubtlessly seen many things, but her strength alone could never avoid fate. No witch would ever be able to defeat the impulse to follow the wind. Utterly dismayed, the grandmother covered Lilith's hand affectionately.

The young witch could tell that even her grandmother, the strongest Soothsayer in the forest, was repulsed by the strange power that suddenly manifested in Lilith's veins.

"I do not want to be banished." Fear like no other clutched Lilith's throat. She wished for nothing but to wrench the gruesome *thing* from her body. Tears leapt into her eyes at the mere thought of leaving the forest—not for an adventure, but because her coven would eventually cast her out.

The most prominent reason that called for banishment was being considered a threat to other witches. If the elder sensed any hint of danger, there would be no escaping it. If

Lilith's power repulsed witches, she would be forced to leave the forest within days.

She was reminded of the vision that Nana had received. It was amusing how a few hours ago, she would have never believed to be in a situation where leaving the Forest of Dahlia was her only option.

"There is only one way," said her Nana. Lilith prayed that it was not what she had in mind, but she knew better than to ignore the direction given by fate.

"I know," she said. She cast her gaze skyward, wishing things could be different.

"You have to leave willingly with Ruby."

CHAPTER TWELVE

Disbelief infested Ruby's chest like ants around the sweetest honey. As a child, she was informed that she was born to protect, not perish.

"You are sending her on a trip to hell," grumbled her father, voicing out her thoughts.

"No," the elder spoke. "It is a trip to find freedom for all."

"She will *die*," he sneered. "Please, there must be another way."

"Farmer," spat the oldest witch in the forest, "please be reminded of whom you are speaking to. This is not a request; it is an order."

Her father fell silent, knowing that he could not sway the elder from her abhorrent decision. If she grew offended, he might have to serve consequences beyond what was deserved. Even Ruby's mother began to tug impatiently on her partner's sleeve.

"Let it be," said the woman, mildly infuriated.

"She is our *daughter*. We cannot lose her to the creatures outside this forest," the father insisted.

"Lower your voice; you are embarrassing us. We will discuss this later," she ordered, and that was that.

Ruby was still very much alarmed and frightened. The voices were absent and did not help calm her nerves, although its life was similar on the line. Typically, it would be sharing her concern or offering Ruby a harsh thought of violence. If the whispers were silent any other time, she would be exceptionally joyful, but not now. Not while they were ordered to dive into a pit of cruelty.

Say something, Ruby pleaded.

What is it? complained the voices.

We are being sent to our deaths. How can you be so calm?

Oh, please, it snickered. *Wait and see.*

Ruby inhaled a shaky breath. She could trust it, but the demon with multiple voices was a master of deception. She would never be able to understand the thoughts of a being who knew her future.

She nodded to the elder's words with a smile, although her heart was bubbling with fury. She did not want to venture into the heart of the kingdom, where the Fort of Morakques was located. She could handle dozens of those pesky creatures but not hundreds.

"You shall go tonight," announced the elder, sending a ripple of gasps throughout the crowd.

"Tonight?" yelled Ruby's father. He was incapable of holding himself back.

"Yes. Ruby shall depart as soon as possible to confront the Morakques while they are weak."

"She cannot have a night of sleep?"

"As I said, farmer. The sooner, the better."

Ruby's heart thumped as quickly as the surge of resentment that traveled through her body. It was not the demon sharing her body that produced the emotion.

"Tonight?" she whispered to herself, startled and horrified all at once.

The elder nodded with a grim smile before retreating into her house for the night. Before vacating the area, witches flashed Ruby sympathetic frowns while ensuring that they stood at least five feet away from her. She felt defeated and despaired as she left with her parents.

"We cannot let her do this," her father declared just as the door slammed shut.

"If you have yet to realize, we have no say whatsoever," said the mother dismissively. Ruby had expected her to say as much.

"Why do you care so little about her?" murmured the father. Their argument made Ruby feel like an unnecessary addition to the room.

"That is not true," scoffed the woman. "She was born to do this; you should have been long prepared."

"There are too many things that can go wrong."

"If she is lucky, she will return in one piece."

"We should not be counting on luck," he disagreed. "Ruby's life matters. To me, if not to you. We should not feed her to the world so simply."

The mother rolled her eyes and gave Ruby a disapproving glare. With a note of finality, she said, "If she does not come back, it just proves how insignificant she is."

There was an unbearable silence that spawned in the moments that followed the mother's vicious words. It planted a thought in Ruby's mind—perhaps, this was an extraordinary opportunity for freedom from her home and mother.

"You are unbelievable," the man grumbled. He lowered himself next to his daughter and rested his hands on her shoulders. He squeezed them gently before meeting her bright red eyes with his glassy brown ones. The painful sight of his tears almost ripped her heart into two.

"Please do not cry, Father," Ruby said, holding back tears of her own. He was the only individual who dared to approach her with love and without a hint of fear. He had a heart bigger than the Kingdom of Dicera, and he was the only reason she feared the trip. If she were to die, her father would never forgive the world for taking his only daughter.

"You have to stay safe," he said, voice wavering with emotions. "You cannot leave me."

"I will not," promised Ruby, although she had no clue how her future would play out.

"You have a lot of power in your blood, Ruby. Use it, and fight." The father tightened his hold on her shoulders and then engulfed her in a hug. The heat of his embrace was warmer than any fire she could summon. "For as long as I live, you will never be alone."

"I will not let the coven down."

"I do not care about this silly mission," replied the farmer. "I just need you to remain safe."

"I will do everything I can."

"You are a strong witch," he said. "Show the world what you can do and return to the forest with a crown."

"I will emerge victorious, Father. Trust me, the Morakques will not stand a chance." She was not certain, but she needed to offer a shred of hope to her father.

"Go on," whispered the man. "Pack your things before the elder comes knocking on our door."

Ruby had tried to weep as quietly as possible when she packed the crops harvested by her father into a pouch she would bring along. She did not know whether to call it an adventure or a journey to death. She was leaning towards the latter, for it was difficult to remain positive.

It was most challenging to bid goodbye to her father, who seemed more devastated than Ruby herself.

When she stepped out of her home, a strong gust of wind dried her tears and nudged her towards the forest's exit. It directed her to stride into a world she had never seen before.

Wait, said the demon after a long while of silence. Although it was not Ruby's favorite *thing* in the world, she was fortunate to be with someone on this treacherous journey.

What is it? Ruby replied, halting her movement.

"Wait!" called a girl while sprinting beside her.

Alarmed, Ruby turned. "Lilith? What are you doing here?"

"I am coming with you." She did not sound joyous about the fact, but she forced a smile to appear eager.

"What?" Ruby's eyebrows knitted together in confusion. There was no reason for this woman who had become somewhat of a friend to resign to a fate that was not hers to claim.

"I have no choice," mumbled Lilith. "I was tasked to find a human healer."

"You are sick?" exclaimed Ruby, perplexed beyond

words. Instinctively, she reached out to grab Lilith's hand to check the beating of her pulse.

An unnatural and menacing cold slithered into her heart. The demon that resided in her mind screeched with wild exhilaration as the feeling soared throughout her body with astonishing speed. As odd as it was, Ruby found it comforting.

The sensation disappeared as quickly as it arrived when Lilith withdrew her wrist.

"What was that?" Ruby questioned, eyes wide and astounded.

"It is the reason I have to leave," the Soothsayer rushed out the words. "I will explain soon. It is dangerous if I stay any longer."

The whispers burst into laughter before the witches could say any more, foreseeing an adventure that was to become books and music and memories.

CHAPTER THIRTEEN

Every few steps felt like stepping into a new dimension. A world blossomed with flora that Ruby had never seen before. She welcomed the creatures of nature to join her on the journey as she admired the glorious sight.

Lilith laughed from beside her as a butterfly landed on the lily lodged in her hair, the sound like summer's gentle touch. The plant had been radiating a strange aura, one that was different from the eternal plants created by Dahlia.

They were not draped in wealthy silks with fanciful embroidery of any sort; they did not have such luxury. Ruby was offered a comfortable pearl-white dress of cotton with rose-gold ribbons around her waist and sleeves as a final parting gift. It was an item purchased by witches who visited villages in disguise. On the other hand, Lilith's garb was similarly simple, only onyx in color with strips of white. It was what she wore when she announced she must leave, and it made her look somewhat like a huntress.

Ruby had yet to figure out why the witch had willingly joined her, but she found no reason to complain. It was fortunate that she had a companion, and the whispers in her mind thought so too.

The witches could not resist gawking at the glorious scenery while following the path. The outside world was said to be unpleasant and brimmed with savagery, but they could only see beauty. Perhaps the trip was more of an adventure than a death mission, Ruby decided.

"Are you inclined to rest?" she asked.

"Sure," responded Lilith. "How long has it been since we left?"

"A few hours. We should find a cave for the night and set off in the morning."

They hiked further into the heart of the kingdom, away from the forest where they spent their entire lives. It was not long before they stumbled across a cavern that looked more like an open mouth. Rocks parted ways to form a gloomy entrance extending deep beyond sight.

"Do you think that Morakques could be resting in there?" Lilith asked as they approached the hollow area.

"They could, but I doubt it. Those who escaped were relatively unscathed," Ruby replied as she glanced at the map in her hands. "A village is not far from here, so they would likely be there."

The map they received illustrated the outside world and was designed by an individual who existed before the young witches were born. On the very right of the paper was cursive handwriting stating, 'Kingdom of Dicera'. It was discovered between two pages of a book about Dicera. Although nobody knew how the locations were obtained, they believed it to be reliable. Anything found within books in the Forest of Dahlia was a source written by witches in the past. They caused a near extinction of their kind due to their recklessness when attempting to understand the kingdom.

Before embarking on her dangerous journey, Ruby dedicated her life to reading every one of those books.

The two witches settled down on the rugged ground and leaned against the rocky wall. Ruby dreaded the night, for she was more familiar with sleeping on bamboo than stones, but the trip required her to do anything to survive.

Softly tugging on the thread in her body, she commanded water to hover over Lilith's hands.

"Drink. It has been a long day," she said.

Ruby was exhausted, too, but the whispers had demanded her to check up on Lilith. Why they bothered to do so was a great mystery.

"Thank you." The Soothsayer eagerly consumed the liquid.

"You have not told me about what happened," Ruby prodded for the explanation. While they traveled towards the village, Lilith was too intrigued by the environment to unravel why she joined the Red Demon's quest.

"Right," Lilith sighed. "I… performed a spell. I had a peculiar reaction to it for a reason I cannot comprehend. It started with a familiar burning void, then something that made me feel alive and powerful. After that, even my grandmother could not touch my skin. She said it felt like I was yanking strength from her heart."

"Have you informed the nature witches?" Ruby was exceptionally inquisitive.

"Yes—three of my Nana's friends. They mentioned the same thing."

"But I did not feel that." When Ruby grazed her finger across Lilith's wrist, it felt like a pleasant shock of cold electricity. She had never experienced it, but she was confident that no power was jerked away from her.

Why? she asked the whispers instead.

Use your head, the demon chided. *You have read about this before.*

I have? Ruby searched her memory for anything that matched the description she was given—a spell, a burning void and the ability to steal strength.

"Wait," she exclaimed suddenly.

The Soothsayer that resided in her head flashed her an image that confirmed her suspicion.

"You were the witch that performed the spell that turned a Morakque into bones?" Ruby was utterly baffled to have found someone who knew of such a spell. She had recollected the contents within the book she read, which indicated a heated vacancy within the chest.

The witch beside her hesitated before admitting to the act.

"Have you been experiencing that void since childhood?"

Lilith perked up before responding, "Indeed."

Ruby paused, analyzing a line that reflected in her mind repeatedly. She sprinted through the memories of the book, thinking of the change in the color of Lilith's eyes.

Suddenly, it all made sense.

"There was a book I read," Ruby started. "Queen Lysandra wrote the autobiography a thousand years ago, and she quoted something familiar. As far as I know, she was the only witch in history who could perform a deadly spell. People had tried it, but without fate's permission, no one succeeded. Her eyes gradually turned black, and she was followed by shadows wherever she went."

"Queen Lysandra?" Lilith repeated as she registered the information.

"Yes, a forgotten witch. She had accomplished far more than Dahlia ever had."

Her companion widened her eyes, startled that Ruby dared to speak that way about the first sorcerer who lived. Dahlia was a person to be worshipped, not hated.

"Lysandra once allied with humans as the ruler of Dicera. She married the king, which gave her descendants royal blood. Many villagers adored the reign of Eara, but Morakques hated that their ruler was a witch and the Queen of Darkness. They saw to it that their sentiments were forced upon the people, which resulted in widespread support for the hunters," explained Ruby. "Any offspring with the blood of previous sovereigns have the right to claim the throne. This created a policy that only allows one child and partner, so there is never a time when there is more than one possible ruler. For example, the child of a king and queen would eventually take the throne, marry somebody, and then conceive a child. This ensures that the royal bloodline dating a thousand years ago continues ruling."

Ruby had gotten all of her claims from books written just two decades ago.

"That is so dangerous," said Lilith. "If that one child dies before marrying, does that mean the royal bloodline disappears?"

"Technically, yes. But there have been times when more than one child was conceived. It is against the rules, but it has happened." Ruby felt proud to have remembered such a prodigious amount of information. She could even recall fun facts: if someone were from the royal bloodline, they would all bear a similar mark.

"Does this mean a witch is ruling right now? If Lysandra is part of the royal bloodline, all of her descendants would be witches."

"I cannot be sure." Ruby frowned. "At one point, something must have happened to the witches and warlocks in the royal bloodline. Perhaps the magic in the bloodline has diminished. Or, someone who did not belong to the throne managed to take it." She was almost certain of the latter because it was improbable for a witch to still be on the throne. Ruby might be uninformed of the present state of royalty, but she was not daft. A witch would not sit idle while their people were approaching extinction.

"I am sure that a witch is still ruling the kingdom."

Ruby was taken aback. "How so?"

"My grandmother once said that Morakques first came together to get rid of ruling witches. Since they still exist, a witch must still be on the throne."

"I doubt it," Ruby said, gazing at the dazzling stars obliterating the blanket of darkness. "While it is true that they despised the witch queen Lysandra and aimed to dethrone her, their resentment towards witches was what truly gathered them. Morakques wish to wipe out the remaining witches to ensure none of us can ever rule Dicera. Besides, if a witch were on the throne, they would fight for freedom and peace between our kind and humans."

Lilith shrugged, seeming too tired for the new

knowledge. She said, "I have never heard of the reign of Eara."

It was a tradition in Dicera for royalty to name their reign after the combination of their names. The reign of Eara, also known as the rule of King Earl Gretea the Forth and Queen Lysandra, was the most prominent in all of history.

"The queen made such a tremendous influence over the kingdom. She was the first witch to exist alongside Dahlia," Ruby said, remembering the wish she had made. She had prayed for a spell that would allow her to leave the protective barrier trapping her at home, and she received it through a vision.

"Why are witches not aware of this?"

"Lysandra was known to be someone very, very…" She attempted to find a word that could describe the queen's writing in her book. When Ruby picked it up for the first time, it looked like it had never been touched in hundreds of years.

"Evil?" Lilith guessed.

"Well, she was vindictive but still managed to have a big heart."

Lilith nodded pensively, then asked, "Why do you think there have never been royals who helped us?"

Ruby felt a pinch of ire. "I assume they believe they are doing us a favor by not hunting us. They are afraid of challenging the Morakques and have grown content with their cowardice."

Lilith regarded Ruby with a contemplating look. "I like

to believe that they are trying and failing. I pray to the wind frequently in hopes that they will be successful."

Ruby smiled, finding it amusing and incredible that Lilith's mindset differed so vastly from hers.

During the brief moment of silence that followed, she called for a few butterflies to grace them with their presence with her ability. The insects looked like they were glistening under the moonlight.

"Have I told you that this is impressive?" Lilith said, smiling at the creatures that belonged to nature.

"You have, actually," Ruby said.

"How do you do that?" Lilith asked while leaning towards the insects for a closer look. "I have never been able to control my magic. When I encounter strong emotions, I trigger it without meaning to." She shrugged. "It has a mind of its own."

A wave of bewilderment slammed Ruby square in the chest. Nature demanded balance, so she was born with the whispers in her mind to share her overwhelming strength. Perhaps, Lilith was given a companion as well.

"Can your abilities express their feelings through voices?"

"No. It is just difficult to control because I have never found a decent method."

"Oh," Ruby muttered. "If it is just your magic, there is a technique I can share."

A grin swept across Lilith's face as she nodded.

"After bottling up your emotions, you can visualize your magic as a thread to be pulled. If you gently tug on it, you will receive a vision that consumes your feelings but does not overwhelm your mind." Ruby struggled mightily with her detrimental abilities before discovering a solution.

"Truly?" Lilith widened her eyes, then dropped her jaw when Ruby performed a simple trick.

Butterflies were lured from the bushes outside the cave to the beautiful blossoms within Ruby's palms. They fluttered towards the plants with fragile wings before landing with grace.

Lilith beheld an expression of astonishment as she held out her hand to the delicate insect. Her hand unintentionally nudged her friend's, but Ruby felt nothing but a comfortable heat that pooled in the body she shared with a demon.

Ruby could have sworn that a few butterflies that she summoned discovered a way to invade her stomach.

CHAPTER FOURTEEN

The uneven ground made a horrid bed.

Lilith struggled to fall asleep due to the uncomfortable floor and the insects that ceaselessly skittered around their homes. For a second after she awoke to the golden rays of the morning sun, she assumed that she was home with her grandmother.

Then the memories came flooding back—the bundle of bones, the goodbyes, and Ruby. She had left the Forest of Dahlia.

Before Lilith set off to the outside world, she had intended to visit a human healer to examine her condition. She accepted that there were no alternative solutions. After all, her power now repulsed witches, with the exception of Ruby. However, with her newfound knowledge about Lysandra and her affinity for darkness, she was beginning to realise seeking human assistance would be no help at all.

"Morning," Ruby chirped. "A horrible morning, but one nonetheless."

"Horrible," Lilith agreed as she sat upright. Her body was hurting all over, and she was undeniably in a foul mood.

"The aches are merciless. I have explored the area and gathered some herbs that might help."

It was a charming act that lightened the Soothsayer's mood by a fraction. It was absurd to believe the angel beside her was formerly feared as the infamous Red Demon. "That is nice of you," she said.

"Do not mention it. Someone reminded me."

"Who?"

Ruby appeared mentally conflicted and said nothing for a moment. Her red eyes were clouded with doubt until she explained, "I was born with another soul which rules over my Soothsaying ability. It is a being with many voices that can control me if I am not careful."

Lilith had heard of such manifestations before, but never conversed with anybody who suffered from it. It was interesting to ponder about.

Two souls with different personalities sharing one body.

It sounded difficult, and those who had to endure such an experience were doubtlessly strong.

"Have you told anybody about this?" she asked.

"No," Ruby responded. "I have decided to share because the whispers like you."

"Truly?" Lilith asked with a small grin. "I am flattered."

"Well, you should be. It is certainly rare for it to care about anyone."

The witches gladly vacated the cave where they spent the night and headed west to the village. There, they could trade for more crops with precious flowers to replenish their dwindling supply. The kingdom viewed magnificent plants as accessories that could be sold for an incredible price, depending on their beauty. With a significant amount of food, they could leave to travel towards the place where Morakques resided—the Fort of Morakques.

They crossed foliage and stunning insects as they tramped, following their map. Lilith halted in her tracks to pick some lovely blossoms beside a narrow stream of water before sauntering into a vast stretch of land.

To their left, the witches could see mountains that grew and shrunk as they walked. It was a scenery that could never be forgotten, for none of them had ever seen something so otherworldly. There were enormous spikes of rocks that nature managed to sculpt into perfection.

They traveled towards their destination with a mix of enthusiasm and dread. Lilith was sure that the village did not exist until constructions and specks that formed human figures came into view.

"We are here," Ruby said, unable to keep the awe from her voice. They had never seen anything like the houses in the village. The residents living within were engaged in a commotion that could be heard from a thousand feet away.

Lilith whispered the wind's prayer to calm her pounding heart. She turned to look at Ruby, who was turning her naturally red eyes to brown.

Before they stepped too close to the village, Lilith grabbed the mirror that she kept within reach at all times. She needed to convert the apprehension in her heart to her ability before it became too heavy to bear.

"Tell me what you see," Ruby said, encouraging her to wield her power.

She closed her eyes before raising the mirror in her palm and recalling the steps she was taught. She visualized her ability as a thread and carefully wrapped a mentally formed hand around the thin line. When she pulled, a vision blossomed in her mind instantly.

Lilith could make out nothing in the first second until the image sharpened, causing a patch of dandelions to materialize in her mind. The flowers would have been beautiful if not for the splatters of blood and the heaviness of anguish lingering in the air.

She gasped as she fluttered her eyes open and returned to consciousness with a future message. However, she was more startled by the sight of her eyes in the mirror than the vision she received.

The whites of her eyes had dark speckles, and the whole of her irises had become an unnatural black. There was no hint of the bright hazel eyes she possessed just a few days ago.

"They have been this color since morning," Ruby said as if such a thing were normal. For Lilith, it was the strangest and most unnerving occurrence. She could barely believe that it was possible.

"Is there something wrong with me?" she asked with a replenished flood of fear in her heart.

"Queen Lysandra had experienced the same thing. It is a change that means darkness is seeping into the soul." Ruby frowned. "I do not quite know what it means, but it *did* happen in history. It might not be a negative change in the slightest."

Darkness. What did that word mean? Lilith wished that she could just call upon the witch Lysandra herself to answer the question.

As she explained what she saw in her vision, the two

young women wandered closer to the village. They had never seen humans who were not witches or Morakques, and their cluelessness might doom them.

Lilith felt exhilarated as they entered the village. The foreign place was lovely and stood in stark contrast to home, where tents were used in place of enormous, complex buildings. At the thought of the Forest of Dahlia, she received a pang of nostalgia.

"Do you miss home?" The question slipped from Lilith's lips.

Ruby was alighted with awe at their surroundings but was quick to divert her attention to Lilith. She pondered before replying, "I miss my father." Sadness marred her face. "He is the only person who sees me. In his eyes, I am not just some valiant protector."

"Not the forest?"

"Well, home is where the heart is, and my heart is here with you." Ruby planted her palm on her chest with an impish smile. "There is not much I miss about the place. Frankly, I felt like a prisoner."

Lilith nodded empathetically. "I understand. You were treated more like a service than a person. It was a mean environment."

Ruby seemed flabbergasted before a pleased grin appeared on her countenance. "I quite like you, Lilith."

"I do hope so. We are stuck together for some time to come."

The two continued ambling, deep in conversation. It took five minutes after stepping into the periphery of the area where a group of homes were closely situated for an uncomfortable heaviness to descend upon them. Lilith was suddenly weakened, as though a substantial portion of her spirit was ripped away.

"Our magic is being constrained," Ruby said. She jerked forward, resembling a being who had a hand slammed onto her back.

Villagers were beginning to stare at the two witches, and Lilith felt incredibly out of place. She knew that if anyone suspected her of being a witch, she might be publicly beheaded. Her grandmother warned her about the fact excessively before she ventured into the world beyond the Forest of Dahlia.

The border was now a distance away, and they could not escape.

"Are you alright?" Lilith questioned. She widened her eyes as Ruby struggled to breathe. It was too late when she realized that they had walked into a trap. The village was not governed by royalty but by Morakques.

"We have to get out," Ruby managed to force out as she doubled over. The strength of her abilities was immense and possibly too painful to steal. The spell in the area was undoubtedly consuming her along with her magic.

Lilith kept her head down as she assisted her friend between the narrow gap of two houses. Mercifully, the villagers stepped away from their path as if Ruby was experiencing a contagious surge of nausea.

"We need to get closer to the border," Lilith panicked. The sight of Ruby's eyes flickering between red and brown was enough to get them both executed.

She racked her brain for a solution that could save

them. All she needed was a safe route towards the side of the village, where they would be unaffected by the enchantment of the area.

If they did not avoid *everybody* in the crowded place where they were trapped, they would meet their end.

Distress filled Lilith's chest as she scanned her surroundings, hoping nobody would approach them.

With Ruby's arm around her shoulder, she paced towards the north. She took only one step before feeling a hand on her shirt.

It belonged to a young man.

CHAPTER FIFTEEN

Lilith was seconds from executing a spell. She was willing to do anything to save her new friend—her coven's only hope.

"Is she fine?" asked the stranger. The boy appeared as fragile as glass, but his twinkling green eyes showed an immense amount of determination and compassion. He had a friendly face, but she knew the art of trickery and the danger of being a sorcerer around an ordinary human. His brown hair was as dark as wood in the shadows, and it suited the shape of his face.

"Yes," Lilith lied. The strain in her voice gave her away, and she could only hope that the boy was intelligent enough to leave. Ruby was slumped on her shoulder, incessantly letting out soft cries of pain.

"Obviously not," remarked the boy dryly. He was dangerously close to her, and every bone in her body urged her to flee.

If he were to take any sudden action, she was ready to strike with magic. It would take merely five seconds to trace symbols on the dirt and mumble an incantation that would make bones out of the boy.

"Here, let me—" The boy attempted to assist Lilith when his hand grazed her skin. Instantly, he drew back and sharply inhaled a breath of air.

Her eyes grew wide. She assumed that her skin only caused a reaction from witches.

"Witch," stated the boy.

Oh, no. Lilith began to sketch the symbols with her feet but came to an abrupt stop when he lowered his back before her.

"I'll carry her," he said. "Quickly. There's a spell in this area that'll temporarily steal your ability." He turned to narrow his eyes. "You wouldn't want your friend to shrivel up and die, would you?"

"What?" she questioned dumbly, casting a worried glance at Ruby. A human would never assist a witch, and it was too risky to count on him.

The boy was growing impatient. He held out a hand, and to Lilith's utter astonishment, a little plant appeared in his palm. "I am a sorcerer, too," he said.

She was reluctant, but she did not have an abundance of time. As she spoke a silent prayer to the wind, she allowed the boy to carry her friend.

They took a wise route that took advantage of the shadows created by houses. Anxiety crept into Lilith's heart with the mere thought of everything that could go wrong. The boy who claimed and proved to be a witch was familiar with the village, and the fact puzzled her. She thought witches only existed in the Forest of Dahlia.

The pressure in her heart had mostly vanished. A sigh of relief escaped her lips as Ruby's state gradually improved. Beads of perspiration had formed on her skin from her struggle a few minutes ago.

"In here," informed the boy as he came to a stop. In

front of them was a small, medieval village house with multiple stories. He set Ruby down on the smooth, stone floor after he entered.

Lilith was still uncertain about his intentions, but a course of comfort seeped into her bones. They were safe at the moment, away from groups of villagers.

The house was a lovely place. There was a shelf of books beside the door and a table littered with papers. Numerous candles were positioned around the room to illuminate the area leading to the stairs.

"What are your names?" asked the boy. His eyes were fixed on Ruby's intimidating red ones.

"Lilith," she said truthfully, then gestured to her friend. "This is Ruby." If the boy was genuine, there was no reason to lie.

"Witches," he muttered as though he could not believe it. "You're not safe yet. It is best in the attic; nobody goes up there."

"Why in Dicera are you stashing us?" Ruby rasped, now able to speak. "Do you fancy keeping us as pets?" Her eyes brightened slightly as she flashed the boy a distrustful look.

"Not in the slightest," he retorted. "The last thing I'd want to do is capture a witch."

"What are you doing now, then?" Lilith asked.

"Saving your lives," he said as if it was the most obvious thing in the world. "This village is no place for a witch. Furthermore, I have many questions."

"Then what are *you* doing here?"

"I've got minimal choices, considering who my father

is," he said, a hint of unpleasantness crossing his face. "Look, we have to go now before he returns."

Upon hearing the panic in his voice, the witches hurried to ascend the stairs. Her current situation dumbfounded Lilith, but the outcome was not necessarily terrible. If the young man were as charming as he seemed, it would be a blessing from Dahlia herself.

"I'll visit the two of you soon," he told the witches after arriving at the loft.

"Wait. You have not shared your name," Lilith reminded. A part of her hoped to trust the boy.

"Marco," he responded before rushing from the attic.

CHAPTER SIXTEEN

Ruby experienced several ripples of anguish that unnerved her more than she would like to admit.

Her body spasmed violently in the aftermath of the pain she endured. It was as if hands were crushing her soul to clutch her abilities. They gripped it with terrorizing force, striving to heave it from its home. It was a traumatizing agony enhanced by the hollering of the voices in her mind.

Although she had calmed down from the situation, the memory remained fresh in her head. Her only distraction was the boy, Marco, whose presence caused a strange reaction from the demon. It became quiet, but it was unlike how it silenced itself around Lilith to heed her voice. This time, the demon was upset and mute.

Can he be trusted? Ruby asked. Only the demon knew if he would lead her to death.

Yes.

It was the only confirmation she needed.

The boy occasionally returned to provide food after she finished the last of her father's crops with her friend.

Lilith seemed to be completely at ease with Marco, although she did not know whether he had a heart of gold or greed. Whether he was keeping them safe out of sympathy or because he would adore the prizes that came with turning in the Red Demon. Ruby thought Lilith's optimism was dangerous, but it made her winsome.

Ruby was skeptical of Marco but had since composed herself after the demon's approval. After all, only *it* could see the future.

At the moment, she did not consider the risks of loitering in an unfamiliar place. At least she was under a roof.

The attic was comfortable. A discreet compartment hidden on the second floor's ceiling led to the satisfactorily decorated loft consisting of a bed, table set, music player, and candles. On two sides of the walls was a small window that displayed the activities of villagers.

Ruby sat on the table, examining the map. At the same time, Lilith gazed outside the glass pane, watching as others got on with their days without the slightest clue about the witches amongst them.

Ruby was awaiting Marco's arrival since he left them with dinner. She had questions that needed answers.

It took half an hour before he showed up once again, this time with two books.

"Hello, Witches," he greeted jovially.

"How is it that you are a witch?" Lilith inquired, still looking into the distance. Like Ruby, she appeared eager to fire her inquiries.

"If you must know, Lily," he said. "My mother had the blood of a sorcerer. She met my father, fell in love, and on one beautiful day, they felt an *irresistible* amount of lust—"

"Lilith," she corrected, "and that is enough."

"You wanted to know." He shrugged with a sly smile.

"Now, it is my turn to ask. Why are witches in the streets of Dakota?"

"Food," replied Ruby. It was not the entire truth, but she was unwilling to say any more. The boy might have proven that he was a witch, but he could be standing on the Morakques' side. And, considering how he was practically unaffected by the spell in the village, he was not a powerful magic wielder.

"Do you not have food in your forest?"

"It is *our* turn to ask a question," Ruby said instead. "Why did you help us?"

Marco placed the books in his hand on the bed before settling down on the chair. His eyes revealed that he was phrasing the sentences within his mind and struggling mightily to do so. Finally, he started, "I disagree with the treatment of witches. My mother was the only witch I'd ever seen. My father did not know what she was, and he was incredibly displeased when he found out. The old man did not even consider the possibility of male magic wielders."

Warlocks were exceptionally rare, but they existed, nonetheless. The first witches were women, and due to the difficulty of receiving a miracle that came in the form of a child, there were very few of them.

"I am not strong," he said, "but my mother told me plenty of things and left me items that could never be found anywhere else." He gestured to the books he had brought along. "My turn. Why do you look like that?"

"Like what?" Ruby questioned, somewhat offended.

"Like *that*. You have red eyes," Marco remarked, then

pointed at Lilith, "while Lily over here has the darkest pair I've ever seen, and not to mention, claws."

"She does not have claws," Ruby snorted, then gazed at her friend's nails. Some color leached from her face. They did not look like the talons he claimed they were, but it was, indeed, unnaturally pointed.

"I was born this way," she said, then struggled for an explanation to describe Lilith's sudden change in appearance. There was no reasonable lie that she could create.

"Darkness," he sighed. Ruby was relatively taken aback that he even knew of the word's meaning.

"You understand this transition?"

"Of course I do," Marco snickered. "It is written all over these." He grabbed one of the two books and flipped to a random page, pointed and read. "Any being with the power of darkness must be banished and restricted from returning."

The witches said nothing, but Ruby knew that both of them had one thing in mind—they had to get their hands on the book.

"I'd like to know what's with the lily in your hair," he asked Lilith. "There's an unfamiliar aura surrounding it."

"I am a Soothsayer; I would not know."

Ruby had not recognized the flower's magic. It differed significantly from Dahlia's eternal plants, but it seemed to possess the same enchantment—it remained unwithered and faultless even as time passed. She did not sense a hint of vileness from the lily.

"That's a horrible answer," he commented, "but I'll accept it."

Lilith gave a satisfied smile before pondering another question. "You mentioned something about your father," she stated. "What about him?"

"Should have seen this one coming," mumbled the boy before standing. For a moment, Ruby assumed that he would leave the question unanswered. Instead, he stood beside Lilith to stare at the busy streets and point at a man.

Driven by curiosity, the witches looked in the direction to see a typical middle-aged man. He seemed as common as one could get until Ruby recognized him.

"He's a Morakque," said Marco with a grimace.

No. He was so much more than that.

Ruby gaped at the familiar features of the man and his hair, styled into a bun.

He was not just a Morakque. He was the current leader of them all.

CHAPTER SEVENTEEN

Lilith was terrified. She had not recognized the man until her red-eyed friend notified her of his status.

Marco explained that his father was a Morakque. The harsh man exploded with rage when he discovered that his wife was a witch. Marco had detailed it with feigned nonchalance, but his despair was almost tangible. Lilith would have offered him solace by embracing him if he was not repulsed by her magic. He explained that his mother was distraught, certain that the Morakque would cast her out. Her distress led to a sickness that claimed her life. It was a story that devastated the witches, although it could be a story of pretense shared to acquire sympathy.

"How did your father react?" Ruby asked curiously. Lilith shot her a warning look, afraid that the question was insensible to Marco's sorrow.

However, he did not seem wounded by it. "Even now, I can't be sure. He isolated himself for a bit, but he remained a Morakque. Once, he claimed he had no choice, but it sounded like an excuse to me." There was a bitter edge to his voice. "Her death must not have affected him much."

"I am sorry to hear that," Lilith said, while, simultaneously, Ruby commented, "I agree."

"It's been a while since her passing," Marco muttered. "I was beside myself with grief and even tried to bring her back with a spell, but nothing in this wretched book works." He motioned to one of the hardcovers.

Lilith was as horrified as she was astonished at the prospect of bringing back the dead. She imagined summoning her mother, then shivered at the possibility of calling upon Dahlia, the first witch to exist.

"What is the book about?" Ruby jumped at the opportunity to ask about it.

"It's a transcription of 'The Forbidden Book of Lysandra', and it is a piece of trash."

"What?" Ruby poked in and smacked her hand over her lips.

The boy rolled his eyes and started to repeat, "It is a—"

"Yes, we get it. How in Dicera did you manage to get your hands on that? It was burned." From Ruby's awe, Lilith knew that the book was a valuable treasure.

"My mother," he said. "She was obsessed with learning about Lysandra's spells, which led to her banishment. She managed to complete two book transcriptions, and she cherished them greatly, which gives me the impression that they are very precious." He leaned closer to the girl with the glistening eyes of a demon without fear. "You seem to know something about Lysandra's book, and that is precisely why I chose to protect you from the villagers who would *love* to tear off your head."

"You want to know about it?" Lilith questioned and extended her arm. He laid the book in her palm, just as she wanted.

"If I didn't, I would have left the both of you in the middle of Dakota."

Lilith decided to believe that Marco was trustworthy. After all, he would have already done something if he intended to harm them.

The girl whose eyes were deliberately becoming the darkest color stared at her nails. The change was mild yet too difficult to ignore, and she hoped that something about her situation was written within the book. She diverted her attention to the priceless transcription she held, designed with a smooth red cover alongside golden stripes, bold words and a thick amount of dust.

She ran her hand over the word 'Lysandra' and pondered about the late woman. The Queen of Darkness. The book must have withheld a myriad of forgotten information.

She flipped through the first few pages, showing notes in cursive and intricate handwriting. It was messy, filled with underlined words and marks, but she understood enough.

It took only a few seconds for her to realize that she was clasping a transcription of Lysandra's Book of Shadows. She could not recognize many of the spells, but she expected nothing less. Her grandmother made a remarkable effort to ensure that she did not learn magic, and she finally understood. The woman was attempting to keep her safe and away from her reserved fate. The path consisted of darkness, and it was something that her coven would never allow.

Perhaps her grandmother knew about it long before she received any visions. Darkness could be a trait that ran in her bloodline; it was a possible reason for her mother's banishment.

There was an uncountable number of spells and their questionable names. The only spell Lilith recognized was a hazardous protection ritual known for taking numerous lives in return for safety. Morakques were said to have used it against royalty. She read each page's titles before flipping, noting that all spells could be used for incredibly evil or selfish purposes.

She recalled something Ruby said about such usage of spells.

Black magic.

The book was dedicated to it. Lilith looked through it thoroughly, flipping through pages that stated the possibility of ridiculous spells like transferring a lost soul into a jewel and even summoning a deceased being from the dead. She paused for a moment when she recognised one of them titled, 'A Bone to Pick'. The sight she beheld was familiar as well, for it was the moment given by her vision. The sorcery was the very one she used to turn a Morakque into bones.

While the book did include spell descriptions, their results were already implied by their names.

"None of those work," Marco chirped, invading her series of thoughts. "I've tried that bone spell because of its promising name. It ended up as a disappointment, as all things do."

"It does not work?" she asked, curiosity nipping at her mind.

"Definitely not."

"Maybe," Ruby interjected, "you are just not strong enough to perform any spells."

"I know I am not powerful," he bit back, "but if it is a real spell, I would know. Nothing would happen, but my power still drains."

"Darkness requires permission from fate."

"Yes, I knew that."

"Face it, you did not."

Marco narrowed his eyes at Ruby. He had a little smile tugging at the side of his lips as he said, "Did you look into my mind, Demon?"

"I could if I wanted to, so you better be careful."

The boy snorted, then waved his hands dismissively at the witch he conversed with. The two had gotten remarkably comfortable with each other, which further proved to Lilith that Marco was as generous as he seemed.

"The two of you can stay for as long as you need," he said. "I doubt you'd be willing to remain for long in the residence of a Morakque, but he is rarely home, and I *do* need friends."

"Are you aware of what your father does?" Lilith inquired after minutes of deliberation. If she were in his shoes, she would be a miserable person.

"In all honesty, I do not know the details," he said with a sigh. "I am mindful that he hunts down my kind with his little squad and kills the witches they capture when they're done with them." He frowned in displeasure. "I have never seen it happen, but I know it does. I cannot bear to watch them perish."

"You do not know of their mission?" she asked.

"No, but I would be grateful to know. Unfortunately, you would have to tell me tomorrow," Marco said. "Goodnight."

The boy did not linger for a reply before leaving the loft without the two books. Just as he left, Lilith and Ruby spontaneously darted to grab the second hardcover. Like the first, it was old and dirty but glamorous in the way only a rare item could be.

Its title was *A Witch's Rules* by Dahlia Ceris. A transcription of a book written by Dahlia that was full of jottings.

The book consisted of every sin that could be committed before the banishment of a witch. Lilith knew that on one of these pages, her mother's act of betrayal would be scribbled down. The first rule stated was about the act of a witch eloping with royalty, followed by forbidden magic. If she had stayed any longer in the forest, she would have been inevitably expelled.

"We were so close to death," Lilith said, going back to staring outside the window. She recalled how Ruby had doubled over in pain and shuddered.

The sky was a continuous dark stretch of nothingness, suspended by the lovely moon and stars. If she were back home in the forest, she would have been dancing on her own, bathing in starlight as if it were made for her. She would have her Nana join her for a quick laugh while a garland of flowers bounced on her head.

She was quiet and drowning in memories when her friend sauntered over to stand beside her.

"We are lucky to have escaped it," Ruby replied.

"I have the sudden urge to hug my Nana," Lilith admitted. It was the only thing on her mind.

"I am sure she feels the same way." Ruby appeared reflective. "We will return after succeeding in our quest."

"Do you think we will?"

"Yes." Ruby sounded so impossibly certain, but her eyes betrayed her.

Lilith was afraid. She had been afraid for a long while, but being trapped in a home that was not hers during such a marvelous night made her realize just how fearsome the trip was. She was missing out on many things for a mission that might end atrociously.

She needed a distraction, a new memory.

She trod towards the music player and randomly selected a song with a classical tune. She turned to Ruby and asked, "Would you perhaps… want to dance?"

With a raised eyebrow, her companion took Lilith's inviting hand. When she danced, thoughts escaped her mind, and enchantments would capture her soul. She would be bewitched by the music and willingly lose herself to it.

The witches swirled and tripped and laughed for what seemed like hours. They shared stories and swayed to the rhythm of the never-ending melodies that played in the background while grasping each other's hands without the intention of letting go.

They blatantly ignored how Ruby could touch Lilith's skin and not feel a hint of repulsion. It was a miracle, and Lilith feared speaking about it would somehow change it.

They were far from home to achieve freedom for their kind. However, as they danced under the striking moonlight, Lilith was confident that she had experienced the best kind of freedom, even though she was lost.

CHAPTER EIGHTEEN

Lilith forgot how many days she dwelled in Marco's home. It could have been a week or even more, but she was unsure because nothing had changed. Nothing but her physical appearance.

"Hello, Witches," Marco greeted as he poked his head into the attic. His sudden entrances had become a regular occurrence.

"Morning," she said with a grin. She sat before the table with The Forbidden Book of Lysandra before her. She had been eyeing two spells for an exceptionally long time.

"Lily, the whites of your eyes are black," he informed casually.

"She panicked about it earlier today," Ruby uttered from the corner of the bed.

The modification of Lilith's features was a factor in wrecking the success of their trip. The traits she inherited from darkness made her look more like a demon than her red-eyed friend. It was a pity that she was not a Concealer like Ruby; anybody who glanced her way would know her true nature.

"I cannot find information that will remove it," she said, despondent. Fate did not plan on taking back the darkness despite her unwillingness to accept it.

"You can't get rid of it, but I might know a solution

that'll help control it," Marco said abruptly, as if finally remembering a piece of invaluable knowledge. Lilith perked up. "An immortality vial—it is rumored to be so golden that it burns your eyes. It can strengthen and assist in controlling your magic, as well as remove it."

"I read that somewhere before," Ruby interjected. "Only its creator, Lysandra, knows the ingredients and spell."

Lilith slumped in disappointment. If only she could bargain with the wind for a chance to speak with Lysandra.

"It is a shame that she's probably a rotting corpse by now," he spoke. Marco ducked instantly, expecting the smack that Ruby aimed for his head. As she began to chastise him for his discourtesy, Lilith returned to the spells she had been eyeing.

She knew that she could not afford to be reckless, for whatever dark conjugations she planned to perform would work. However, the promises of the results were too tempting to refuse. Their names were 'Reach Out to a Loved One' and 'Reach to the Dead'. She wanted to speak with her grandmother, and she would love nothing more than to uncover the mystery of her mother. The woman was ejected from the forest and would be inescapably killed by the dangers of the outside world.

"What are you looking at?" Ruby asked, lowering herself to scrutinize the witchcraft Lilith wanted desperately to execute.

"Don't mind her," Marco said. "I caught her memorizing multiple hexes that are pure evil, so do not ask and do not anger her."

Indeed, Lilith had studied fatal spells that could twist the guts of a person. She prayed that she would never use them, but the trip she embarked on demanded additional precautions.

"I want to do this," she decided. The room went quiet.

"It's dark magic," he said. The boy was wrong to think that the single line could convince her to decide otherwise.

"It is simple, and it certainly is not evil. I just hope to see how my coven is doing."

"What if something happens?" Ruby asked, sounding too concerned. She was possibly the only person who could change Lilith's mind. "Darkness is not something to be played with. It is dangerous."

"I know," Lilith said, "but I will be careful."

"Fine, but do not lose yourself in it." Ruby looked uncertain and against the idea. Lilith knew it was not intelligent, but she craved to attempt another spell within the book. It would indicate that she genuinely was poisoned by the forbidden enchantment of darkness.

With the help of Ruby, she dampened her hand and wrote down the symbols on the page. Then, she spoke out the magical incantation.

Nothing happened.

Marco was stifling a scream as he hid behind Ruby, but nothing bizarre transpired. Contrary to the usual drain, Lilith felt her power strengthen, but she perceived no spark of sorcery.

"It does not work," she said, slightly disappointed.

Just as everyone was sure that it was a failed attempt, black mist erupted from the table and formed a smoky circle. Lilith jumped back, then gazed in wonder as the gap within the shape became a motioning image. She could recognize the woman and the house it displayed with outstanding clarity.

"Nana," she mumbled. The girl refused to prolong the image by chanting the incantation, knowing the risk of doing so. Darkness was a complex thing, and it was better not to dive into its depths.

Her grandmother looked well but tired. She was studying the senior's exhausted features when the smoky mirror-like phenomenon vanished into nothing.

"That is…" Marco was speechless.

"It is crazy," Ruby murmured in astonishment. "I have never seen anything like it."

"It is quite extraordinary," Lilith agreed. "It is overpowering and alarming, but it feels—"

She halted upon the enthusiastic yelling outside the house. Curiosity urged her to stand and peer out the window.

"What is happening?" Ruby asked.

Marco faltered as he looked outward from the clear glass pane to where his father was positioned with a sickening grin. A terrifying blast of fear crossed his face.

On a wooden block beside two houses were two robust villagers holding down a miserable woman. A group of commoners surrounded the area with radiant and reassuring smiles, as though they were doing Dicerians a tremendous favor.

"What are they doing to her?" Lilith questioned, although the truth was reflected before her eyes.

The woman struggled to escape while shrieking over the cheering. She sounded like a vulnerable animal, resigned to a dreadful fate due to a committed crime. However, the petite woman looked far from a monster; nothing would be atypical if she were to walk the streets of Dakota as a villager.

"I know what she is," Ruby said under her breath. Although they knew nothing of the situation, it was patently unpleasant.

"Criminal?" Marco asked quietly, as though speaking too loudly was a sin.

"No," she replied. The woman was bellowing and crying as the men slammed her head on a slab of stone.

Lilith felt a spike of fear attack every bone in her body as she, too, understood. The woman had a bracelet with a shimmering obsidian stone around her wrist, which inadvertently revealed everything a Morakque needed to know.

"If she's a witch, why isn't she doing anything?" Marco muttered.

"She could be a Soothsayer," Lilith explained as another wave of anxiety washed over her. She had to do *something*, anything.

Yet, the sorcerers could only watch as the Morakques' leader ascended the wooden block with a massive and formidable axe. Lilith could discern the bloodstains on the wickedly broad bit and the merciless silver cheek of the weapon.

"We have to do something," Ruby exclaimed anxiously.

"A spell," Lilith said, frantically flipping open the

transcripted book once written by Lysandra. In her state of panic, nothing was present in her mind.

"We can't." Marco reached out to stop her but lunged back as his hand grazed hers. "Calm down. Your skin is heating up," he started, then glanced at his blistering skin and cursed. "You must not give away our position. It's a risk, and we might go down with her."

They returned their stare to the witch outside. Ruby gasped as the Morakque held up his axe, then forcefully brought it down. There was no time to do anything as it severed the neck of the witch into two.

Lilith's vision blurred at the sight. At what just happened. At the thundering applause and whooping that followed the public *execution* of her kind.

The villagers in Dakota celebrated the death of the innocent. They believed that being born different was a crime.

Sobs sounded from beside her. The emotions bubbling within her heart were on the brink of explosion, and she knew Ruby felt the same. Wrath, fear, disdain, and sorrow built on the strength fed by darkness, calling out to her immense buried power.

"You have to leave," Marco voiced out her thoughts.

"Now," Ruby said with blazing eyes. Yet, her voice was so different from her own—it echoed with numerous voices of different pitches.

"I'll miss both of you," he said, on the verge of weeping. He turned to grab the two valuable books in his possession and handed them over to the red-eyed girl. "Take this, and please, stay safe."

The power escalating in her heart was becoming too difficult to control. If she and Ruby stayed any longer, the house would be engulfed in flames.

He fumbled with the door that led downstairs and began to bawl. "Goodbye, Demon," he told Ruby, then looked over to her. "Lily, you shall not dare forget me." As he opened the trapdoor, he said, "Good luck with your mission."

The witches nodded, distancing themselves from the boy who had taken them in when they most needed it. They were about to leave when he blurted, "Wait!"

The girls swiveled around to look at him.

"I'll catch a carriage and meet you in Elymore—the town closest to the castle. It's safe for witches."

"Why?" Incredulity seeped into Ruby's voice. Lilith found it odd too, for leaving meant putting his life in peril.

"I won't laze around while the both of you waltz into danger. My father ought to know that I will never follow in his footsteps."

The image of the beheaded witch flashed time and time again in Lilith's head. She inhaled sharply, then forced a smile for Marco, her friend, one last time.

"We will achieve freedom for our kind," she promised, then scrambled outside and into the wilderness beyond the bounds of Dakota.

CHAPTER NINETEEN

Ruby clasped Lilith's hand as if letting go meant losing her forever.

The demon was an awakening, raging creature inside her body. The terror summoned by the headless witch had shredded away the intellect she might have once possessed, leaving just sheer instinct to guide her movements. Immediately, she reached out for one thread in her heart—the Soothsayer thread—and pulled. As much as she loathed the whispers, its presence provided her with some manner of reassurance.

Her emotions spiraled like an endless tropical cyclone, the memories flooding her mind again. She had seen a witch's death before, but never the act of beheading. Never the sight of people born the same way as she, celebrating a tragic demise.

She had never witnessed anything more traumatic.

The now-dead witch was fighting and weeping, yet her cries for help were silenced by gleeful yells. Her head had soared in the air, face permanently fixed in an expression of agony. Her blood splattered the ground like blossomed petals, painting the village path scarlet under the glaring sun and vermillion under shadows.

The crowd applauded.

They applauded for a cruel death.

Nausea crawled in Ruby's stomach, much worse than the one she had received when she first saw a witch's death. Then, it was a spear to the heart, surrounded by witches who grieved for the dead sorceress. Now, it was an axe across the neck, surrounded by villagers who *detested* the dead magic-wielder.

She had never felt such intense emotions.

She sprinted away from the village with Lilith's hand in hers. It had burned Marco, but it felt cold in her palm.

Ruby was on the brink of eruption.

She had tried to bury the building pressure within her and simply feed it to the threads. She thought she could gently tug on them and return to her calm state. However, there was too much power. A gentle pull would never work; her magic was too profound.

She had books in her hands while Lilith carried the map and a pouch by her side. Marco had assisted them in selling the flowers they had arrived with and earned them a handful of coins.

They wandered deep into the wild behind the village, where shrubs and towering trees were dense.

Ruby was blinded by her tremendous power and the dread of releasing it. It was enough to ruin the kingdom, and the demon wanted nothing more than to use it.

Consume it before it consumes you.

She stopped, swaying wildly before lowering to her knees. Lilith fell with her, panting.

Ruby's vision blurred, and it took a moment to realize that it was tears that blinded her. She dropped the book, crying as she dug her hands into the woodland ground.

She could have saved the woman. She could have killed the Morakque right there, in front of villagers. It would have landed her in fatal danger, but she could have done *something* to help. Instead, she watched in silence.

"I can't..." Lilith said between gasps. Tears streamed from her eyes and seeped into the earth like a perishing waterfall.

An infuriated storm of misery attacked Ruby mercilessly. The emotions were still enhancing, and the whispers were rapidly increasing in volume. What was once soft voices became a cacophony of screaming.

Release it, chanted a voice.

If you are so fond of dying, allow me to take control, said another.

She did not know what Lilith was enduring, but she could imagine her struggle. The Soothsayer already struggled with control; for her, an abundance of power would be impossible to tame.

Ruby watched her friend in anguish as she continued to gasp for breath.

Lilith had her eyes squeezed shut and her hands clenched into tight fists. Perhaps she was already receiving waves of distorted visions, or she was still attempting to calm herself. Whatever she was withstanding, it looked unbearable.

Ruby could barely focus on anything with the chaos in her mind, but still, she tried to fix an unwavering stare on her friend. It allowed her to observe the most startling event.

Her friend fluttered open her pitch-black eyes, and the distress drained from her face in an instant. From Lilith's back, three human-like figures burst into existence. They looked like shadows created by inky smoke. They moved gracefully, like real people with flexible bodies.

Disbelief stole Ruby's tongue. She refused to look away even as her head flooded with ardent and intolerable noises. The demon was delighted, and she could not comprehend the reason.

Her friend was still panting but had gathered enough strength to approach Ruby and engulf her in a tight embrace. Ruby was still sobbing as she tried to dismiss the commands of her abilities and the howling of the voices.

Release your magic.

Do it, or eternal pain will rip you apart.

There was no other way. She tried to push it down, to forget and to calm herself. *Nothing* worked. She could only pray that releasing her powers would not result in a royal disaster.

With a shaky, illusory hand, she reached out to the threads in her heart. They were filled to the brim with emotions—*power*.

Please, Queen Lysandra of the Eara Reign, she thought as she gripped the strings connected to abilities in her heart. *Do not let me doom the world.*

She jerked the threads.

At the movement, the whispers praised her and silenced their bawling. However, the demon did not instantly seize control like the greedy animal it was. It merely offered a contorted vision of a boy—Marco.

The emotions that swelled within her chest bloomed and withered, like letting go of a hefty sack after decades of bearing its weight. The world before her eyes flared with colors—a mix of tangerine and marigold. Flames fired from her fingertips and leapt to the woods, incinerating the leaves that surrounded her. A strained cry escaped her lips as a ripple of agony thundered in her chest before evaporating.

She was burning the kingdom's grounds, but the lack of emotion in her heart did not give her the capability to care. Only her mind spun with concern, but it was slowly diminishing.

As another wail sounded, this time from the memory of the headless woman, a cord of lightning split the sky in half and produced a brewing, unnatural storm.

It started with quiet and cold droplets that kissed her skin, then progressed to become a downpour. It extinguished the fire and spattered the ground relentlessly, like a determined act of vengeance towards the flames.

Ruby was still heaving after returning to a decent state of mind. With the last of her remaining strength, she called upon plants and their leaves to save the books and map from the furious storm. It was the least she could do while she was still conscious.

She turned her head to the side, where a line of wild creatures was situated. She had summoned them meaning to. The animals watched with stillness as Ruby drowned herself in what felt like an ocean of tears. Her abilities had stolen her emotions and energy, but somehow, the despair remained.

Sorrow is a gift, told the whispers when they were but a child, soothing like the generous mother she never had. *If sadness ceased to exist, happiness would be worthless.*

Fatigued and stripped of magic, Ruby drowsed off into a slumber in the solacing arms of Lilith.

CHAPTER TWENTY

Lilith gazed at the shadows surrounding her. They became a cocoon of smoke, made from the phenomenon that haunted her. It was a mystery she could not grasp. The dark figures seemed like intelligent beings with minds of their own, and she could not comprehend the purpose of their existence.

She had fought to conceal her ability as the power in her heart stretched thin, then erupted to form the silhouette-like creatures that ceaselessly followed her like pets. Was she the master of them, or were they the master of her?

Maybe darkness was another ability she possessed, for they were not spells but a core power that she could utilize. It became a fraction of her soul, despite how much she wanted it to evaporate into nothingness.

Lilith stroked Ruby's hair like an affectionate lover. For the young woman to create a ferocious storm that could brew throughout the entire sky of Dicera reflected the stupendous number of emotions clutching her heart like a persistent pest. It had been several hours since she dozed off in Lilith's arms.

From a raging hurricane, Ruby's feelings had calmed to become a dying storm.

A soft breeze that carried the scent of nature wafted

through the air and lifted a few strands of Lilith's hair. The phantom hands of the wind reached out to one of the precious books Marco gifted and managed to turn the hardcover to a certain page. The current of air halted.

Peering at the book, Lilith found her eyes settling once again on the spell titled, 'Reach to the Dead'. She knew better than to even consider performing it, but the incantation lingered on the tip of her tongue and the symbols on the tip of her fingertips. She wanted to speak to her mother so badly.

One of her dark figures approached the book and then traced the symbols on the moist dirt floor. They could not touch the earth, but Lilith could see the ghost of the symbols she had memorised written on the ground. Even her shadows were urging her to seek the mother she could barely remember.

The dark figures could not speak, but their actions were clearer than wielded words.

"What are you?" Lilith whispered to them, knowing she would only receive silence. She doubted that the ghosts could comprehend what she said.

The Forbidden Book of Lysandra remained on the page as if begging her to carry out the spell. Even fate wanted her to visit her mother.

And when fate called, no individual could disregard it.

The world seemed to stand between her and the book. Logic compelled her to turn away, but a stronger sensation tugged at her heart. Suddenly, she was back in the Forest of Dahlia, following the push of wind to the still water of the pond.

The page revealed its complexity with its additional notes, warning that the spell was not necessarily used to visit the soul of a deceased loved one. Instead, any lurking and dead being could be called upon if they were in the same bloodline as the witch who began the conjuration. Lilith also needed a sort of insight into whomever she planned to summon. The spell was unlike many others, for it required ingredients. Two ingredients that Lilith possessed—a mirror and a blood obsidian.

It was tempting.

She positioned Ruby's head against a tree and grinned as one of her shadows stayed alongside the sleeping witch. They had taken an intriguing liking to Ruby.

"Should I do it?" Lilith whispered to the wilderness. The only response she received was the wind's whisper.

With one spell, she could unveil the mysteries surrounding her mother. Lilith would know the explanation behind the woman's banishment, her grandmother's protectiveness of the truth behind it and her unknown father. The information she had sought her entire life depended on a single spell that only she could perform.

She made up her mind.

Lilith traveled north for a few minutes to an empty area with little vegetation. Two dark forms followed behind her with glee and gestures of victory.

She had not yet grasped the danger behind her affinity for darkness, but perhaps she would acquire the knowledge soon enough.

As the witch inscribed the symbols into the dirt, she mumbled the wind's prayer. Nothing could prepare her for the encounter with her mother. Still, she relied on the familiar words for an embrace of calmness.

Lilith placed the mirror with its engraved obsidian before the symbols, then stood back to inspect her work. She released a shaky breath, then spoke of the line to trigger the spell.

Her heart was thundering in her chest like a sprinting metronome as pessimistic thoughts swamped her mind. If her mother failed to recognize her and refused to answer her questions, despair would crush her like a ton of castle bricks.

She held her breath and waited patiently, trapped in the silent world of her panic as seconds ticked by.

Then, as abrupt as an earthquake, ebony smoke flared from the mirror's surface and obstructed her vision like an opaque wall. Slowly, the wind dispersed the haziness and exposed a standing woman enveloped in darkness with the confidence of nobility.

Lilith waited for all of the fog to vanish, but it never did. It took a moment to realize that the woman she summoned created darkness of her own.

Lilith felt her breath hitch in her throat as she studied the figure who was supposedly her mother. The woman had wavy, sparkling amber hair that reached her calf and eyes that mirrored hers—utterly black. Her skin had a ghostly shade, as though she was near-transparent. She wore a long and elegant gold dress with an intricate red design sewn from the most talented set of hands, glistening bright against the shadows behind her.

"Mother?" Lilith managed to choke out.

The witch situated in the middle of the symbols

scanned her surroundings with a wicked smile before looking at Lilith.

"At last," the woman spoke. Her voice was honey-laced and delicate, yet a petrifying touch to her accent made the phrase sound like a curse. "My little descendant. It took a thousand years for fate to find the perfect soul."

"Mother?" Lilith repeated as she stared at the glorious witch. She looked more like a goddess created to be worshipped.

"Oh, child," said the older sorcerer. "You must be confused." She used her hands of blood-curdling, sharpened nails to lift her ravishing dress and dip into a graceful and practiced curtsey. "I am Lysandra."

CHAPTER TWENTY-ONE

Lilith had heard plenty of rumors about the first Witch Queen of Dicera. Much of it came from Ruby, who adored Lysandra for her ability to rule during the reign of Eara—the first and only time witches experienced freedom. Despite being a soul of darkness, commoners and nobilities showed reverence towards the woman.

Yet, she was unable to prevent a group of cruel and jealous villagers: Morakques.

Lilith refused to believe that the legend from all those tales was standing before her, where her mother should have been.

"I had anticipated my mother to materialize," she said, hoping there was an explanation for Lysandra, of all witches, to appear.

"Well, then. Good for you," the queen replied as she studied her appearance in the mirror with glee.

"Why?" Lilith tilted her head, bemused. The queen's nonchalance was beginning to irk her; the woman was gazing more at her reflection than the witch who brought her back into the world of the living.

"Have you not realized?" Lysandra lifted her head to look her descendant in the eyes. "If you could not summon your mother, she is most probably still alive."

The perception planted a seed of disbelief in Lilith's

chest. It was a revelation that lifted her spirit but puzzled her greatly, for she had doubted the possibility every time the thought crossed her mind. No witch could venture into the outside world and survive, yet her mother might have done just that.

"You are certain?" she asked.

"It is either the truth, or I am wrong," said the queen. "And we both know that I am *never* wrong."

Lilith could not decide if her ancestor was merely confident or overly conceited, but she leaned towards the latter. She had to convince herself that the woman was the greatest queen to exist, no matter how narcissistic she appeared.

As elated as Lilith was to discover the news about her mother, she found it unfortunate that she could not receive answers to her endless questions. Furthermore, she was not mentally prepared to face a queen. Must she curtsey or get on her knees? Was there a little gesture of respect that she was not aware of? How should she address the first witch to exist?

Yet, she was aware that the opportunity was as golden as Dicera's crest. The queen could be the only being who beheld secrets about the kingdom and the art of darkness.

"I would be grateful if you would allow me to inquire about my current state," Lilith said, cringing at the tone of her words. It was too quiet and uncertain.

"You may drop the formalities, descendant," the queen said with a snort. Even the sound to express her derision seemed absurdly poised. "Before I answer any questions, I would appreciate a favor in return."

Lilith nodded with uncertainty; she could not refuse a queen, but it would be ill-fated if she were given an impossible task.

"The spell you performed is a pesky little thing. It is not necessarily temporary. For now, only I can choose if or when I leave the human realm. As long as I am close to you, I can stay for as long as I wish," the queen explained. "I would like for you to escort me to Dheeksha Cave, and in return, I will hand you the information you desperately seek."

Lilith agreed. The assignment seemed simple enough.

"Flawless," said Lysandra in delight. "Now, what is it you would like to know?"

There were so many questions that the young witch would love nothing more than to ask.

"What is this darkness?" she began.

"It is a curse and a blessing. It comes in the form of spells and can only be manipulated by those who have fate's permission. It is as powerful as the combination of all core magic and clearly, the most dangerous," said the queen. She sat down gracefully on a massive rock, and the shadows that followed her figure created a throne-like seat for the queen. "Do you not feel the delicious strength that washes over your senses every time you use dark magic?"

"Indeed," Lilith said, craving the explanation.

"Darkness does not drain you. It consumes you." Lysandra curved her lips into an impossibly magnificent frown. "It demands balance by gradually eating you up and overtaking every piece of your soul. It is a sickness that will soon descend upon you if you use it too carelessly." Her words were sharper than swords crafted by the most talented blacksmiths, yet the cultured twist of the words on her tongue made them as blunt as the weapon's back.

Fear corrupted Lilith's chest like blossoms during spring, gripping her as mercilessly as a prisoner in manacles. She had not expected the consequences to be so grave. She masked her terror with indifference, but her emotions were wholly displayed by the cloudy shapes of her living shadows, making themselves as small as possible.

"Your transformation is speeding up due to that." The queen pointed to the lily in Lilith's hair. "It is poison, and the darkness has already seeped into your soul." She spoke as if it mattered little to her. As if Lilith's death would not halt her bloodline. "You need not remove it now. It will come in handy in the future."

"Are humans able to touch my skin without burning?" Lilith asked, curious.

"Yes," responded the queen. "Sorcerers with too little power are repulsed by darkness. Which, unfortunately for you, is all of them. It was not always like that; the curse was planted by my greatest friend."

"Will I perish to darkness?" It was another question that could crush her soul.

"Possibly. If it consumes your soul, you will die." Lysandra shrugged. "You see those little puppets alongside you? They are your servants for now, but too much darkness will make them your master. They are you, but without sanity. Your soul will be wiped from the world and replaced with a chaotic creature whose only wish is to destroy. That is the cost of power."

"Is there a cure?" Lilith needed any information that was positive and not a threat to her life.

"There are two," revealed the queen with a sigh. "The first is death. It will allow you to remain in everlasting control of your ability. It has been a millennium since I discovered the second cure." The elder glanced at her shadows, and as if by command, they shrunk to become vial-shaped. "A golden vial of immortality."

The spell to create an eternal individual was said to be exterminated information. Nobody was able to replicate it.

"You did not take the immortality vial?" It was unlikely that the witch who created the concoction had not used it for herself. Yet, Lilith knew the woman had passed on. How could an immortal die?

"I did consume it," said the elder. "I produced some with fate's permission and ingested it with my husband. It prevents ageing and the degeneration of our cells, but an arrow to the chest will kill you all the same."

It was not her place to ask about Lysandra's death, but Lilith was indeed curious. She had many inquiries but plenty of time to collect replies. Perhaps, bringing the divine queen of all witchcraft back into the world of the living was a blessing from the wind.

She lowered herself to retrieve her mother's gift—the mirror. She swore that one day in the future, after her mission with Ruby, she would seek her mother in the kingdom. They would be alive and free and happy.

"Where is your third shadow?" Lysandra asked. They were gentle words twisted into a queen's demand.

"Back there." Lilith motioned behind her, where Ruby rested. "It decided to stay with my friend."

The queen guffawed as if there had never been a better joke. "Impossible!" she declared. "Unless the both of you have a bond finer than the relationship between witches and magic, it is a myth."

"Then I suppose we have an extraordinary connection, then."

"What is her core ability?"

"Everything," Lilith stated. The queen lifted her head in a silent demand for an extended response. "She controls elemental magic and is a Soothsayer as well as a Concealer." It *did* sound somewhat ludicrous for someone to behold all magic known to an ordinary witch. Darkness was the only ability that Ruby lacked.

"Impossible," remarked her ancestor again. "I do not accept lies. Deception is the worst kind of art and the nastiest way that words can be weaved."

"Why do you assume it is impractical?" Lilith was a tad bit offended to be regarded as a liar.

"Oh, my descendant," Lysandra uttered. "I created darkness because I was greedy for power. I wanted to possess every existing ability but discovered that it was impossible. The scar you carry on your side is proof of my attempt to control all affinities at once."

The scar. Lilith wondered if her grandmother knew that it was passed on by their ancestor—the only being in history who could manipulate darkness.

"Fate had given Ruby another soul to share her body," the young witch said. "It is possible." She led the queen southward, where the exhausted young woman was slumbering, yearning to prove the elder wrong.

However, she found nobody snoozing against the bark where she had left her friend.

"Ruby?" Lilith called.

Before she could so much as blink, a figure obstructed her vision and firmly grasped both of her wrists. "Where were you?" asked the red-eyed witch. Behind her was a dark cloud of a human's silhouette.

Lilith froze as her gaze bounced from Ruby to Lysandra and back again. She predicted Ruby's countenance to morph into one of bewilderment and distress, mouth agape and red eyes flaring after spotting the very visible queen at her back. Not only was Lysandra striking because of her actively shifting shadows, but her attire also heavily juxtaposed their drab surroundings.

"What were you looking at?" Ruby asked testily to prevent Lilith from brushing aside her question, unaware of Lysandra's presence.

Only Lilith could see the Witch Queen, then.

"I ventured a little down north."

"You could have gotten caught!" snapped Ruby. "Do not *ever* scare me like that again."

Lilith grinned. "I am fine, am I not?"

"Swear it."

"I swear," Lilith laughed. She glanced at her ancestor, who could inevitably sense the overly prodigious magic travelling within her friend's heart. The thousand-year-old witch looked intently at the skin-to-skin contact between the two fated friends.

"This is no laughing matter." Ruby rolled her eyes.

For once, Lysandra did not behold the countenance of indifference but, instead, genuine astonishment.

CHAPTER TWENTY-TWO

The witches ventured further west, passing evergreens and delightful blossoms. Passing the serene flow of unbothered streams glistening under the evening glow. Passing the rough ground of intricately woven protruding roots and littered branches.

The heat engulfed the young women like a second skin, coaxing a sheen of sweat.

Soon, Lilith would have to tell her friend about the knowledge she received from her ancestor, who would not stop talking. *Forgive my insolence*, she thought, *but I'll very much like to seal her lips.*

"Your puppets are attached to someone else," said the queen, glancing disapprovingly at Lilith as though she were the mother of her shadows. "Feed them fear by feeling fear. Teach them to respect a queen." The elder had not ceased blabbering unnecessarily and had been mentioning a queen's role over and over. She voiced it with such certainty that Lilith believed for a moment that being the second possessor of darkness meant a bright future.

As they tramped through the greenery towards the Fort of Morakques, exhaustion began to emerge. It crept into Lilith's bones like a spider, intertwining webs of weariness that made her feel unbelievably brittle. She had never roamed so far and long.

She was famished but disregarding the words of a queen was rude. She nodded to answer the elder's statement; the mere action took a prodigious amount of energy.

They were hoping to stumble across a wild creature for food, but they experienced no such luck. Although the young witches had gold with them, they dreaded purchasing anything from nearby villages. Entering such public places could be fatal.

Ruby had offered plenty of water, but their thirst was impossible to quench. They needed nourishment before continuing their seemingly endless journey.

"We have to purchase food," Ruby said, heaving. She settled down on a log, depleted.

Lilith nodded, her senses and thoughts made chaotic by hunger. She would do anything for a bite of roasted boar.

"And how, exactly, would you do that?" Lysandra questioned, circling around Ruby. The girl had no clue that the queen she worshipped was standing so close. "The closest village is ten minutes away. It is busy with villagers, and your eyes will simply give you away."

"We cannot," Lilith blurted, understanding her ancestor's explanation through her muddled brain. "I am not a Concealer. I would blatantly give us away."

"Then I will go on my own," Ruby said, grimacing.

"Remember what happened in the Village of Dakota. Roam only the perimeters for stalls; they should be free from spells that seize your magic," Lilith reminded. "Be careful, please." She was exceptionally afraid. It was such a terrifying risk, but they were on the brink of starvation.

Her friend grasped the map, then glanced at Lilith with a grim expression. It made a wave of fear corrupt her chest and turn her stomach.

"I will," Ruby assured, giving Lilith's hand a gentle squeeze. There came a fleeting quiet, the air heavy with the chance to rescind her decision, but Ruby did no such thing. Instead, she closed the distance between them to plant a feather-light kiss on Lilith's cheek.

Then, the red-eyed girl began her short yet dangerous journey towards the village. It was heartbreaking to see her petite form disappear into the misty air, pass trees and plants and skittering insects. Her footsteps faded from thumps to muted pats.

Lysandra was quiet for a moment, watching her descendant's expression as it twisted into a look of concern.

"She will be fine," she said.

"How can you be so sure?" Lilith did not wish to offend the woman, but she was beginning to descend into a foul mood.

"You forget," said the queen with a sigh. "Just like you, I possess the gift of darkness. Moreover, I have mastered the skill." She used a sharpened nail to tuck a strand of hair behind her ear. "If somebody is near death, I can feel it."

"How did you figure it all out by yourself?" Lilith questioned. Her throat became sandpaper, hoarse and painful. No amount of water seemed to cure it.

"I had a millennium, dear descendant. Paired with my undeniable intelligence, it is hardly a surprise."

She wanted to snort, but she lacked energy. Instead, she nodded with weariness clinging to her eyelids.

"You must not sleep," said Lysandra in a tone of reprimand. "I hope to speak."

"What is it?"

"I do not understand how your friend exists."

Some weight was lifted from Lilith's eyes upon hearing the statement. She was under the impression that the queen knew everything and possibly more.

"She was born after a ritual with an immense sacrifice," she summarised. "Her power is mentally shared with another soul in her body, as I once mentioned. It has voices and a mind of its own."

"What an uncommon creation of nature," commented the queen, then glanced at Lilith's three shadows. They were silent, but their presence remained, playing a game of tag around the bark of a towering tree. "You have no doubt felt a bond—a connection with her soul," she said. "In the history of witchcraft, overpowered witches never lived during the same reign. It is almost impossible; the chances are too slim, considering the only and last potent witch was me."

Indeed, Lilith felt something unique around her friend; their first encounter had displayed as much.

She let out a shaky breath, her mind still raging with concern like an untamable storm.

Lysandra sighed, slitting her eyes at Lilith's display of worry. "You are being dramatic," she stated. "As a queen, you should not allow something so trivial to leave you so bothered."

"Queen?" Lilith asked incredulously.

"Yes. You have a heart that belongs to royalty. So act like one," the elder chided.

Lilith bubbled with silent fury at the thought of her miserable situation. She was famished, Ruby could die obtaining food for them, and she was being infuriated by a dead queen she accidentally summoned. It was ridiculous. It did not help that Lysandra had been speaking in riddles with an ancient accent that she could barely understand.

Feeding the senior with questions could be the only way to avoid any sort of rebuke.

"Did I perform necromancy?" Lilith asked. It was the first thing that emerged in her mind.

The woman fell silent for a precious second before answering, "Yes. I created it lifetimes ago to speak to my parents. There were consequences, but I died before I could serve them."

"Does every spell have a story behind it?"

The queen's mouth twisted into a graceful downward curve. For once, Lilith saw the imperceptible sad features that painted her ancestor's face. A time-worn sorrow that remained there for a millennium, the expression so distinct that it seemed practiced.

"Indeed." Lysander smiled wistfully. "Every single one. I wrote a book about it titled The Reign of Eara. I hid it long ago."

"Why?"

"It would be dangerous if released to all witches. They would know how to create spells and core abilities, and it could doom the world."

"You mentioned consequences. What are they?"

"As I have said, my descendant, it is darkness consuming you. With every powerful spell, it gains more control until it becomes you."

Lilith shuddered. It sounded inevitable, and judging by the carelessness in which she had been performing black magic, it probably was. She refused to ask fate to show her death, for it might terrify her.

She sighed, looking at the three dark figures that had already become a familiar presence. They were playful things, chasing and tripping and laughing. Yet, they made no sound in the slightest.

Lilith returned to brooding over Ruby's absence.

The queen pinched her eyebrows together as she glanced at her descendant as if she were nothing more than a child, which she was, in Lysandra's eyes. "I will help you."

Lilith was about to clarify, but no explanation needed to be served. With the simplest flick of her fingers, the millennium-old witch called upon a swirling dark phenomenon in the shape of a royal wall mirror. In the shape, a vivid image began appearing from nothingness. Starting as a blurry view, it gradually transformed into a detailed landscape. In the middle of the ethereal creation, a speck—no—a *person* began to form.

Ruby.

Lilith gasped, turning to the queen with astonishment shining in her eyes. "How?"

"I am an intelligent being," Lysandra replied.

"How do you still possess magic when you are dead? Will darkness not consume *you* too?"

"No," uttered the queen as though it were the most

absurd thing she had ever heard. "As you mentioned, I am dead. In my current form, I can perform certain magic without consequences."

Lilith smiled, a portion of wrath withering away like a plant in winter. She gazed at her friend as she traveled from an empty patch of grass to a lively village celebrating a festival full of vibrant lights, then to a store along the edge, selling mouth-watering food. Safely, she saw Ruby return to the forest.

She let out a sigh of relief as footsteps echoed and the queen's magic faded away, leaving tendrils of dark smoke loitering the area.

"Thank Dahlia," Lilith whispered.

"Dahlia?" blurted the queen, staring at her descendant with slight amusement. "Is that what you young witches say during this reign?" Lysandra let out a quiet laugh. "When I see her again, I will be sure to enlighten her."

The young witch barely gave her ancestor a shred of attention, too focussed on the return of her friend.

"You are back!" she exclaimed, unable to keep the relief and excitement from her voice.

"Yes," said Ruby, relieved. She, too, was afraid for her life. "I might have eaten some of what I purchased on the way back, but there is plenty more." As she settled down on a log with Lilith, she used her nature affinity to gather a pile of sticks. Then, she allowed flames to leap from her fingertips to create a comfortable fireplace.

After eyeing the succulent meal she was to have, Lilith stared and tilted her head at Lysandra, attempting to scrutinise the queen's wariness as she looked at the fire. The expression was disquieting.

It took a moment before the elder returned Lilith's stare with a string of peculiarly chilling words. "Be careful, my little descendant," she said. "A storm is brewing."

CHAPTER TWENTY-THREE

Ruby eyed her friend, who was staring into a blank space with intense calculation. It was unlike her to be detached from the world.

"Is something wrong?" Ruby questioned, biting into a loaf of something delicious. An explosion of sweetness flared in her mouth, paired with the perfect touch of tenderness. While she was in the village, where innumerable illuminated hues were scattered to celebrate an unknown festival, she struggled to choose which food she wanted. She had never seen any of them, but their scents were so divine that they stirred even the demon in her head. She could only select what she hoped was the most appetizing with so little money and an abundance of choices. At times, she discovered, an abundance of choice could be as damning as none.

She took another bite, savoring the eruption of flavor. It was a shame that she had not learned the names that belonged to the baked and cooked nourishments she had purchased.

In the Forest of Dahlia, she ate farmed vegetables and captured animals. With her nature ability, she was often empathetic and steered clear of consuming the latter.

"No," replied Lilith, hesitation evident in her tone. Then quickly, she added, "Well, actually..." She quickly looked away to the side, where two of her shadow-like figures were attempting to climb a tree to no avail. One of them was seated beside Ruby, who was clueless about what they were but was skeptical that their owner knew herself. Their presence was sudden and an utter mystery.

There were three of them with the same physical appearance—a dark and flexible human-shaped silhouette formed by something that appeared to be a smoky, moving artwork from strokes of a brush carried by a talented hand. However, Ruby could tell one apart, for that special figure dedicated a large portion of time following and lingering around her.

She is hiding something from you, sang the previously quiet voices in her head, sounding sly as a fox. Ruby already figured as much.

"You can tell me anything." Ruby shrugged, as if she did not already know everything about her friend. They had been sharing an overwhelming lot of truths and stories, for they only had each other in their journey.

"You are bound to get mad," Lilith said.

Ruby cast an intrigued look at her friend. She dipped her head, then took another bite of her tasty meal. "Enlighten me."

"While you were asleep in the forest, I wandered north to perform a spell."

She jerked upwards, eyes widening. "What?"

"I know, I know. I should not have been so careless without understanding the consequences of using darkness, but I know them now."

"I suppose you had somehow injected knowledge into your head?"

Lilith laughed, staring in the direction of a small log. "Contrary to your assumption, I summoned the dead."

The casual way she delivered the confession startled and pushed Ruby to think that her friend was joking. Yet, her nonchalance was proven to be anything but a joke when partnered with her grim expression.

"You cannot be serious," Ruby spluttered. Her anger caused the fire before them to flare brighter. "You must be out of your mind!"

Lilith frowned. "Well, I mentioned you would be upset."

"How can I not?" Ruby exclaimed although she was not quite fuming. Perhaps just a little disappointed that her friend did not know better. "Have you forgotten that necromancy is heavily forbidden and dangerous? Using your new, mysterious ability could severely harm you."

"I know it is foolish, but I was trying to reach my mother," explained Lilith. A pained sigh escaped her, and it delivered a punch straight through Ruby's heart.

Ruby heard about her friend's mother countless times and knew how much the woman meant to Lilith. Although it did not make her choice any more reasonable, it made it understandable.

"Did it work, then?" Ruby asked. She heard of necromancy but never believed in it until now. It was absurd like the rumor of a subtle message in Dicera's crest.

"I—" Lilith paused, grimacing.

"Oh, just spit it out. It cannot be worse than performing *necromancy*."

"It is not bad, just a little shocking," she confessed, then cast a glance at an empty space. "I summoned a queen."

"A queen?" Ruby gaped as she followed her friend's gaze to the area occupied by an unnatural stillness. She was aware of many queens from the past reigns, recorded from witches in plentiful books. "Which one?"

"Queen Lysandra."

Ruby almost lost her grip on the food she held. She opened her mouth to say something—anything—but she was left speechless. *Naturally*, if it involved Lilith, it had to be the most ruthless yet calculative queen in history that followed her around. Queen Lysandra from the reign of Eara, whose name caused a slither of awe and fear to emerge within those who recognized her. She was a powerful and intelligent witch who succeeded in creating a short moment of peace as the ruler of the kingdom and darkness. The ability's strength was as great as all core powers combined.

"I have learned many things from her."

"She told you?" Ruby said, choosing her words warily. She could not risk offending the queen she secretly worshipped.

A small, somewhat confident smirk twisted Lilith's lips. "Indeed, for I have the power to end her lineage."

Ruby froze again. Suddenly, she was too full even for the delicious food she had bought.

It was little information withholding a significant amount of absurdity, so baffling that she could barely wrap her mind around it. It meant a great deal, considering the amount of knowledge she gained from the books she devoured. Gradually, she released the shock of the discovery to grasp the news more firmly with understanding.

Lilith was a descendant of Queen Lysandra, the most powerful witch to ever exist. The thousand-year-old was also following her around and handing out vital information about her new ability.

Perhaps, this was an encounter and blessing given by fate. It was beyond fortunate to be able to seek the only person who understood the art of darkness. The only person who knew *everything*.

Unable to shake the awe that surrounded her friend's circumstance, Ruby decided to ask, "So you know the mystery behind your three shadows?"

"I do." Lilith nodded. She seemed to delve into her mind to recall. "According to Queen Lysandra, they are either servants or masters. They are drawn to power, which I suppose is why they adore you so deeply."

How similar those shadows and the soul sharing Ruby's body were.

"How do you regard them?"

She cast a look at the three figures she summoned, faceless and without a heart but very much alive. "They are my equal."

Ruby was taken aback by the response. Throughout her entire life, she had never thought of the demon in her mind as an equal. They were friends and enemies in many aspects—they fought for control within their minds, and their thinking perpetually contradicted each other. Although she was the rightful owner of her body, the demon would always hope to obtain it. It was why Ruby would never see it as her equal and hence would never call it by name. She doubted that would ever change.

No matter, whispered the voices, hearing her thoughts as loud as fanfare trumpets, *You can shun me, despise me, but the end of our story will remain unchanged.*

The demon's whispers reminded her many times of its greatest desires—rule and ruin. It yearned to attain respect, and it would do anything to show that it was capable of bringing the world to its knees. No matter the cost, whether it be destroying the very world it planned to reign or annihilating every Morakque who threatened them, the demon would do it.

Ruby knew that its dream to rule was impossible.

Sure, Ruby replied sarcastically.

I can see the future, Ruby, it reminded her, as if she did not know already. *Want me to prove it?*

No, thank you.

The whispers let out a cacophony of sighs. *Khaos will agree. We share the same ambitions, the same heart, the same bond.*

Before Ruby could question, Lilith interrupted their silent conversation. Watching her three creatures of darkness, she concluded, "I have decided to name them." She turned to her friend, a smile painting her features. Somehow, the light expression removed an unknown weight from Ruby's chest.

"Here is a little fact: the ability of darkness does not necessarily mean evil. Instead, it means a taste of chaos and violence. Everything in the world is touched by chaos—a hint of messiness. Without entropy, life would be devoid of twists and thrills. Hence, I have decided on—" Lilith smiled wider, fixing a stare at the silhouette beside her friend, "—Khaos."

"Oh," Ruby said. Something was caught in her throat, and she discovered it to be yet another wave of shock.

"Yes! It is perfect. Its uniqueness highlights that these three creatures are far from ordinary."

"Indeed, they are," Ruby agreed. It was the truth, for such forms of shadows only existed once in the entirety of known history.

I am unique, too, said the demon cheerily, *for someone like I have never once lived. Some witches have a voice that manifests in their minds from time to time, but I am more than just an occasional visitor. We are special, Ruby, and we shall live as such.*

Its voice slowly faded into softness, sounding like the swishing gust of wind that would rouse leaves into action. It had quietened itself upon hearing the voice of Lilith, who began sharing all she had learned from the queen.

"That means you cannot use your ability so carelessly," Ruby exclaimed the obvious when she heard of its possible consequence.

"I am aware, but it is difficult when the ability grants us significant power."

Ruby glanced at The Forbidden Book of Lysandra, lying harmlessly on the ground. "Then only use it when necessary, and even then, you must ensure it is wise to do so." She sighed, realizing that this quest to seek freedom and peace in the world could be more challenging than she once thought.

If Lilith were to be possessed by the shadows surrounding them, she would no longer be herself. Instead, the creatures starving for chaos would take her place. That was far worse than the attacks of the Morakques.

It might be too late to notice, but they did not have an eternity to loiter.

Time was an essential element to achieving their freedom, and it was running out as profusely as blood from an open wound. Day by day, they approached the location of their possible death.

It was a pity. Ruby was the strongest witch in Dicera, and with the addition of Lilith, a witch just as powerful, they could heal the world. They *would* cure it, but nobody in the Forest of Dahlia noticed. They might have sent them for the mission, but they provided too little for the young women who had barely ever stepped into the outside world. It was a death trip.

They needed a plan on their own.

For the next few weeks, they traveled on foot towards the Fort of Morakques as if they would never reach. Ruby did not wish to arrive where their lives could be taken in the bat of an eyelid, but she barely had a choice.

They were silently delaying the time for their planning, but they could not wait any longer.

"We have to start today," Ruby said, although her friend must have already known.

Lilith nodded reluctantly, then lowered herself to trace a single character in the dirt. "This is the Fort of

Morakques." She gestured to the shape. "I imagine excellent security around the location. They are using captured witches to create a spell that keeps magic out of the area, so the two kinds are likely separated for the witches to avoid affecting themselves."

Agreeing, Ruby added, "There are two locations we have to locate—the fort and where they keep sorcerers." She drew a second circle in the dirt, keeping a distance from the first. "Remember the Village of Dakota? The spell works most prominently in the middle, not anywhere along the border. The witches are unable to cover the entire area with their protection spell."

Lilith frowned. "Marco's father resided in that village although he is a crucial Morakque. I do not suppose that they stay the night within their fort. They simply meet and plan there during the day."

"We should explore the place at night," Ruby said, latching onto her friend's suggestion. She grabbed the map and skimmed through it, then fixed her red eyes on the location they were to visit. "The place is relatively close to the castle," she noted, adding another circle in the dirt.

"We need to discover where they keep our kind first. Without witches in the picture, we do not have to worry about any protection spells."

Ruby allowed a small smile to invade her features. The witches who escaped their capture gave them valuable clues—it was close to the Fort of Morakques, and they were often visited.

"We have little time on our side," Lilith said, echoing

what Ruby was fretting over, "but we have to take some time to observe Morakques. We need to be sure of their routine."

"We should first assist the captured witches. They are bound to be weak, but we *have* to help them or at least stop their spell before risking going anywhere near the Morakques."

Lilith contemplated. "How can we bring all the witches safely back into the Forest of Dahlia?"

Khaos, all three of Lilith's shadows, converged into one and shrunk into a grey cloud that began to swarm around the circle representing the castle. They helped Ruby recall, "On top of rescuing witches, we were sent to seek assistance from royalty." She pointed to the castle. "We should head there instead of the forest."

Lilith broke into a smile. "The royal family might have enough resources and a solution to escort us safely back home."

"Yes, but why would they aid us?" Ruby asked glumly. "They have clearly made no such effort since the dawn of time."

"Think positive. We have never once asked for help, either."

They spent the next hours finalizing the plan.

It was tedious but crucial, for their lives depended on it.

"To gain freedom, Morakques have to be defeated," Ruby said.

"Or, they can accept us for who we are," Lilith remarked, always the optimist. "We will proceed step by step. First, rescue our kind by sneaking in and breaking them out. Then, we lead them to safety. Afterwards, we strive for freedom."

"If somehow, we succeed, what will we do after?" Ruby questioned softly, staring at the fire she had created. Her eyes sparkled with the tangerine-colored glow of the searing flames, giving her ruby eyes a glimmer of intimidation.

"I think fate will undoubtedly change our plans. By then, we will know," Lilith said, turning to face her partner in their possible endeavor to change the kingdom. She tucked a strand of her companion's loose hair behind her ear with a gentle smile, one that caused an eruption of heat to flare in Ruby's stomach.

"Soon," Lilith said, almost in a tone of promise. Then, she leaned in and kissed the tip of Ruby's nose.

The demon living within Ruby's head released a shriek that was neither painfully shrill nor unpleasant. It sounded *happy* for her.

She noticed its behavior around Lilith but never entirely understood it until she pieced everything together. A bond tied them together from their very first encounter. While the demon was attracted to Lilith's power, it also relished Ruby's constant joy in the presence of Lilith's hopeful spirit, accepting character, and curiosity.

They were a fated pair from the beginning.

CHAPTER TWENTY-FOUR

"Do you think our plan will work?" Lilith asked the Queen of Darkness, who was fanned by shadows as she rested on the edge of a log.

She spared the young witch a glance before she returned to sharpening her nails. Lilith bore the claw-like trait as well, with the edge grown unnaturally long and invaded with blackness. If her Nana were to see her in her current form, she doubted the senior would recognize her. Lilith looked poisoned but not ill. Demon-like, but she felt like the same Lilith she always was.

But who was she kidding?

Of course, she had changed.

A trip to the outside world ensured that. Lilith was bound to undergo changes from the second she stepped out from her forest into a place where she was portrayed as evil.

"Why are you asking?" questioned her ancestor, eyes brimming with boredom. "You are still a Soothsayer. If you wish so desperately to know, simply use that ability of yours."

Lilith knew that, too. As time progressed, she had somehow begun trusting and familiarizing herself with the queen's blunt words. Something about them was reassuring in a way she could not explain.

"I am afraid I will not like what I see," she said,

frowning. Her eyes darted from her ancestor to the morning sky, beginning its ascend deliberately. It was still fairly dark, but the day would approach soon enough.

"Then do not seek it," said Lysandra as if the answer were obvious. "Save your energy for darkness. You will thank me later." Khaos perked up in excitement.

Lilith considered the response. She received countless warnings about an event that would soon happen, and her curiosity was in a wild state.

"Alright," she said after some time. It would be foolish to disregard a being who knew much more than she.

"Splendid!" said the elder cheerily. "Now, I would like to know of the current world." The twist in her tone made it sound like an order.

"You are asking the wrong witch." Lilith barely knew about Dicera. All the information she gathered was from Ruby, who read more books than she managed to see throughout her life. Still, heeding the queen's demand, she said all that she had learned.

"Morakques are a pain," muttered Lysandra bitterly.

"If only all Dicerians agree."

"You, little descendant, can make that happen." She shrugged. "After all, having the ability you currently possess makes you my heir. With that status, you can grant the commoner's wishes and gain respect."

Lilith laughed at the suggestion. She was nothing but a little witch on an impossible quest, balancing on a single thin thread like a weighty animal on a collapsing bridge. If the queen was certain that Lilith could be the Queen of Darkness, she was royally mistaken.

"In this day and age, our kind is hated. Morakques have influenced them," Lilith said, thinking of the act of decapitation in the Village of Dakota. It was a hideous memory, but it helped her learn how cruel the world was and how wary she must be to survive.

"Do you know why that is?"

"Ruby says it is because humans are afraid of being seen as weak. They are simply wicked."

"What do *you* think?"

Lilith mused, "I think they harbour prejudice against witches because they do not know any better. They do not believe in peace because we have lived too long without it."

There was peace once, she remembered, during Lysandra's rule. Then, the Morakques' envy of witches' powers led to disharmony. It had been generations since then. It was well past time people understood that only unity could forge a flourishing future for Dicera.

"Why, yes. Remember, there is no good, and there is no evil. There are simply different sides and perceptions. This will eventually lead to opposing ideas on the same subject." Lysandra grinned, a captivating curve on her lips. "I must say, humans can be remarkable."

"What makes you think so?"

"Hundreds of moons ago, I met a man. He was not a warlock, nor was he merely a villager, although I was once under the impression that he was." Wistfully, she stared into the distance. "He was a prince, and he treated me like a queen, as he should. He made me believe that peace was possible, and hence I achieved it with his help." Her smile turned grim. "I miss him terribly."

It was not the first time Lilith heard of this tale between the queen and King Earl Gretea the Fourth—a romantic but tragic story that ended in two different deaths.

"He is in a better place," Lilith said. It was what Nana always told her when a sorcerer met their end.

"Oh, but he is not," Lysandra commented, sounding remarkably certain. "I handed him a golden vial of immortality without any words of advice. He does not know how to get it out of his system, so he is alive but in a daily state of misery. I will find him soon enough, and when I do, I will not let him go again."

The young witch gawked. Nobody mentioned that the king from a thousand years ago was still alive and roaming the Kingdom of Dicera.

"How will you find him in this mess of a kingdom?"

"He is not a wandering man. His body is resting in a cave, unable to decompose. If he were to be given water, he would wake. But I plan to take his soul with me to another realm, away from this world where he is trapped," said the elder, revealing the reason for her need to visit Dheeksha Cave.

Lilith did not know what to expect after death. She caught herself pondering about it several times during the trip, thinking she was bound to be caught and murdered. Her ancestor knew the answer, but she was too anxious to discover the truth.

"You wish to know, do you not?" asked the old witch, reading her mind flawlessly. "For centuries, Dahlia was with me in the kingdom as a travelling soul without a physical body. I cannot say where we will go if we choose to leave, for I do not know myself. I refused to leave this kingdom without my king because I knew that one day, you would perform the spell."

"How old are you, exactly?" she blurted before she could stop herself. She regretted the words as soon as they rolled from her tongue, realizing it was rather rude to phrase her words so boldly.

The queen did not consider her insolence. Instead, she answered, "Let's see… I was born early in August, about ten centuries ago, perhaps more. It is easy to lose track of time when you are dead."

Lilith nodded in awe. She doubted that she would want to live for such a prolonged period of time without the presence of someone else.

"Now, enough of the endless questions. You must wake your friend and get ready. I sense people."

She gulped, turning to the slumbering Ruby. She reached out to lay a hand on her, but a thundering load of footsteps already woke her up.

The red-eyed witch narrowed her eyes. Not at the rising sun, Lilith realized, but in concentration. She was listening to the voices in her mind.

"Should we run?" Lilith asked, eyes widening as if she had done something wrong. If they were found by Morakques, they would have no other choice.

"No," her friend said. "I can deal with them."

Lilith nodded, a lump forming in her throat. She trusted Ruby, but they could not risk endangering themselves. If things were to go out of hand, she would have no other choice but to reach out to darkness.

Her shadows were just as alarmed as she, but they did not cower.

"There is something I have not mentioned," Lysandra said suddenly. "Even now, your dark figures can possess your body. They cannot stay for long since you still hold the leash to control, but they have that ability."

Lilith bit back a groan. Of course, she would only receive such vital information now when her life could be gone in a matter of seconds. Her heart was attached to a single piece of string, dangling helplessly within her chest. She knew it would dip into her stomach when Morakques came into view.

The young witches waited for moments that felt like a decade. Then, after the sound of footsteps changed from soft pattering to wild gallops, Lilith began to properly worry. How did they find them?

"Careless girl," sighed Lysandra, too composed and calm. "It is inevitable; anybody would be able to see your fire."

"Why did you not say anything?" Lilith was bewildered.

"I did, though I should not have. I cannot poke my finger into fate's business." The queen chuckled, the sound practiced and gentle, but it had an edge like a sharpened blade. "I cannot wait to see how this plays out."

In the blink of an eye, a row of humans gathered in front of the young sorcerers. They ranged from teenagers to the elderly, from commoners to nobles. With a quick scan, Lilith noted that there were two dozen of them—a number that Ruby could easily deal with. However, she would need to be perpetually prepared for any sudden attacks.

The few humans carried spears with them, a display that confirmed her assumption. They were indeed Morakques, and they seemed ready for a fight.

Seemed.

Some of their expressions deceived them, showing a quick flash of fear. It took a moment for Lilith to grasp their reason. These Morakques were not facing witches, but instead, *demons.* Two of the deadliest in the entire kingdom.

They scanned wary eyes across Ruby, then Lilith, then Khaos. Their shock almost drove them away,

"What are you?" muttered a Morakque, softer than the whisper of winds. As if a single wrong word could wipe away his existence.

Ruby attacked.

She was against the idea of lingering and answering questions from people who only desired a witch's death. Yet, she needed to be wary of her surroundings—a forest prone to fire and flood.

Lilith simply watched as Morakques began to choke and suffocate before spitting out mouthful after mouthful of water. Her friend was handling the situation with ease, flicking hands recklessly and expeditiously. She felt her stomach tighten at the death that was beginning to dawn around her. Wishing to distract herself, she fished out her mirror to perform a quick Soothsaying spell.

An image swirled in her mind, then showed a disturbingly clear image of a spear soaring in the skies. Then, another flickering vision as it pierced her friend's stomach. Profuse crimson flowed as ceaselessly as a waterfall. The sight was almost too much to bear.

"Ruby," Lilith gasped right as she disconnected from the vision. Her eyes searched the area with gripping fear for anyone holding the weapon.

Ruby was rapidly preventing Morakque after Morakque from attacking, diminishing their strengths. All of them were still alive, though weakened.

Lilith knew why. Her friend was trying not to trigger the 'demon' she claimed lived in her mind by only using one element. Unless Ruby wanted to incite destruction and a massive amount of death, she could not risk using multiple abilities at once.

A hurricane of incantations Lilith memorized surfaced in her head. She knew of the consequences and how careful she must be, but her life and mission would be affected without Ruby. She needed to do something, whatever it might be.

Lilith started to sketch symbols in the dirt with her feet, the spell fresh in her mind. Her eyes darted from one Morakque to the next, counting a total of twelve with spears. She had to eradicate them all quickly before one of them stabbed her friend.

She shut her eyes, then muttered the words as terror flooded her system.

Lilith was too horrified to see the damage of what she did. A series of groans filled the air, then utter silence. The pause was so unnerving that she felt the need to run.

"Wonderful," uttered a voice—no—*voices*. They came from Ruby but sounded like what would belong to a mythical creature. The syllables of the single word echoed as if spoken in a spacious cave, and a trace of danger trailed it like a loyal follower. It sounded both menacing and gentle, a mix of ruthlessness and love.

It was not Ruby who said it but the demon that resided within her.

Lilith opened her eyes, looking around with a pang of unexplainable guilt in her chest. The Morakques she targeted had their spears plunged into their own flesh. The spell had made them turn against themselves.

Then, she looked at her friend.

Ruby did not appear like herself. When she spoke, Lilith felt a shiver down her spine.

"It is time for change," the voices announced gleefully. "Let us rejoice at the impending war."

CHAPTER TWENTY-FIVE

When Ruby returned to her body, disorientated and missing a portion of her memories, panic seized her at once.

She did not allow the demon to control her body, but it disregarded her as if she were nothing more than the wind during a stormy day. If it performed any sort of sorcery that demolished land and animals and plants, a handful of consequences would soon be served.

Glancing around the area with the red of her vision evaporating away, she caught the sight of Morakques. The area was filled with them—they decorated the ground like rocks on forest paths and painted a masterpiece of scarlet. Everywhere she turned, the brilliant color stared back with a terrifying smile as if taunting her with its ghastliness.

Did I do this? she asked the demon, eyes unwavering on the liquid that oozed from the Morakques' wounds. The weapon they brought along was stuck steadfastly into themselves as if somebody had yanked it away and used it against them.

No, the whispers said.

She released a sigh of relief; it was not her who performed such a gruesome task. Then, as sudden and hefty like boulders launched from a catapult, a wave of dread engulfed her. If she did not commit the murders, then it must be…

Oh, but Ruby, you need not worry, interjected the demons amid her thoughts. *We played a part in the killing.*

Color washed from her face as she whirled around to find Lilith blinking furiously as she stumbled. Shadows were gathered around her form, vaguely forming three figures. They were still in a position that resembled kneeling. They had their heads hung low in respect as if praying to a goddess they worshipped.

"What happened?" Ruby asked. She refrained from eyeing the Morakques, frozen in a state of terror.

"I killed them," Lilith muttered, sounding in a daze. Her lips wobbled as she stared at the symbols traced on the ground.

A spell that could take out a dozen could not have been something simple and without cost, but Lilith stepping in might have just saved her life. Again.

"We have to leave. Now." It was a short order, but it was crucial in every aspect. Although the witch of all abilities still had plenty of questions and swirling thoughts, she knew that lingering was not a choice.

Swiftly, they grabbed the items of importance and the leftover food, then continued with their journey. They were close to their final location, with their plan still fresh and untouched.

They quickened their footsteps as they walked, exchanging only a few words and responses. The day was still in its early hours, and so they had many more left to go.

The map directed the witches further away from their homes and nearer to death.

The apprehensiveness that built within Ruby's stomach told her as much.

You are such a pessimist, complained the voices. *You are seeking freedom for your kind and possibly more. Be a little more positive; it makes a world of difference.*

She did not truly view her mission from another perspective, one that looked at the bigger picture.

She had never delved into the thought of succeeding, for she did not know how it looked. If she used her imagination, what exactly would it be like? When the witches were released, and the Morakques wiped out, her kind would explore the outside world without fear of torture. They would see the gloriously broad mountains and vibrant flowers that bloomed with pride, festivities with floating lanterns and radiant lights that illuminated the land. Humans would finally realize that witches were not potion brewers with pointed noses who craved bloodshed.

If freedom were to be achieved, the world would be different in many ways. Ruby could dance freely with Lilith amongst humans, surrounded by cheer. She could share enchanting fairy tales with children and delight them with magic. She could read books to her heart's content and converse with her father in a kingdom of peace.

At the thought of her lovable father, Ruby's heart ached with longing. She missed him dearly and unfailingly carried his support with her wherever she went. He, along with Lilith, was her beacon of strength and hope.

The witches stopped for just a moment to visit a pond where they could rinse their hands and bodies of grime. Then, they trudged along dense forests and abandoned buildings and rivers with weak bridges from morning until midnight.

With every passing moment, Ruby thought of how their quest to find peace could heal the kingdom. She stayed away from the thought of being obliterated, feeding herself with confidence. She believed in herself and Lilith. Together, they were witches who could break the world and fix it again. The world was plagued with misunderstanding, and she was sent to find the cure.

Ruby was not going to die. She would not.

If the demon in her mind wanted power so badly, she would acquire it and then use it to mould the kingdom into a delightful home.

Ruby swore to do everything within her capabilities to fight for freedom and find a route for Lilith to escape her terrible fate of dark consequences.

Yes, hissed the whispers like a ghost dressed in shadows, haunting youths at night. *Remember, you are capable of great things.*

Déjà vu slammed into Lilith's chest as she lifted her head, taking in the sight of Dicera's only castle. She did not know who lived within the building of gold and ruby, but the place felt like a home she had never seen.

No, she realized. She had seen it before, multiple times. Tens, hundreds, perhaps thousands of times. Several visions resurfaced in her memory, all showing the same towering building.

She stood a great distance away, yet she could almost

hear the calling voice of the gargantuan castle. It was calling her name and Ruby's with a sound carried by the gentle breeze, quiet yet audible. She wondered if her friend heard and felt it too, like a ghost-like hand nudging her towards the castle as if welcoming a guest—*no*—a member of a family.

A breath hitched in her throat. The sight of gold infused with strips of vermillion was such a bizarre yet fitting combination, one that she saw and forgot over and over again.

"Did you know," Lysandra spoke while Lilith's thoughts wove a web of emotions, capturing awe and delight in the form of prey, "I designed Dicera's crest, and they have never changed it?"

"You did?" Lilith asked, tearing her attention from the castle with much effort. "The rumors said as much. They even claimed that you added messages within it."

"Indeed," said the queen, striding through the cloud of Khaos and separating them into three. She left her descendant's side and continued the journey. Lilith's shadows returned to her back, fanned out like a peacock's tail.

The route to their final destination was just a few minutes away, but the witches could not resist halting in their tracks to gawk at the building waving at them from afar.

Lilith turned to Lysandra just as the dead sorcerer flicked her hand. A swirling mist of darkness wandered to a fruit from an outstanding tree and seemingly yanked it, causing it to drop beside Ruby's feet.

"You can do that?" asked the younger witch, baffled.

The queen shrugged with an air of insouciance. "I did not know either. I did it solely for my enjoyment."

Ruby lowered herself to grab the fruit, finally diverting her attention away from the castle. "The trees bear fruits that we can use for food. When we are close enough to the Fort of Morakques, we will conceal ourselves within the forest until we are certain of their routine."

Lilith nodded. It was exactly as they had planned.

She was fatigued, but their fight for freedom would not end right as they arrived at their location; it was far from over. Night had dawned long ago, and they had planned to stop due to the dimness, but they were so, so close. Only two hours away. Ruby summoned flames to dance at her fingertips to provide light but stopped as soon as she realized that the brilliance of the castle could cast patches of illumination upon their path. She carefully relied on her ability to guide them only after it grew too faint.

Located six miles away and on the same horizontal stretch as the building was another source of radiance. It was not reflected by the glorious moonlight from the blanket of darkness above but by fire. It was another monstrous structure but much plainer than the castle. It resembled a high-rise stone building surrounded by a blaze, alive and snapping. Unlike magnificent gold, the stones were dull and grimy, like an abandoned grave. Its builders had no intention of offering it an aesthetically pleasing design; it existed merely as a stronghold.

The Fort of Morakques.

Its walls cast a long, ominous shadow across the

massive land that stretched out before it. On the yard's right stood a stone platform, its surface worn smooth by the countless feet that had trod upon it.

Lilith was taken aback by its aura of resilience.

"This is it," Ruby confirmed, frowning.

They trudged on towards it, weaving through the trees. They would remain in the forest for the next few days before their rescue attempt. They had to figure out where the witches were kept.

Although Lilith's mind might be willing to show the future, she did not seek it. Whatever the end, she promised herself one thing—she would not let Ruby die. She would unleash the darkness building in her body despite the consequences.

It worried her to know that Ruby would do the same in a heartbeat.

"We have reached," Ruby said firmly.

"Indeed," Lysandra said, although the witch could not hear. "Now, it is a great time for lessons."

As poised as a goddess, she rested upon a jagged platform encircling an empty, ghastly depth to nowhere. A wishing well, old as the hills with moss and fern trickling its sides like the cascade of droplets. It was concealed along undergrowth beneath a bloomed linden. Lilith was slightly mystified by the sight of the ancient structure; she could not imagine how it was constructed. Lysandra mistakenly took Lilith's confusion as an urge for clarification on her statement.

"Child, you are royalty. Yet, you do not know the rules

and all that revolves around your future life," Lysandra remarked with a disapproving look.

"The rules back then were different; the world has evolved," Lilith answered defiantly. It would be a waste of precious energy. The Queen of Darkness' status was not recognized amongst Dicerians; nobody would heed her command even if she could drop into a perfect curtsey.

"There are things that will never change," commented the queen.

"Well, is it not too late? We must sleep."

"No," responded the queen stubbornly. "Their daily meeting starts around the afternoon. I can provide you with two hours of knowledge before you visit the darkness of unconsciousness."

Lilith blinked. "How do you know about their meeting?"

"I am a genius, my descendant. I know everything." She rolled her eyes as if baffled that the fact was not yet known. "Now, do not spoil my reputation with your impertinence." Lysandra, in all her immortal glory, appeared more like a mother reprimanding a toddler. "You will do well to respect your elders."

Grumbling, Lilith agreed, clueless as to what the lesson entailed. Yet, she felt a hint of anticipation despite the ache in her bones.

Then, for the next few hours, she was given a myriad of advice from the first Witch Queen to exist. She made sure that Ruby was included in the session, for if one of them were to rule, the other would undoubtedly be strung along. They acquired the most bemusing information that seemed unnecessary in all aspects. They learned about the significance and definition of well-embellished royal outfits, the differences in golden threads, the statuses of those that must curtsey, the most polite manner to respond when asked to dance, and the most proper way to speak. They also found the most valuable way to wield magic and strengthen it within the body before utilizing it.

Lilith gazed at the beams of moonlight as she attempted to sleep after she was taught. Her memories replayed the several ways to lower herself to greet and gesture for assistance, like mentally preparing herself for a test that was to come.

Her shadows twirled as if following the wind's command, like smoke from a heated bath. Lysandra, on the other hand, was nowhere to be seen.

"You cannot sleep?" asked a voice beside her. She did not need to turn to recognize its owner.

"I am scared," she said. It was a raw but firm confession that escaped her lips, filling the air with the weight of uncertainty.

"I am, too," Ruby said. "It is just a few more days before..." She paused, unsure of the unforeseen future, although they had the ability of foresight.

They needed a voice to reach out to the masses to rally support. People should be aware that Morakques could be defeated. Moreover, the Dicerian royal family would doubtlessly be grateful to the witches if they helped protect the crown. The support of royalty would provide them with influence, and they could work from there.

Since the Morakques only hoped to eradicate witches, they might have no other choice but to fight.

"We can do this," Ruby said. Their plan was ambitious, but it was promising and possible.

The royal family had been struggling to triumph over their neighbors for the longest time. Although the sovereigns knew that Morakques wanted nothing more than to take the throne and remove the kingdom of witches, they could do nothing. Especially since commoners and even nobility looked up to Morakques so much.

"The queen claims that I am the new ruler of darkness," Lilith said, chuckling at the absurdity of the statement. "Yet, no one knows what that means."

"That is untrue, actually," Ruby said. "There are many books with the title, so people *do* know about it. However, they regard it as a myth because nobody believes in a person followed by shadows. If anyone were to see you in your current form, they would recognize what you represent."

Lilith turned, slightly bewildered by the fact she was never told. "What should I do with the title?"

"The Queen of Darkness is known for winning wars, inciting chaos and providing souls with darkness in the form of sleep and death. It is something that humans came up with, but I believe that in a few days, everybody will be awed," Ruby shared a proud grin on her face.

"If I truly bear the title, I would want someone to rule alongside me."

"And who would that fortunate soul be?" Ruby asked, a lopsided smile igniting her face like a lantern in the night.

Mischief removed the weariness in her eyes and shaped her features into one that belonged to a goddess.

"A very beautiful woman," answered Lilith. "My equal and soulmate."

"Soulmate?" Ruby repeated. She propped herself on an elbow, casting a shadow over her companion. Her eyes lingered on the eternal lily that was never removed from Lilith's hair, then skimmed down to her lips, then the torn piece of sewn fabric at her side that revealed a stark scar. The birthmark was mentioned in many, many books indicating a descendant of the most powerful witch.

"Yes," said the Queen of Darkness in a whisper that could be heard a mile away. It was but a murmur, yet it was fetched so far by the tense air and expressed such a profound yearning.

"That is intriguing," remarked Ruby with voices that resounded in the forest. Around them, the greenery, the serene flow of a nearby river and the flamboyant blossoms under pale moonglow were silent witnesses with unperceivable eyes. "I like that."

Lilith watched the figure hovering over her. She had the sudden urge to lick her lips and disregard her need for sleep. Her heart was chaotic within her chest, like a creature trapped in a cage with the keys dangling a few steps ahead.

"Do you find joy in teasing me?" she asked, tilting her head to the side.

"I do."

Lilith lifted herself just slightly to reach out for the red-eyed witch, snaking a hand around the back of her neck to pull her closer. Khaos gathered by their side with pure elation at once, concealing them in darkness like a thin blanket.

Their lips were inches apart.

"You dare be so impudent to your queen?" Lilith asked.

"Were we not equals?"

The Queen of Darkness paused, contemplating. "Right," she muttered. "How careless of me."

Before Lilith allowed herself to be selfless, she leaned in.

Their lips met, forming a destructive burst of chemistry. The kiss was brimmed with passion and longing and everything that had been building within their souls since they met.

Once, in the Forest of Dahlia, they existed separately—a Soothsayer and the Red Demon.

Now, they were one.

CHAPTER TWENTY-SIX

Morakques approached from diverging gravel and cobblestone routes which blended seamlessly with the dirt of the forest ground. A handful passed by the witches without noticing their presence, leaving behind the forest as if it did not contain the two beings who might soon ruin them.

They left the witches behind like a dark scarf on a winter floor that would eventually trip them.

Ruby stayed silent as she watched commoners and nobility pass by—people who could be parents, siblings, and lovers. For the first time, she learned that there were women within the Morakques. At the sight, Lilith stated that if she were to truly rule one day, she would ensure that equality prevailed.

With each hour, Morakques flooded into their fort.

The witches spent the day observing their foes like assassins, taking notes of their routine. Morakques would return for meetings in the afternoon, then wander the field in front of their stone structure to train and converse. Ruby compared the fort to jail and Morakques to prisoners, for they needed to return daily and did not seem thrilled but instead upset. She wondered for the first time if they *wanted* to be who they were.

Every once in a while, a few of them would head

towards the castle. In all, Ruby was certain that there were at least ten thousand Morakques altogether, loitering the field and within their building.

Ruby and Lilith spent only a few more days noting every little detail until they felt the need to move on. They discovered that there was an assembly every evening for all Morakques, which provided them with the opportunity to collate the number of enemies they would face.

As the scintillating golden sun that rivalled the gilded castle began its descent, the meadow area began to form rows of people. There were announcements and conversations that the witches listened to daily, unbeknownst to the Morakques.

"The Queen," the leader, whose name the witches learnt was Wei, sneered, "has been sending her royal guards to spy on our business."

The man stood tall and imposing on the platform, his brown hair pulled back into his signature tight bun at the nape of his neck. A few stray strands fell across his forehead, adding to his rugged appearance. The wrinkles on his round face gave him the look of a weathered sailor used to navigating treacherous waters.

A gasp rippled throughout the great crowd, and Ruby imitated their shock with a laugh. Picking up all the details of their enemies led to them figuring out who belonged and who did not.

"There is an undercover amongst us, and we will figure out who it is," he continued. "It would be appreciated if we are careful with our words until the guard is captured."

Lilith chuckled, then slapped a hand over her mouth to

silence herself. Although Wei was Marco's father, his constantly irritated demeanor set him apart from his son. He was utterly clueless that the man closest to him was under royalty's command.

They watched as the Morakques began to take their pledge of allegiance before speaking about new inventions and discoveries.

"We have to know where they head every two hours," Ruby muttered, gazing into the distance. She attempted to ask the demon for the location, but it refused to speak. "It may be where they are keeping the sorcerers."

"I have an idea," Lilith whispered, turning to Khaos. "I will send one of them to have a look, then allow that shadow to seize my body and tell you."

"Is that not dangerous?"

"The queen claims that as long as three of them are not controlling me, nothing horrid would transpire."

Ruby nodded grimly, then watched as a shadow left like colored mist, as imperceivable as the tiny movement of leaves when touched by the wind. The being that cannot be caught wafted away without the softest whisper of goodbye, leaving traces of swirling darkness. Lilith diverted her attention away only after it disappeared out of sight.

The air became tense after arriving so close to the Fort of Morakques, so close to the end. Ruby was unsure what exactly was ending—a chapter of their lives or the entire book. Their beating hearts were balancing on a plank, a step away from the dark ocean that wanted nothing more than to swallow them whole.

"I am pretty sure the royal guard will be imprisoned

soon enough; his presence is too obvious," Lilith stated, eyes trained on the man. His collar was improper, his face too serious, and his overall appearance screamed loyalty instead of hatred. Morakques were driven by wrath, for it was what empowered them.

"Have more faith in the poor man," Ruby said. "He has been hiding in their midst for days."

Lilith snorted, then listened in on the assembly talk. She learned about people in the royal family just by doing so.

It took a moment before the darkness that wandered away on its own finally returned, drifting freely like darkening clouds with swirling smoke in the place of raindrops. Ruby glanced at her companion, who returned the look with reassurance.

The shadow seemed to have anticipated the moment for a lifetime. From a human figure, it became a python-like haze before disappearing into its temporary body.

Lilith's eyes flickered once, twice, then all traces of her were gone. The quiet calculation behind her gaze was replaced by a violent hunger, and her nails grew terrifyingly sharper.

"Hello, Khaos," Ruby stumbled on her words just slightly. There was an odd sensation in the back of her head as if the demon in her mind was battling to leave. To bridge the distance between itself and the shadows that were also made of fate's attempt to balance the world. It had a determination that alarmed her, reminding her of the last time it managed to escape.

"Queen," greeted the shadow, forming a smile as it

dropped to a curtsey—the graceful dip meant for the highest-ranking royalty. Ruby had never seen such a cruelly edged smile on Lilith's face, nor was she ever called such an unbelievable title.

"What did you see?"

"A shed guarded by six Morakques—two outside, four inside. It leads underground to a dungeon with many, many witches in cells. They are not injured but instead weakened. I believe they can still run if needed," it reported in Lilith's voice, although it was evidently not her. Whereas she would raise her chin in confidence and speak in a gentle but commanding tone, the shadow used her voice as a weapon. It was sharp and savage and could pierce as effectively as a dagger.

"How many witches?"

"Dozens."

Ruby nodded, contemplating. If the place was constantly guarded, it would be difficult to release the prisoners. "Thank you."

Another sickening grin was plastered on her face. "Of course," it said. "Tell Faye I said hello."

The true name of the Red Demon made her heart skip a beat. It had been years since she heard of it. Knowing someone else had that knowledge made her feel a certain way—as if she was annoyed that it was no longer something between her and the whispers. Something that made them friends.

For why? The demon snorted (if the sniff of absurdity could be labelled as such) in its voices. *You think I am a creature that deserves no name.*

Ruby did not know why it mattered so much, either.

"Alright," she answered Khaos after a long pause, her voice as dry as sandpaper.

The shadow nodded, then seemingly yanked itself from Lilith's body. It retracted, escaping as a form of dark mist. Gradually, the glimmer of kindness returned to the Queen of Darkness, a stark contrast to the wickedness that overtook her face when Khaos was in control. She was dazed for a second before hope clouded her features.

"Did you receive any important information?" Lilith asked.

Ruby nodded, then told her about the underground prison and its captives. The news was not startling, unfortunately. They knew how cruel Morakques could be simply to reach their goals, and they could do nothing but fight their crimes with crimes.

"We need an effective way to sneak in and save them," Lilith said, contemplating.

"But there is no way to go unseen and unscathed; it is guarded at all times," Ruby complained. It was true; their daily observation fed them with the fact that the place was always guarded by Morakques, who switched their shifts constantly. If the witches were to kill them, it was likely that another would come within the next ten minutes. That was not enough time to break locks, hurry the prisoners out and cover their tracks.

They did not possess the time to sit around and wait, either. With every passing moment, Lilith was at risk of death from her darkness. She needed a cure, and that was only possible if they were free from Morakques.

Lilith pursed her lips. "We can barge in."

"No," Ruby retorted.

"Fine. We will mull over it during the night."

The sun began to set, and the Morakques were beginning to head home. Ruby realized a few days ago that not all Morakques left; a few stayed in the stone building, and at times, they camped in the field. The witches had buried the books they traveled with in case the hunters stumbled upon them.

"Is there a cure for your darkness?" Ruby asked, nestling closer to her companion. It was a cold night, and Lilith's presence provided her with physical warmth and another type that pooled in the pit of her stomach. It churned with an ocean of nervousness and excitement that created little flutters. The irresistible blend of feelings made her magic near its edge. Sometimes, it came so close to bursting that she had to call upon growing flowers to bloom so that it could drain some of her emotions. It worked for a moment until it came back in yet another wave.

"No," answered Lilith. Ruby's heart sank. "Queen Lysandra said that darkness will never leave. The fates gave it to me, and it is impossible to get rid of it. However, there is a way to gain control and never die from it."

The red-eyed witch pulled away to glance at Lilith's expression and immediately missed the heat. But she had to make sure it was true. "How?"

"A golden vial of immortality."

Hope drained from her face almost immediately. She had read about it many times before. "That is impossible to get."

The young queen shrugged. "You never know."

Ruby sighed, glancing at the moon that was now hanging with pride in the sky. Another wave of feelings hit her hard in the chest, and she tried to swallow it down. This time, it was sadness and worry. "I cannot lose you, Lilith."

She wanted her companion to say anything. Perhaps reassure her by saying that she was not going anywhere, and promise she would try her hardest to achieve the impossible and live. Yet, all she received was a frown.

"I will try," the response came late. It was probably the only and best thing Lilith could say.

The distress built and built, and Ruby made no move to suppress it. Her well of magic was so immense that it affected her feelings so easily, and she was tired. She was worn out from having to be careful just so she would not be caught and murdered. So, the young witch did nothing even as her emotions overwhelmed her.

Then, before she could even think of the risks of her action, familiar red smoke shot from her fingertips to bloom another patch of flowers. It was not all she did; magic unintentionally blasted from her hand right after. Ruby realized a second too late that flames danced on the forest ground, travelling and spreading and becoming something much bigger than mere specks of shimmering light.

Lilith gasped, but she did not run. "Ruby!" she scolded. "You could have hurt yourself."

Ruby smiled sheepishly in reply, then gazed at the fire that made her eyes glisten. She traded a small portion of her emotions to create two little whirling figures from a memory that was engraved in her mind. It was the day they danced to the rhythm of an instrumental song in the loft of Marco's house, giggling at each other's faces as they stood so close together. Ruby had felt Lilith's rapid heartbeat against her chest. They twirled and accidentally tripped once or twice, but they always returned hand in hand.

For a moment, Lilith was entranced. She looked at Ruby—*truly* looked—and appreciated every slope of her profile, every dip of the everchanging shadow cast by her blaze, every strand of auburn hair. Then, the more reasonable part of her mind worked her mouth. "Our lives are on the line, and you are putting on a grand show?"

Ruby reached into the part of herself that supposedly withheld the leash to her magic. Lilith had relayed a message from the previous Queen of Darkness. Lysandra said that a witch's power came from the mind, for it possessed the ability to control our emotions. Since childhood, she believed the heart was responsible instead.

Cease the fire, Ruby said mentally. She could feel a connection with the fire she produced, like a bond tying her consciousness to the flames. It was almost too easy. All she had to do was imagine the disappearance of the flames.

"Morakques are bound to come after seeing the fire," Lilith said, a hint of panic in her tone. "We have to go. Now."

Barehanded, the witches broke into a sprint. They dashed through the pebble-filled routes of footprints, passed the watchful eyes of wildlife, and wandered further away from the hunters' fort.

For a moment, nothing but the soft crunching of shoes against leaves could be heard.

Ruby was not in *such* a hurry, mostly because she doubted that the Morakques could catch sight of them. If they did not notice a member of the royal guard in their midst when it was so painfully obvious, she was doubtful that she would be caught.

The witches halted in their tracks, glancing around the area.

Ruby turned to face Lilith. "They are not going to search—"

"*Monsters!*" exclaimed a voice, breaking the serenity of the forest. Ruby widened her eyes, then swallowed, pressing her back against the tree's rough bark while Lilith did the same a few feet away. Her breaths came in short pants, distracting her from the anxiousness that now gnawed at her insides like persistent flies on a lion's mane. From watching them for the last few days, she had not thought that the Morakques were observant enough to spot them.

She was wrong.

Lilith muttered the wind's prayer under her breath, casting her eyes skyward. Her shadows had imitated her emotions and shrunk in fear.

An eerie silence settled. For the following seconds, nothing happened. Ruby only allowed herself to sigh after a long moment passed.

It is fine. Everything is fine, Ruby told herself.

How sure are you? questioned the demon.

Now is not the time, she said, trying to block out its voices.

Oh, but it is. Here, let us count together. Three.

Ruby bit her lips, shutting her eyes to focus on her

thoughts and not the voices that resounded as loud as horns in her head. They filled the entire space of her mind, leaving no gap for anything else.

Two.

She glanced around. Nobody.

One.

She looked to her right, where Lilith stared at Khaos. The shadows were beginning to split into three, reassured that Morakques were nowhere close.

Zero.

A hand clasped her left shoulder, and a gasp left her lips. Terror bubbled in her throat as the world paused.

"Found you," mumbled a gruff voice.

A sensible part of her concealed her true appearance before turning, reshaping her features and changing her red eyes to hazel ones. If the Morakques knew that they captured the Red Demon, imprisonment would be a blessing. She was the biggest threat to them and hence would likely be immediately executed.

She looked at Lilith quickly, and apprehension coiled in her stomach. Both of them were held by Morakques, with little way to escape. She could eliminate them easily, but that would be too much of a risk. One sound from them or one mistake from her would lead to an army of Morakques investigating. Then, she and Lilith would be as good as dead.

Without the Concealer ability, Lilith hung her head low. One glance at her eyes and the Morakques would know.

"Found who?" Ruby asked, innocent.

"Filthy witch," he sneered. It was too late to pretend. "Nobody else would lurk in a forest with clothes such as yours."

Bile rose in her throat as dread colored her face.

"Come with me." The man shoved Ruby without sympathy. She gritted her teeth at the treatment, although she could not expect anything more generous. The man yanked her hand, and she decided that was it. Making a mental note of his bearded face, she promised herself that he would soon be nothing but ashes.

She followed unwillingly as the Morakque led her towards his fort, then made a sharp turn. "Found these pesky creatures loitering in Hollow Forest," he said to a friend as he forced her into a shed, then underground.

The dungeon was lined with torches, similar to those surrounding the fort. They were the only source of illumination in the gloomy place, where cells each held up to three weary individuals. Ruby was unable to gaze into the prison long enough to tell if they were witches. A pungent odor wafted into her nose, and she scrunched up her face in a grimace.

"In here," said a voice, then both Ruby and Lilith were thrown into a dark and grimy cell. The clinking of metal was heard, then another wave of silence.

Ruby lifted her head just slightly, then waited until the guards who carelessly hurled them into a cage left their sight. She looked to her side, catching the coal-black eyes that belonged to the Queen of Darkness.

When their eyes met, they came to a spontaneous, startling realization.

Perhaps, being confined was the best opportunity they had to rescue the witches.

CHAPTER TWENTY-SEVEN

Lysandra was angry.

"I cannot believe you are willing to rot down here," she snapped. "You are a queen, for Dicera's sake. You live in a castle, not a cell!"

No, she was furious.

Lilith's lips were sealed shut, listening to the rants of her dead ancestor. Lysandra was evidently out of place with her exquisite gown, voguish a thousand years ago, and perhaps even now. She belonged in a ballroom with a king wearing a suit just as fancy, not in prison.

On the other hand, Lilith looked like the perfect captive; her clothes were muddy and torn and exceedingly unroyal.

She might have understood that being captured allowed her and Ruby a better chance at saving the trapped witches, but she wanted nothing more than to leave the horrid dungeon. Multiple iron bars, three brick walls and a high ceiling blocked any chance of escape. The only light source was the torches with flickering tangerine fire, throwing shadows that danced to an unheard tune on the ground. Lilith's own shadows loomed at her back. Thankfully, they were intelligent enough to scatter and blend into their surroundings when Morakques passed by.

"How long are we staying in this wretched place?" asked Lysandra, huffing.

Lilith glanced outside the cell she shared with Ruby. The four guards never seemed to stop talking. They were perpetually distracted, but they would be alerted if they heard something out of the ordinary.

"Not very long, I hope," muttered Lilith under her breath.

After guiding the witches out of the dungeon, Lilith and Ruby were to head towards Elymore, the town closest to the castle and safest from Morakques. There, they hoped to be granted an audience with royalty.

Ruby was already looking for loose bricks that could be removed. First, they needed a way that allowed the witches to be aware of their arrival.

"I found one!"

Lilith raised an eyebrow, thankful for the discovery. Lysandra paused in her reprimanding.

"Is it possible to remove it?"

"Of course," Ruby answered, then flicked her fingers in a fraction of a second. As if it was hammered from the other side, the brick quietly fell into her palms. Lilith widened her eyes, impressed.

"What ability did you use?"

"Nature. I asked the trapped soil between bricks for assistance."

"The soil responded?" asked Lilith flatly, the insanity of it urging her to laugh.

"I used Queen Lysandra's method."

Lilith had yet to try the technique of imagery made into

reality introduced by her ancestor, mostly because she hoped to reserve every shred of strength for the future. If she used her ability, whatever emotions she might have would drain. She thought of what exactly she felt at the current moment—the eternal anger towards the Morakques, concern for the future, and most prominently, her love for Ruby. They were strong feelings that she kept hidden so she might not lose control over her powers like she used to.

"It is helpful," Ruby commented, glancing at the brick she held.

Lysandra made a sound of pride behind them. *I know, right?* The words were written on her face.

"Is there anyone in the cell next to ours?" Lilith whispered, approaching the witch who was contorting her face back into her own—red eyes, sharp features, full lips.

Ruby nodded in reply as she stepped to the side, allowing Lilith to look through the gap where the brick once was. They had to be quiet and extremely careful. While the guards were busy speaking, they needed to pass on a message.

"Psst! Hi."

Lilith could not see those on the other side of the wall, but she knew that she caught somebody's attention by the sound of shuffling. Yet, she received no response. She skimmed through her mind for a solution that could immediately gain the trust of a witch, like speaking in a code that only her kind would understand.

Thankfully, the hole in the wall was beside the corner and difficult to spot. It gave Lilith a little more time to ponder without panicking.

At last, she decided to whisper the prayer to the wind, for it was only known to witches. The string of words was frequently spoken, and Lilith knew that any witch would understand the words.

She only received a response after a few seconds, coming from a weak and croaky voice belonging to an old woman. "They caught you too?"

"Is there anybody else sharing your cell?" murmured Lilith.

"Few others."

"Ruby and I were sent by the elder to rescue the captured witches. I will need as much information about your stay before we can proceed."

There was another moment of silence that Lilith took for shock.

"There are a few dozen witches down here. Every day, a few of us are taken out to perform spells and be experimented on. The room is just down the corner," the old woman said, so quietly that Lilith had to strain her ears. "There is honey and pewter and more—ingredients for spells. The Morakques figured out the use for all of them. They use us to defend themselves against the royals and detect the witches in their midst."

Frowning, Lilith looked at Lysandra. "Are there spells that work against witches? Something that poisons us but not humans?" she asked. She had never heard of such a thing, but it was possible.

"Of course." The former Queen of Darkness was certain. "Not poison, exactly. Some spells harm witches and only witches. However, there is a chance to overcome it if you are strong enough." She shrugged. "What can I say? I was intelligent enough to create powerful, undefeatable creatures."

Lilith recalled her time back in the Village of Dakota. She was wrong; she *had* come across the spell before. It was claimed to be a protection spell for those against her kind. She shuddered as she revisited the memory of Ruby, panting and tormented as magic was yanked from her.

Lilith spent the next few minutes asking the woman questions and listening, gathering as much information as possible before returning the brick to its original position. She had to know enough of the dungeon's layout and the confined witches to produce and polish a decent plan.

"What have you got?" Ruby asked.

"Not much, but enough. The witch I spoke to promised to tell the rest of the witches in this prison to ready themselves," responded Lilith. "We need to be escorted out of our cell by Morakques to play a part in performing the protection spell. With all of the witches gathered there, we can make our escape."

In the meantime, Khaos would explore deeper into the dungeon, then return to report what they saw by responding to simple yes or no questions.

"We should split up after escaping with the witches," Lilith suggested. She received the reaction she expected. Ruby immediately adamantly shook her head and refused the idea. "Ruby, I understand why you are not thrilled about this because neither am I. But we must be more practical about this."

Ruby looked unconvinced. Lilith sighed and

continued, "The more people we have in our group, the slower we will travel, and we need to move as fast as we can. If we split up, I can go alone to retrieve the books that Marco gifted us, while you can take the head start with the witches towards safety. They are undoubtedly exhausted, and going together to grab the books would only waste their energies. We cannot afford that."

Ruby's frown was profound, but she was no longer passionately rebuking the idea. Lilith finished her explanation for the necessary split, saying, "Besides, you know the direction towards safety, and I will have the map. I will meet you in the safe territory." She looked at Ruby with a determined expression.

Ruby did not appear pleased when she responded, "You have a knack for persuasion."

"So you agree with the plan?"

"I hate that you will be traveling alone. It is not safe."

"I can command darkness."

Ruby grumbled, "Fine, but only because Queen Lysandra will be accompanying you. I doubt she would appreciate harm coming your way."

Lilith smiled radiantly, looking at her ancestor. Lysandra was still murmuring curses for having to be within ten feet of grime. "She is currently frustrated with this place."

"This place *is* horrible," Ruby agreed. "The voices want it destroyed."

"We can make that happen," Lilith said. It did not sound like such a terrible idea.

Ruby grinned approvingly. It was short-lived, for it

faded just as the sound of agony reverberated throughout the dungeon, like groans that belonged to a dying horse. It bounced off the walls and made Lilith's ears ring.

Iron creaked, screeching filled the air, a thump, then silence.

In front of the two witches laid a Morakque—no—a royal guard. Lilith recognized the man and allowed empathy to cross her features. However, she knew long ago that he could not hide amongst Morakques forever.

A string of profanities escaped the man's lips, followed by moans of pain. Lilith wanted to help but paused as soon as he lifted his head. He gazed into her eyes, which were infused with the color of coals and dropped his jaw. All signs of pain disappeared for a slight moment. Then, he looked into Ruby's red eyes, and the color drained from his face.

He opened his mouth like he wanted to scream, but no sound escaped.

"What in Dicera," muttered the man, keeping some distance between him and the girls. The sight of a grown man from the outside world cowering before a witch would have made Lilith laugh, but she could not afford to terrify the guard any more than she had. She predicted his arrival, and he came at quite a convenient time. With his help, Lilith and Ruby could learn about Dicera's royalty and how to secure an audience with them.

Currently, the witches' main goal was to carry out the rescue and then escape unscathed without Morakques knowing that the most powerful witches had entered their dungeon. The hunters could not know that the Forest of

Dahlia was now without their Red Demon and thus, unprotected.

"Hello," Lilith said in a whisper. Her voice belonged to a girl, not a demon.

"What are ya?" demanded the guard, fear and distress clouding his eyes like dancers entering a ballroom. His terror made his accent impossibly thicker.

Lysandra stared at the man, who looked in his mid-thirties. "Insolence," she said disapprovingly. "He should really learn some manners. You *are* his queen, after all."

Lilith managed a smile, then glanced at Ruby to do the same. Her companion rolled her eyes before mustering a forced grin.

"A witch," answered Lilith. She was not ashamed of what she was, and she said it in a tone that showed him what she thought. "Not all sorcerers look like my friend"—she gestured to Ruby—"over here. Do not worry. We will not hex you or anything. Instead, I would love to assist you in return for a favor."

"Assist?" repeated the guard, baffled. "I came knowin' there was a possibility of getting caught. My comrades will come by tonight if they sense anythin' wrong; I ain't need rescuing."

Lilith's mind spun, disbelief dropping her jaw. Her heart was alighted with pleasant surprise at her luck. If the man was going to escape with the help of other guards...

"When your friends come along to rescue you, release all witches as well," she said, shooting Ruby a victorious glance. This would make things simpler. They would no longer need to navigate the way because the guards and witches would be heading in the same direction towards Elymore. Lilith added, "In return, I will save your life by not killing you."

Ruby tried to hold in a laugh but failed miserably.

Lysandra, on the other hand, beamed. "I am teaching you well."

"Treason," spat the guard, barely sounding intimidating. "You people are despicable."

"No, I do not think so," Lilith said and smiled, gesturing to the scar on her body. The scar that showed she was a rightful heir to the Dicera throne. It did not mean she would be queen, but it represented as much.

The man's jaw was now touching the floor, his eyes brimming with so much emotion that it bewildered Lilith. "Are you alright?" she asked. She could not help it.

"A witch?" he asked disbelievingly to nobody in particular. "The queen is a witch?"

She raised an eyebrow in confusion.

The guard was silent for the next minute, and Lilith decided not to push for an answer. It did not matter. She was not the Queen of Dicera, nor did she think it was possible still.

"Will you help?" she asked, overwhelmed by the silence.

"Eh, do I have a choice?" he scoffed.

"Yes. I can offer an additional favor on my part. When I become queen in the future, I will give you a great position." Lilith hoped that he did not see the wavering confidence in her lies.

Strangely, the guard believed her. Lilith was thankful,

but she could not help but feel that it was strange. He did not put up more of a fight. "I will help you, Lilith."

She widened her eyes, and Ruby snapped her head in the guard's direction quicker than a heartbeat. A fusion of confusion and terror corrupted Lilith's chest like a swarm of attacking bees after its hive was demolished. A lump formed in her throat, and she did not know why the reaction dawned. Perhaps it was the shock of a human knowing the name she never shared. Or perhaps, it was because she already knew deep down what he would say next.

"It's your name, is it not?" he asked, sounding too certain to be wrong. "Lilith. The daughter of Queen Emeline, the current ruler of Dicera."

CHAPTER TWENTY-EIGHT

Her mother was alive.

The fact alone was not shocking since Lilith discovered as much. But to know that her mother was the Queen of Dicera? That changed everything.

She did not even consider the possibility because of how incredibly slim it was. The thought had slithered into her mind once, then was dismissed without hesitation. She could not believe that her mother, Nana's daughter, was the ruler of Dicera. The obstacles on the path blinding her from the truth suddenly vanished, like mist clearing from a grove. Answers that she sought her entire life were laid out so plainly just by one discovery.

Nana must have known.

The woman ensured Lilith received very little knowledge about her magic because it would be effortless to find out with a vision or spell. What did her grandmother think Lilith was going to do anyway? She was not *that* reckless; she would not put her life on a thin thread to venture out of the forest.

Lilith swallowed a gasp when another revelation crept into her mind. There was only one explanation for her mother's banishment from the Forest of Dahlia—her mother eloped with royalty (the current king, for Dahlia's sake). It was the very first rule in Dahlia's book, 'A Witch's Rules,' and she broke it.

"Ah, another one of my descendants following in my footsteps," Lysandra chimed. "We *are* scandalous, are we not? I cannot say I am not proud."

Lilith did nothing but stare into the guard's eyes, which made him uneasy after a moment.

Queen Emeline. That was the name of her mother—the Witch Queen. It was almost too good to be true.

"Our plan," Ruby whispered, echoing Lilith's thoughts. "It is complete."

If Lilith's mother was the queen, she would most likely agree to help witches if it was asked of her. Although Lilith doubted that her mother would recognize her, she knew, *somehow*, that woman she did not know loved her.

"My mother spoke of my name?" Lilith asked with hope clinging onto every word. She did not know why it meant so much to her.

"Ay, of course," the royal guard replied as if the response was the most obvious thing in the world. "You are the lost princess." He leaned against the brick wall, keeping his gaze unwavering on the Queen of Darkness. "As ya might know, anyone with the royal bloodline has the right to the throne. So, there is a policy that ensures royalty has one child only, no matter what. Your birth was celebrated almost two decades ago, and then nobody ever heard from you again."

Lilith refrained from gawking. She knew so little about the outside world, but she was apparently such a big part of it. She wondered if the other witches knew about her mother.

She suppressed a snort at the number of titles she bore like a crown on her head—Queen of Darkness, lost princess, possible future queen of Dicera, and descendant of the most powerful witch to ever exist. If fate believed that she deserved to carry those names, she must not neglect them.

Looking to the exit of the dungeon, she noted that a guard had been replaced by another. She was using them to keep track of the time, so she would not be carrying out her escape in daylight.

"When are your comrades coming?" asked Lilith.

The man was still sensibly wary, but he replied either way. "Eh, probably an hour or two after they realize I stopped handing in reports."

"May I ask if Elymore is safe for witches?"

"I'd say so," said the man. "Once you reach the land that the royals own, it'll be safe for you. Telling Morakque and royalty territory apart is easy. Uh, this separation of land happened hundreds of years ago when Morakques' influence became undeniable. The royals went negotiatin' a pact with them. Agreed to give up the land so the hunters won't go mixing round with those loyal to the crown. Don't know what they were thinkin', but the change's irreversible." He ran his fingers through his hair as unsaid words painted his face.

Lilith knew that he had many questions and doubts. She could only imagine the weight on his shoulders for being the first and only Dicerian who recognized Lilith as the lost princess. Her lips formed a tight line as she attempted to figure out the look plastered on the soldier's face—bafflement, bewilderment and fear. There was something else, but she could not put her finger on what it was. It seemed like a mixture of relief and concern.

"What is it?" Lilith asked.

"Nothin'," he replied immediately and must have noticed how horrible of a lie it was. "Uh, it's just… I guess I always had an inklin' that the queen was a witch. I've been assigned the role of her guard for almost a decade, so it's only normal that I catch on to things." He wet his lips, seeming to be in a mental debate with himself. "The queen bears the mark of royalty just like you, so it should've been obvious. I don't know why I doubted it for so long. I think it's because I kept believin' all witches have horns."

Lilith tried stifling a laugh. Ruby did not even try but immediately quietened when Morakques turned heads in their direction.

To be fair, Lilith thought that Ruby possessed horns once, too.

She retreated into a corner, where the removal of a single brick would reveal the witch in the next cell.

"I am going to perform a soothsaying spell," Lilith told Ruby and the royal guard in a hushed whisper. Lilith needed to know if she could trust the guard with the escape and perhaps receive some hints about the near future. There was a lump in her throat that could not be swallowed, like a rock obstructing the flow of a river. She bore many titles, but she was born with only one—Soothsayer. She wondered why she was afraid to look into the unforeseen future when she had done it so many times before.

"A spell?" blurted the guard quietly. Cold fear flashed across his face, painting it as white as a ghost. He went impossibly paler after noticing Khaos. Two of them were floating above Lilith's shoulder and one was above her head.

Ruby chuckled at his expression. "I would suggest that you be careful. She is going to create a potion that will scald and corrode your skin. Imagine it like little insects."

The guard widened his eyes and pushed himself against the wall, believing every word.

Lilith rolled her eyes, but a smile lingered on her face. "She is kidding."

The guard was not convinced.

Lilith let out a quiet sigh, then fished out her mother's gift—the mirror—still by her side as always. The Morakques were absurdly irresponsible for not checking their prisoners for possessions. Not for the first time, Lilith wondered if they were truly committed to their role.

She was stronger than the last time she saw the mirror, and now she could *feel* the obsidian on the frame. It was like a tugging leash attached to her heart, connecting her magic to the rock. Once, she could only seek the future with the presence of the obsidian or when she was strengthened with a spell. Now, she knew her ability would flare to life even without the glimmering scarlet stone.

Fluttering her eyes shut, she used her mind to imagine what the future might bring. Then, as expeditiously as a heartbeat to the next, it distorted and became a moving image of pounding footsteps and heavy pants, a flurry of movements and emotions. The thrill of running was so apparent that she could smell it.

Abruptly, the vision shifted into another. Lilith looked to the side as she ambled, eyes settling on Ruby and the smile that brightened her face. She could feel her lips curling, mirroring the smile. Behind them were a dozen guards, all with Dicera's crest sewn onto their uniforms. There were witches, too, walking alongside the soldiers as if they were one.

Then, the second vision dissipated and became a third. It took a moment for Lilith to realize the scene had changed from a forest to a broad and open field. There were warriors around her, both dead and alive. Khaos was there, lingering quietly while people screeched and yelled and cried.

Before she could glance around the area for Ruby, she returned from blinding daylight to depressing darkness. The cage came into view gradually, and two pairs of expectant eyes were fixed on her.

"Is he a snitch?" Ruby asked.

"No," Lilith said. From what she could infer, the escape was bound to happen, and so was a battle. She gulped at the word and the grotesque images it brought to mind. It was a suitable name for a sort of weapon crafted to eradicate, filled with spikes and chains that could sweep its opponents off their feet.

Ruby grinned, satisfied. "Great. Now that I know you are no traitor, what is your name?"

The guard furrowed his eyebrows as if baffled by the question. "For why?"

"If we are to escape together, I think your name deserves to be known."

"Des." He was hesitant for a moment before asking, "How about yours?"

"Ruby." She grinned. "Or Your Majesty. Both works."

The guard snorted, then looked at Lilith. She shrugged in reply. "*If* I ever were to rule, Ruby would be by my side as my queen."

"I see. Well, the law *does* expect a coregency—"

Ruby shot upright suddenly, and his words halted. Lilith looked questioningly at her companion, trying to read her unsettled expression. Her eyes dimmed to a hazel color, and she sharpened her features in a flash, causing Des to let out an accidental shriek.

"Look down, Lilith. Hide your fingers," Ruby whispered, and Lilith did as instructed. "Morakques are coming."

It took only a second before said Morakques came into view, filling the dungeon with the sound of clinking—metal against iron bars.

"Come out, Witches." Lilith had her eyes cast downwards, but she recognised the voice. It belonged to the bearded man who hurled Ruby into their cell.

Slowly, she stood. It was a blessing that nobody noticed her unnaturally sharpened and dark nails yet.

Ruby followed her lead, trailing behind obediently until they were out of the cell. The Morakque's rough hand was around Lilith's wrist as if she were harmful.

The clanking of the cell doors rang out, then only shuffling of feet was heard as she entered a separate room.

From the corner of her eyes, she could see Khaos. She wondered if the Morakque would think the shadows odd if they were more noticeable.

"In here," he shoved. Then the sound of doors slamming shut echoed in the room. Lilith did not dare to lift her head, but she could see multiple feet on the ground. The room was already occupied by people, presumably witches.

"Hello," uttered a woman's voice.

"What is this place?" Ruby questioned.

"Here, you will assist the Morakques by casting a spell that harms witches in several villages."

"And why do you think I will agree to that?" Ruby remarked disdainfully.

"One word from me, or one press of this button, and you shall perish." Lilith pictured the woman gesturing arrogantly to the button she spoke of. It was likely a handheld device. Humans outdid themselves with their mechanical inventions. There was a slight pause before she spoke again, "You. Stop looking at your feet."

Lilith felt her breathing hitch. If she lifted her head, there would doubtlessly be a commotion about her strange characteristics. The woman overseeing the Morakques' protection spell would alert every guard within the dungeon.

Her mind raced for a solution. She needed time. She needed to tell these witches in the room about her plan. She needed a way to silence the threatening woman.

An idea struck her mind.

How could she have forgotten? She was the Queen of Darkness, ruler of death and sleep.

She closed her eyes, Lysandra's voice resounding in her mind. Using her technique, she flicked her hand while visualizing her aunt falling unconscious. The room was still silent, and then a thud sounded. Quiet gasps were heard from the witches in the room.

Lilith knew that she had done it. She dismissed the bubbling urge to smile, for she had not entirely succeeded. Yet.

Slowly, she looked up. The faces of her kind came into view, and she tried not to mirror the grin on Ruby's face.

"What are you?" whispered one of the witches. Fear laced her words like venom on a snake's fang.

"My name is Lilith," she said quietly, not exactly answering the question. She looked into the eyes of everyone surrounding her, who stared back in utmost terror. Some of their eyes paused on Khaos and the cloud of darkness they formed behind her. More had their unwavering gazes on the mark Lilith bore by her side that was now helplessly exposed. They whispered amongst themselves, both awed and scared.

She looked at Ruby, who nodded back at her. "We are here to help you."

Their murmurs subsided. "Are you… a witch?"

Lilith stared back, bemused. "Yes."

"But, aren't you the queen's child?"

"I am," Lilith said, then pondered about what better response could inform the witches of all they needed to know for now. She would have time later, but she needed the witches to listen. She needed trust, even if she had to lie to obtain it.

She lifted her head. "I am the heir to Dicera's throne, a Witch Queen who will lead a future reign—the Reign of Ruth."

CHAPTER TWENTY-NINE

Ruby knew that Lilith was uncertain of her words. Although the Queen of Darkness spoke with conviction that could fool all Dicerians, Ruby heard the slight shake in her words. A tremble that only she understood.

In the past, she faced the elder in the Forest of Dahlia and vowed to protect all witches from the Morakque's purges. She did it so many times, but doubt nipped at her mind no matter how strong people believed her to be.

She resisted the urge to reach for her friend's hand. The demon within her mind was practically begging for her to do so.

Oh, come on, you coward, it said. *Just one touch. Do it.*

Ruby ignored it, trying to build a veil between them. She focused on the reality outside her mind, where witches looked between Lilith and her, bemused to the very core.

"I will explain later, when we leave the Fort of Morakques to Elymore," Lilith said. She looked at Ruby, who lifted the concealment spell on her face. As if a wall of fire arose in front of their toes, they shot back as one. It was their first reaction after realizing that they were staring into the eyes of the infamous Red Demon.

Ruby knew it was not a compliment to be feared. Once, she was troubled by how people failed to see that her demon was another soul on its own. She was lonely and trapped in a world of misery. Yet now, she could not help the giggle that rose from the pit of her stomach. It was not funny, but rather amusing, that witches feared her. They were the people who fed her all the power she had, after all.

Imagine being afraid of a monster you created, the whispers agreed.

"I was tasked to save our kind by the elder," Ruby said. Fleeting expressions flashed in the faces of witches—understanding, gratitude, relief, and confusion. "We have no time to spare; our plan is in action." She glanced at the shelf by the side of the room and gestured to the items for spells atop each section. "Grab as many of those as possible. If we encounter difficulties on our journey, they will be helpful."

Some witches were stiff and unmoving, as if they could not believe help had arrived. The others sprang into a blur of motion, rushing to gather items.

Ruby sighed, allowing a second of relief. She turned away from the individuals to take in her surroundings for the first time since she was brought into the room. The smell within the enclosed area was better than the odor that rented the air in the narrow walkway between cells, but the quality was not any better. The walls were coated with dust, soot and even smears of red. The splatters of dried liquid were traced to the ground as if someone was massacred right where she stood.

"Hey, are you alright?" A hand closed around her, entwining fingers delivering a warmth that, for a second, convinced Ruby that all was fine.

"I am," she responded, although she was not. No matter

how much comfort she received, the thought of the future leeched onto her mind like an ear's constant ringing after a deafening sound. The demon knew, and its tone when regarding the future did not serve her with anything positive.

Lilith knew she was lying but said nothing. Both of them needed a great amount of time before ever feeling *alright* again.

The room was filled with the noise of shuffling, heavy breathing, and hushed conversations. Ruby was holding her breath, knowing that something horrible was bound to happen.

She morphed her features into one that was not her own, then waited and waited, all while squeezing Lilith's hand tighter.

Her heart was speeding with every passing second. Anxiety was stroking her heart with calloused hands, bearing sharpened nails that could only belong to a demon. The serenity in the air was unnerving, for silence seemed so unlikely in such a dreadful time. Somehow, nothing happening became more terrifying than the only other option.

Moments stretched into an eternity. A lump rose in Ruby's throat as a myriad of wrecking thoughts sprinted across her mind. Perhaps, the royal guards were not coming. Or worse still, the Morakques—

A deafening bang exploded from outside, sounding like an eruption of chaos. Witches released gasps and yelps of shock, some losing their grip on the ingredients they held. Vials shattered, footsteps thundered, screeching and bellowing began, yet nothing was louder than the violent thumping of Ruby's heart.

"Follow our lead and be wary of your surroundings," Ruby yelled over the noise. "Do not hesitate to use your abilities!"

Ruby fluttered her eyes shut without wasting any additional time and visualized plants rising from the ground beneath. Flowers burst from under the earth and pushed the door open, detaching it from its hinges. It landed on the Morakque guarding the door, the impact shattering his bones.

Ruby rushed out, glimpsing the royal guards that flooded the area with their bright uniforms with Dicera's crest stitched onto their clothing. The cell's darkness did not allow her to observe any details from her brief look. However, she noticed the determination that painted their faces as distinctly as the outlines of their darkest shadows.

She mirrored the look as she led her kind down the hallway. Begrudgingly, Lilith released Ruby's hand and rushed to a wounded Morakque on the ground and delved into his pocket for the keys to the cells.

Ruby watched as the guards stepped out of her way as if given the instruction to avoid her. She grinned, feeling as powerful as a gust of wind.

The ground seemed to shudder as if the air in the dungeon were frigid and beginning to glaze the floor with a thick patch of winter snow. The witches were riding a rapidly moving tide of the shiver that marched on the blood-stained flooring. The place let out a low rumble, starving for a meal.

Ruby knew that every pause thinned the thread that carried the weight of all witches and royal guards. She continued with the plan, instructing the witches to follow her while they escaped through the mouth of the shed. Soldiers swarmed out with them, an army with sorcerers. What a strange collaboration it was.

Des gestured to the group of royal soldiers with wild actions, pointing and uttering words that left his lips in an incomprehensive babble. Perhaps it was Ruby's mind that refused to understand his words, for it was spinning. There was too much uncertainty and too much danger. She was worried sick for Lilith and could not grasp anything worth celebrating.

I have a solution to rescue our people, the elder had announced back in the Forest of Dahlia. That time felt so distant now. It was as if the speech was delivered ages ago. *We need a witch who will bring the freedom that our kind desperately seeks by requesting aid from the royals. We must see to it that all the captured witches who live return home to us.*

Ruby was so close to rescuing the captured witches who were waiting impatiently for death within the Fort of Morakques. Yet, her mind was glued steadfastly to the fact that Lilith could die. She *would*, and Ruby did not want to accept that. She embarked on the quest to release witches from their cells and seek freedom alongside her companion. Accomplishing it would not be satisfying without her other half.

She needed a cure for the darkness that would consume Lilith. She needed a vial of immortality.

It is humorous how you wish to rid of her darkness in fear that it will control her, the demon chimed in with voices that resounded ceaselessly in her thoughts. *You have not considered the possibility of* me *controlling* you. *Permanently.*

You would not, Ruby replied.

What makes you so sure?

Ruby did not know the answer to that. Instead, she shoved the conversation to the back of her mind and continued sprinting with all the previously captured witches following her trail. The scenery around her became a blur of colors, with blossoms of pink and red and purple merging and creating illusions that messed with the head. Shrubs reached out from the ground, resembling hands rising from a grave and wildlife under cover of darkness watched with sparkling and visible eyes that stood out like a sore thumb. She was thankful for the light that managed to illuminate her paths and her surroundings.

After what felt like hours of travel, the castle finally came into view. Its towering walls and spires rose above the horizon like a beacon, compelling Ruby forward with each breath. A sudden gust of wind pushed her in its direction. She felt a connection with the gargantuan building, like an animal in the form of her heart, tethered to a tree in the form of the castle.

The witches were not safe until they entered the territory of royalty. Ruby suppressed a derisive snort. If royalty ruled over all villages in the kingdom, her kind would be safe in many more places. She would be able to enter freely without her magic being yanked away.

The guards were beside her, closing the distance

between the towering gold and red structure. Ahead of it would be Elymore.

Ruby's mind wandered to Lilith, and she fought the urge to stop dead in her tracks and turn back. They did not plan to meet in Elymore, but instead, in the safe territory— the land governed by the royals of Dicera. There, witches were relatively safe.

Ruby knew that the royal guards and witches had an overwhelming ocean of questions, and she would have to answer them in waves until they were but a calm sea.

Her heart was almost pounding out of her chest. Still, she continued pushing one foot in front of another, again and again and again until they reached the border that Morakques could not cross. Morakques were prohibited from entering the area due to the pact made centuries ago, which made it safe for her kind. Ruby was rather impressed that the agreement still stood.

Telling the two lands apart was almost too obvious. Whereas the Morakques' land was dark and depressing, the royalty's area was breathtaking.

Ruby slowed to a halt and then faced those who followed her. They looked weary with faint colors appearing on their cheeks.

She calmed herself, then shook the negative thoughts that roamed her mind. She could not bathe in her success yet. With her was a large group, but it did not include Lilith. She knew that the Queen of Darkness could protect herself, for she was improving in power immensely. Yet, she could not help the slither of concern that resided in her chest.

Ruby glanced back to where she had come from, hoping that her friend would appear.

The space remained empty and quiet.

She began speaking about her quest to her kind, hoping it would distract her from gazing into the area that stretched beyond sight. Yet, her eyes kept drifting back even while delivering her words. Even the royal guards were listening, hooked on every word.

"Lilith and I plan to bring everybody into Elymore, where we will be safe," she was saying. "We do not know if Dicerian royalty will be willing to help us to return safety to the Forest of Dahlia, or relocate all of us to a protected area, but fear not, we will seek an answer from the people who rule the kingdom."

"You are going to speak to the queen and king?" gasped a voice. "What if royalty sides with Morakques? Our heads could be gone by dawn!"

Ruby did not spend her entire life reading and equipping herself with knowledge for nothing. She was sure that royalty and Morakques had bad blood that began because of their differing outlooks towards witches.

"The rulers do not work with *Morakques*," said a guard. The way he spat the title for the people who despised witches summoned a smile on Ruby's face. "Queen Emeline does not tolerate those creatures. Villagers across Dicera might support them, but that will soon change."

Almost everybody looked at the soldier who spoke.

"How would you know?" asked a witch as politely as she could.

"Her Majesty said so herself. She is so certain that

change is arriving, and she is always right. It is almost as if she can read the future."

Ruby felt the grin on her face widen. She was sitting on a *juicy* load of information. But the thought of the woman brought her attention back to Lilith.

You do not have to worry, said the demon. It was the only phrase that Ruby could understand in the incoherent mumbles of the voices. She was getting great at ignoring the relentless and never-ending murmurs in her head.

Is she coming? Ruby questioned.

She will always come back to you, whispered the voices just as the sound of crunching leaves filled the air.

Ruby saw a smoky darkness exit the seaweed green forest first, followed by Lilith.

"You are safe," Ruby breathed as a figure approached her.

"As are you." Lilith smiled. She carried the belongings that they had buried in the ground, the books almost tumbling from her grasp. Ruby helped to grab half of the items.

"We can continue our journey to the town," Ruby said, loud enough for everybody to hear. It was just a short distance away.

She surveyed the large crowd of witches and guards, then allowed herself to feel just an inch of contentment for doing it—saving her kind. They were safe, for the time being at least, and that was enough.

"Let us go," Lilith said, intertwining her fingers with Ruby's.

Ruby sighed in relief as she held Lilith's hand again.

She memorized its perfect size as if it were made to be molded into hers. The contact made her stomach flutter, and her skin burned with the most pleasant sensation.

Spontaneously, they moved towards the town, two similar smiles on different faces.

CHAPTER THIRTY

Lilith did not know what to expect of Elymore. Perhaps the townspeople lived in houses as incredible and gold as the castle. Their heads might be too high in the clouds to even notice witches storming into their area.

She could not imagine living so close to the castle, to be able to exchange one glance for an astonishing view. The monumental structure where dignitaries lived looked just as it did in her visions. It startled her to know how familiar she was with something that she had never seen in person. It must have appeared many times, and she had forgotten them like they were nothing but vague dreams. They were not.

She saw them now, replaying over and over in her mind. The brick wall that protected the building, the exquisite external design, and the crest. The soldiers were wearing the insignia on their shirts, pinned and pridefully shown to all with eyes that linger. Lilith imagined it to glimmer under the touch of sunlight like the finest jewels used for spells.

The crest hinted at something at her very soul, reaching somewhere she did not know to exist.

As the first house in Elymore entered her sight, her thoughts took a drastic turn. What if the people despised living so close to the castle, for having royalty as neighbors cast a shadow so dark that they lived not wealthily but terribly?

Ruby's hands were still held in hers as if neither of them wanted to let go. Lilith had too many things wandering her mind to consider what the red-eyed girl meant to her. They journeyed and experienced and learned together. Lilith was certain that she would not want to embark on a quest with anybody else. Were they officially lovers? The question tugged at her mind as relentlessly as thick mist, but she removed it and focused on what was before her.

The village. Royalty. Her mother.

She wondered on many occasions what she would say to her mother if the woman were alive. It did not seem possible, but still, she allowed her imagination to sway her into a different world.

Back then, all she wanted was to fire questions and receive answers. She would ask her mother how she was coping and silently hope for the woman to return the question. She wanted to share about her Nana and how dull life was in the Forest of Dahlia. Now, she had so much more to say. Her adventure was chapters long, and it could take days to speak of every little detail.

Beyond her mother was her mission to achieve freedom for witches. She would have to stand her ground against Morakques.

She felt nervous and confident, but the latter feeling diminished as she felt a burning sensation in her chest, as if a hole had formed in her heart. She knew an explanation for that odd sensation now—darkness. It had swirled and resided within her soul for as long as she remembered. She had brushed it away so many times that it became simple to do so. The darkness would eventually consume her, and death was going to visit. There was no escaping that fate.

She glanced at Lysandra, who matched Lilith's pace even though her dress was constantly in the way. Her ancestor was quiet, which would be a blessing on many occasions. She did not want to admit it, but the words and dry jokes of the wise witch were growing on her.

It was odd that Lysandra did not speak. She was *sad*. She and Lilith shared the same demonic black eyes that left no place for emotions to shimmer within, but the young sorcerer knew. Was it because she would end Lysandra's royal bloodline? Or was it because it had been long since the queen entered an area that once belonged to her?

Lilith carried on walking as thoughts crowded her mind. As they approached the town, heads began to swivel, and curious stares pierced into them like sharp daggers.

She did not bother to hide her eyes or nails. People would assume the worst, but it made no difference. In the end, she was going to die protecting those who were afraid of her.

The witches around her might be frightened by her appearance, but she would stop at nothing to fight for the freedom they deserved.

The flames from the town were luminous and scattered with colors. It seemed like a place where conversations took place even on the darkest of nights, but it was quiet. Almost deafening.

The sun was only beginning to rise, but everybody was awake. Lilith caught a few eyes peering at her through the windows of houses that looked far bigger than a hut. She half-expected a wave of screams to engulf the place, but nothing happened. People just stared, trying to make sense of those who were evidently not royal guards.

"Witches," said one of the villagers. It was a small boy who uttered it, and he had not done so with a sneer. Instead, he said it in awe, as if he had dreamed of seeing witches since the day he was born.

People were whispering now—a stir in the quiet village.

Lilith slowed to a stroll, darting her eyes from one house to another. There were differences between the houses in Elymore and the Village of Dakota. For one, those who lived nearer to the castle had homes that reached for the skies. It was nothing like she had seen before—two or even three rooms stacked atop each other like balancing stones. The roofs were all unique, some flatter and more colorful than their neighbor's.

Could the townspeople design their own homes? Lilith would love to do that.

There were flickering flames between every house, throwing a dancing shadow on the clean concrete ground that was not peppered with specks of blood. It was a far cry from the Village of Dakota. There were no lanterns and sounds of festivities either, although the place was so full of light.

Marco's house was the biggest in his wretched village, yet the building would be the smallest if placed in Elymore.

The shops were not mere stalls but instead rooms of their own. Glass stood in its shimmering glory, displaying what was inside the stores. They sold food that Lilith never tasted, clothing with unfamiliar styles and accessories. Back in the Forest of Dahlia, bracelets and necklaces were made out of flowers and taut strings. Lilith could barely believe her eyes when she noticed glittering jewels in the place of flowers.

"This place," Ruby muttered, "is surreal."

Indeed, it was. Perhaps it was because the witches were exposed to nothing in the outside world, but it did not matter. They were experiencing and observing it now—the adventures and dangers outside their forest.

If Lilith were to imagine the world in fifty years, her mind would wander to how Elymore looked. She remembered having the same surge of astonishment when she first saw the red and gold castle in her vision.

She did not know what exactly the villagers were gaping at. It could be simply because they were witches. But she was certain that it was because she and Ruby looked like demons that originated from every child's nightmare. Furthermore, the scar on her side, which had been passed down from Lysandra, bore a baffling message: Lilith was an heiress to the throne.

The group behind them trudged along like loyal followers. The witches were just as awed as Lilith was, for they had never seen anything like the town either.

The whispering grew louder until the people's voices were audible.

Lilith could hear every word. The disbelief and amazement in their tone startled her. She anticipated more fear to arise among people. Usually, witches scared them. It was why Morakques wanted to get rid of every living sorcerer left in Dicera.

The locals of Elymore were unlike those who resided within villages like Dakota. They were not taught to despise her kind and celebrate the death of sorcerers. For once in a very long time, she felt a hint of safety.

People did not back away or cower. Instead, they *waved* as if witches were their friends. Lilith smiled as a ripple of reassurance joined the crowding emotions in her chest.

For Dahlia's sake, she failed to notice the emotions she felt. They were like stacking bricks that exceeded the clouds, unstable and moments from toppling and destroying everything on land. Her mind was so filled with thoughts that she practically ignored the burn in her heart. Her current situation caused distress and misery, love and hate, reassurance and worry all at the same time.

I can control it, she told herself. For now, Khaos remained obedient, but she knew that she would lose against the darkness eventually.

She squeezed Ruby's hand. *I am sorry*, she wanted to say, *for I will break our promise.*

They strolled deeper into the village, their eyes ceaselessly glancing from stores to houses to the castle in the distance. Lysandra took the opportunity to drift away from the group and explore on her own.

Suddenly, a booming voice rang out, "Hey! You made it!"

Lilith's heart swelled with joy at the sound, and as she turned, she caught sight of Marco. In the time since they had last seen each other, his hair had grown longer, adding a hint of maturity to his boyish charm. His cheerful shine remained. While Lilith and Ruby were disheveled from their journey, he was as well-kept and lively as ever.

"Marco! We missed you," Lilith said, beaming as he approached her.

"Who wouldn't?" he replied. "Look, I left home a few days after you fled, and I gained some information. We should sit down so I can share them, preferably in that cafe." He pointed to a store.

Ruby informed the royal guards that they would be right back. She and Lilith handed the items they had on hand to Des before Marco rushed them into the shop as if they were pressed for time. All the while, he babbled about the perfection of the cafe's delicacies and how often he visited with his mother in the past.

The store was thick with the aroma of freshly baked breads and pastries that Lilith had never seen. The place was cozy and inviting, with its walls painted with shades of sunshine. There were framed photographs hung on them, displaying a variety of buns. The plump man behind the counter and the customers on their wooden seats stared at the witches' entrance with shocked expressions, but no one demanded that they leave.

"Hold on. You're going to love me for this," Marco told them and left after guiding them to a table. When he returned, it was with three porcelain plates—two balanced on his hands and one on his forearm. On each was an identical bun. They were small, round, sprinkled with a dusting of powdered sugar and had a slightly golden crust.

"What is this?" Ruby examined the food on her plate as if it might be poisonous.

Lilith nudged Ruby's side. "Oh, just eat it." She took a bite, and her eyes went wide at the burst of sweetness.

"Exactly what Lily said," Marco responded, shoving the entirety of the bun into his mouth. With his mouth full of the pastry, he said, "It tastes like a cloud if it were edible. It's immaculate."

Ruby picked it up, sniffed it, and then ate it. She chewed for a moment before nodding approvingly.

"See, I knew you'd like it," he remarked smugly. "Now, before we get down to business, I have to ask"—he tipped his chin at Khaos, floating behind Lilith—"what in Dicera are those things? They're creepy."

"Well," Lilith said, glancing behind her shoulder at the three dark clouds of human figures, "they are my shadows."

"They're alive," Marco commented with exasperation. "I don't even understand this world anymore."

"Me neither," Ruby chimed in. "Now, business time."

"Oh, you're no fun," Marco grumbled. "Fine."

He leaned forward in his seat before he began, "We all know Morakques have been hunting witches forever, and the royals show displeasure but do not interfere—that is apparently how things have always been. But recently, the witches in the Morakque's prison vanished with a royal guard.

"Some Morakques believe that this meddling with their business is unacceptable, and when a handful of them are indignant, the others blindly agree. So, they have decided to launch a coup to prevent what they fear most—witches amongst humans and aiding royalty. They've gathered an army to march down the castle."

"An army?" Lilith was horrified. She never intended to start a battle because she knew of its dire consequences. She and Ruby had thought that it would only ensue if Morakques realized that all witches were freed by royals. Only then would they have nobody to hunt. The witches certainly did not consider the smallest interference from royalty to be an act of war. "How did you find out?"

Marco grimaced. "Being my father's son has its perks, I suppose."

Lilith's heart dropped as she realized how foolish she had been. She should have known that war was inevitable from the vision she received when trapped in the Morakques' cell. Moreover, what was it that Ruby uttered when possessed by the demon in her mind?

Let us rejoice at the impending war.

This fight was destined to happen.

Lilith felt a deep sense of hopelessness. She had somehow believed that it would be possible to convince Morakques into putting aside their hatred for peace.

"Morakques clearly hold tremendous power in Dicera. Would you say it is more than that of royalty?" Ruby asked.

"I'd say equivalent." Marco sighed. "It's strange. Morakques could have started a coup before any acts of war took place. In theory, they have a chance of overtaking the throne with the witches they had confined. But there were always these petitions to prevent war as if they themselves dreaded it."

"It is war," Ruby deadpanned, "not a festival."

"Yes, yes, I'm not daft," Marco huffed. "I'm just saying that it's almost like the Morakques are starting to realize what they're doing is wrong. I guess if you've dedicated your entire lives to committing an ongoing mistake, it'll be all you know."

"What, do you suppose they will suddenly turn over a new leaf?"

Marco ruminated on the question. "Maybe."

"It is unlikely."

"But possible," Lilith considered. No matter how possible, however, it was too late. Nobody could stop the impending battle. She felt crushed. "If only I could see my Nana once more before this battle plays out."

Ruby looked gutted. "The witches back in the forest have got no clue about any of this." She fidgeted with her hands. "I wonder what my father would say. I miss him terribly."

"This is all so sad," Marco said. "I loathe my father."

Ruby looked back at him with raised eyebrows. "Because of his status?"

"Yes. But mostly, I despise how he treats me well, because it makes it easier to forgive the despair he caused my mother and me."

Just as he finished speaking, Lilith noticed that the townspeople around them had descended into silence. The halt in their words was so jarring that Lilith felt compelled to peer out the window beside her.

Lilith half-expected an army of Morakques to attack with spears and arrows, but the thought quickly dissolved when the townspeople outside began lowering their heads—one by one and without a word.

Their attention was no longer fixed on the witches.

Lilith's mouth dried as she excused herself from the table and left the cafe.

Approaching from the direction of the castle was a woman wearing a casual gown that reached her knees. There were fine gold embellishments on the clothing, sewn in a way that sent a message. Lysandra described it once— an intricate swirl of glimmering gems forming the shape of fallen leaves.

It meant the highest-ranking royalty.

Lilith did not need any more explanation or convincing to come to a conclusion that made her heart almost leap off a ledge. It took everything within her not to yield to the overwhelming urge to *explode* with power, especially when the woman instantly quickened her footsteps after her eyes met Lilith's.

Because it was not just an ordinary queen who was bridging the distance between them.

It was Queen Emeline of the Dicera Kingdom— Lilith's mother.

CHAPTER THIRTY-ONE

If someone were to ask Lilith how she thought Queen Emeline looked, she would imagine her own face on someone else's. Perhaps not identical in appearance, but at least similar. If the word 'queen' was added into the mix, she would picture a crown and an icy stare that brought people to a halt.

She had not seen many queens throughout her life, but she *did* spend the last few weeks with Queen Lysandra. It was not wise to compare a queen who was believed to be the best in history to her mother, but it had not stopped her from envisioning sharp lines on her mother's face that warned others never to cross her.

When she heard the name Queen Emeline, a woman radiating confidence came to mind.

She did not anticipate her mother to look like… she could not describe it in words. Like a bird trapped in a cage but still free to screech and chirp—a queen that could give orders from a distance but never eye to eye. The woman looked like any typical woman on the street, like an assistant baker or item seller. The only thing that made her look different was the dress she wore that bore the royal emblem of Dicera. No crown, no confidence, no coldness.

But then again, most queens did not look like their status. It was their blood and voice that made them worthy.

"Wrong, my descendant," Lysandra said as if she could hear Lilith's thoughts, appearing beside the young witch without warning. "A queen looks like whom they represent. My older descendant over there"—she pointed to Queen Emeline—"lacks power. It is simple to tell. You are so incredibly fortunate to have summoned me, Lilith." The woman seemed to be done with her little speech until she spoke once more. "You, little descendant, will be the greatest queen to ever exist."

Lilith almost snickered at that. She did not show disbelief on her face, but she knew an impossible statement when she heard one. Her mother was a queen for a decade or more, so she did not *lack* power. Furthermore, Lilith did not know what being a queen entailed.

"Must I repeat myself?" Lysandra asked. "You have the heart and mind of a queen, dear. Your mother only has the heart for love."

Of course. Lilith had already figured that her mother had eloped with the King of Dicera. Perhaps the woman had no interest in ruling. It would explain why the Queen made no changes to the lives of her kind, when so much power was in her hands. *She* lacked *power*, Lysandra claimed. Not physical or mental strength, but the will to fight for what she wanted.

Despite the thoughts that churned furiously in her mind, her heart was still racing. Despite everything, she could not ignore the fact that the mother she had sought for so many years stood so close to her.

They were only ten feet away from one another when Queen Emeline paused.

Lilith wanted to hug the woman, tell stories of her adventures, share about Ruby, and ask about the life of a queen. Yet, she was rooted to the spot and speechless. She was *worried*, she realized. It was hard to tell when her chest was so filled with crushing emotions. What if her mother was afraid of her? What if her mother did not want to accept her? What if her mother was not convinced that she was her daughter?

She inhaled sharply, staring into the eyes of the queen. Lysandra would say that such audacity was insolent, but her mother said nothing. The woman stared back, eyes glittering and wide. She must have seen the scar on Lilith's side.

Then, as if Queen Emeline needed any more convincing, Lilith showed the mirror she had kept since birth—a gift that she never dared to part with.

"Lilith," whispered the queen. Lilith made yet another comparison: when she first heard Lysandra's voice, she felt a burst of panic. Maybe the power and twist in her ancient tone caused it, or the way the senior lifted her head and seemed to stare right through Lilith and into her soul.

Queen Emeline was different. She did not display her power through words. Her voice was soft and laced with honey, filled with emotions and vulnerability. Lilith would never be able to match that tone; her voice was more of a demand.

Lilith did not know what to say. If she was told that her mother would stand in front of her two days ago, she would never believe it.

"Mother," Lilith said. She almost winced at the loudness of it in the quiet town.

They stared. A few seconds passed before Queen Emeline darted forward to close the gap within them.

Lilith stilled. Her mother was going to embrace her, and she would love nothing more, but a slither of panic wove into her mind.

A witch cannot touch her. She would steal their power and burn their skins.

Stepping away would be disrespectful, but she felt like she could do nothing else. Ruby, who had left the cafe to stand beside her, had not noticed her predicament, and Lysandra…

Lilith looked at her ancestor. The old witch knew. Amusement flickered in her features, and her black eyes shone impossibly bright, waiting and watching. For Dahlia's sake, the woman was *entertaining* herself with Lilith's dilemma.

Stuck between the ridiculous decision to step away or burn her mother, Lilith ran through the things she *could* do. It would be exceedingly disrespectful to do anything but accept the hug.

So, she did nothing.

She stood still as she anticipated the warm embrace from the mother she never had. Before she could blink, she felt hands on her shoulders, and then they were gone as if they were never there. Lilith wondered if they were just phantom fingertips.

Her mother was rigid, but this time right in front of her. Her face was painted with silent agony, but that was all she conveyed. Lilith did not know if the pain she caused was excruciating, but her mother made it seem like she simply pricked her finger on a thornbush.

The woman could hide pain so splendidly. Perhaps that was the attribute that made her worthy of the throne.

"I am sorry," whispered Lilith, too softly for the townspeople to hear. She could explain everything, but she needed time alone with her mother. Ruby reached out to hold her hand after seeing the regret and yearning on her face.

Mother. That common word seemed so unfamiliar.

"Come with me," she said, then glanced at the people around her daughter. The guards had their heads lowered, but the witches were as clueless as farmers without the soil to plant. The queen's lips thinned, and then she uttered, "Treat this as a home; you are safe here."

Lilith smiled. At least she accomplished something for the witches.

"Come," Queen Emeline repeated, casting her gaze downward. Her eyebrows furrowed at her daughter's hand, firm and unmoving within Ruby's. "Both of you."

It pained Lilith to admit that she could not fully trust her mother yet. It might take time, but it would happen. Hopefully.

Tentatively, Lilith and Ruby followed.

"Where are we heading?" Ruby questioned, sounding dubious of the mother's intentions. Lilith would have been offended if she, too, were not skeptical.

"I do not know," Lilith replied. For all she knew, her

mother could be leading her to a volcano she had not known to exist.

A wave of suffocating worry lumped in her chest, seizing her mind and creating thoughts with pointed edges—overwhelming and loud, as if piercing the inside of her head.

"If this goes badly," Lilith said, pausing as if her concerns would become a reality if she said her next few words aloud, "I want you to run."

Ruby turned, a look of bafflement on her face. Lilith had already predicted the expression before she spoke her words. Taken aback, Ruby whispered back, "No."

It was a single word that carried hefty stubbornness.

It was annoyingly understandable. If Ruby requested the same of her, Lilith's reply would be the same.

"Fine. Let us just hope this goes well," Lilith muttered.

"But where is the fun in that?" interjected Lysandra, her voice a scream in the silence that surrounded them. It made Lilith jump. Ruby narrowed her eyes in confusion.

"You are saying things will go awfully?" Lilith asked, voice barely audible.

"I said nothing of the sort," explained the queen with a dramatic gasp. "I am simply implying that you should be ready."

"For… what?"

"The end is sooner than you realize."

Lilith shuddered. End of *what*, exactly?

The two young witches followed Queen Emeline to an empty patch of land with lush greenery and mosses before realizing where they were heading.

The Dicera castle.

Lilith's breath hitched in her throat as the tugging in her heart became more persistent. She was unsure if its cause was her overpowering emotions or her proximity to the breathtaking structure.

She frowned, recognizing the sensation that followed, for she had experienced it many times in the Forest of Dahlia. It crawled her skin like unseen ladybugs, causing her to flutter her eyes closed. She hoped that the feeling would somehow cease on its own.

She knew better.

When she felt the creeping itch that traveled through her body, she knew instantly that she was seconds from losing control of her ability.

No matter how much power she gained, Lilith would always be a Soothsayer. That part of her was tingling and enraged, clutching the opportunity to reveal itself.

She had never been this strong, and she knew immediately that her visions would spiral so violently that she would suffer lost memories. She hoped that darkness would not erupt from her soul when she inevitably lost control.

"Are you okay?" Ruby questioned. "Your skin is warming."

"No," Lilith gasped quietly, the world becoming a swirl of green and red and gold.

She could hear Lysandra sucking in a sharp breath as her magic yanked her into the future world. Oddly enough, her surroundings remained almost identical.

Suddenly, she could not tell the difference between

reality and vision as they merged into a flawless image with uncanny similarities. Only after a moment could she tell them apart. Although she was situated in the same position, Ruby was no longer beside her. The ground was no longer lush and beautiful but instead stained and peppered with the scars of war. Splattered on the grass was liquid as red as her friend's irises.

The world distorted to become nothing but shadows and a thick red mist, then screaming and agony and pain. Lilith's head spun as she heard wailing and screeching and bellowing, maniacal laughter and yells of satisfaction and vicious celebration. Everything came so rapidly.

It could have gone on for seconds or minutes or even hours. Memories of her chaotic vision came and went. She could have sworn that she saw a speaking jewel, Marco, his father and her Nana again, but nothing was certain.

Her emotions drained as visions crossed her mind. She remembered none of them, except one.

It was the last thing she experienced from that loss of control, and it was a feeling—a crippling promise that could only fit the description of one word.

Death.

CHAPTER THIRTY-TWO

Lilith's heart was pounding.

Emotions still swirled within her, but a great portion was taken away. She gave a sigh of relief, no longer feeling heavy and suffocated as if smothered with the kisses of death. It took a moment to realize that her uncontrolled visions had stopped.

"Are you ill?" asked her mother, genuinely concerned for her daughter.

Only Nana and Ruby knew of her loose leash on her overpowering abilities. Lysandra had not given Lilith much insight into it, so it was a mystery with an answer she did not plan to seek. After all, she discovered that her need to know was overshadowed by the desire to survive. Soon, her life would be pilfered by the darkness that threatened to seize her freedom.

She sought many things, but control was the most important.

Perhaps, it *was* possible to leash onto the phenomenon that planted itself in her soul. She glanced at Khaos, the three of them huddling around her form like a second skin, making Lilith appear like a silhouette from afar even under the touch of glistening golden sunlight.

"No," she replied after a moment. "I am okay." Her

mother nodded skeptically before walking once again, every second bringing them closer to the castle.

Never releasing Ruby's hand, the witches continued their journey. It had been a long adventure that led to discoveries and love and pain, but it would inevitably end; all things did. She pondered about the end of her story—would it be a tragic death or one that carried smiles? Since there were no other options, she hoped it was the latter.

She turned to Lysandra, who was gazing at the castle ahead with such yearning that Lilith felt a pang of sorrow. A thousand years ago, the former Queen of Darkness lived in and ruled over the same land she currently stood on.

"Hey," Lilith muttered, too soft for Ruby to hear. "I am going to die, am I not?"

Somehow, she knew that Lysandra was listening.

"Oh, do not be so dramatic," the queen chided. "Though, it is a great possibility."

Possibility? Was her death not guaranteed? Fragile hope fluttered in her chest, thin and brimming with life like the elaborate designs on a butterfly's wing. It was an explosion of color in darkness and a surge of emotions in her empty heart. She refused to delve into her series of thoughts following her current circumstance to avoid an attack of profound emotions. Yet, she wanted nothing more than to allow hope to flow through her veins. It would cure her uncertainty and fear, then give her a reason to imagine a future life.

She prayed for Lysandra to say nothing more. She wanted the former queen to leave that spark of faith alone.

However, asking Lysandra to stay silent was just as impossible as living for another thousand years.

"Possibility is an overstatement, actually. Of course, you are going to die; one day, you will get too tired to carry on living," she said. She uttered the words without a hint of pity, and Lilith wondered if her ancestor cared that her bloodline was bound to end.

Lilith wanted to fight the answer. She did not expect to survive for an eternity, but she hoped to live long. She experienced too little freedom to simply leave.

"Do immortality vials still exist?" Lilith asked. She knew very little about them.

The queen was oddly quiet for the next minute, walking as though Lilith asked nothing. Then, as softly as the whisper of winds, she muttered, "No."

Disappointment nipped at Lilith's bones. Death was inevitable, she knew that. She steered away from upsetting thoughts, telling herself that what mattered was how much impact her purpose would bring to the world before it happened.

"However," Lysandra continued, "I know the ingredients needed to create them."

Lilith was tired of false hope. Its rise was a majestic sensation, but the fall of sorrow and devastation was not worth it. "How?" she questioned.

The old sorcerer answered, "First, we head to Dheeksha Cave. But you must be aware that those golden vials come with multiple problems."

Lilith bit back from asking, and it required very little effort. The castle offered the perfect distraction. The witches were granted entrance through the gate attached to the brick wall encircling the castle. A roar sounded, and then a satisfying clink. The young witches exchanged a glance while withholding their awe.

Golden walls streaked with red stretched from the ground and seemingly beyond the unclouded sky. The polished stone pavement below their feet was tainted with dirt due to the filth under their shoes. No one was staring, but Lilith felt watched and blamed for the dirt that painted the ground.

When she was first told about the castle, Lilith imagined the interior to be illuminated by golden flames, licking the walls and decorating the rooms with a glimmering sheen. She least anticipated the absence of fire. Instead, the area was brightened by inventions with names she might not be able to pronounce. Lamps that were peppered everywhere contained an orb of white radiating the floors and reaching out to touch every corner.

The inside was grand, and she could barely believe that it existed. The space was broad, dangling the opportunities to dance and laugh and celebrate in front of her face. The tiles on the ground extended from the entrance to various rooms ahead, glistening as if they had been washed a million times. Portraits lined the walls, bordered by golden frames with labyrinthine designs, joining and ending on the bottom, where Dicera's crest was engraved.

High above, standing candles were attached to small silver plates that quite literally hung with a complex structure. Lilith gaped at it, refusing to understand how that crown-like invention was able to fasten itself on the ceiling.

Tearing her eyes away, she studied the tiniest details of the building. She could not stop sauntering because something unique appeared with every second.

Suddenly, she halted.

Her mother continued with her strides, and Lilith had to push herself to follow. However, her eyes were trained on a portrait that caught both Ruby's eyes and hers.

It seemed to stand out from others. Royalties in other portraits sat with a gentle or awkward curve to their lips, eyes sparkling and faces prepared. Women wore gowns with serpentine patterns that made them look identical to the ladies in the pictures beside them. Yet, the image they stared at was an artwork that painted something else.

The portrait depicted a woman with a sly and demonic appearance, said to be the greatest queen to ever exist.

Lilith looked to her left, only to find Lysandra gone. Frowning, she glanced back, then to her right, then up. Her mouth curled into a mixture of bafflement and awe as she watched the witch—the *thousand*-year-old sorcerer— swinging on the chandelier above. She gawked at her ancestor, who sat as gracefully as though she were on a throne, using clouds of darkness to cause motion.

She saw the sadness now. The Lysandra in the portrait looked only a few years younger, seeming joyous and content. Her eyes were a swirling pool of black that captured souls, yet even *they* sparkled in the painting. Her grin was both devilish and immaculate, as if it belonged on her face and no one else's.

The mentally older sorcerer had a hint of sorrow etched

on her face. It was as if she experienced too much and could only manipulate humor to conceal her true feelings.

Her dark eyes had seen grim and crumpling bodies; ravaging effects from acts of vile intentions; love that ended in nothing but shattered words and an eternity of nothingness; and pain that Lilith could not imagine. It reflected the devastating and majestic life of a heroine.

Lilith thought of her own story then—her story with Ruby—and an unintentional smile twisted her features. There were no good or evil sides in the Kingdom of Dicera, just different perspectives. They were villains in the story of Morakques, and she decided with flames in her eyes that she might as well be the best of the worst.

After all, her mortal life balanced on an unstable rod, and nothing would matter after death.

"That is her?" Ruby questioned.

Lilith glanced at the witch in the portrait. "Indeed."

"She is beautiful," commented Ruby, and she was right. The woman in the picture looked like a seductress—a beautiful viper with lethal venom.

"Thank you, dear child!" the sorcerer replied from above, although the red-eyed girl could not hear.

"She is grateful for the compliment," Lilith told Ruby, then flashed her ancestor a grin. Lysandra smiled back.

To keep up with the Queen of Dicera, the girls quickened their steps and passed by countless golden pillars lined with intentional cracks of vermillion. The hallway resembled a museum with various artifacts belonging to the deceased arranged for display.

They were led to a closed door, and for a moment, distrust brimmed in Lilith's heart.

Behind that door was a cell enclosed by iron bars, one that was no better than the jail in Morakque's territory. Blood painted the walls in hideous dots of color, and marks were engraved into the floor as if previous prisoners attempted to wreck their nails by scraping at the stone ground. The room stank of death and hatred and rot.

Lilith shoved the unsightly thought to the back of her mind, trying to inject a hint of faith for her mother. When she resided in the forest, meeting the woman was her only goal. Despite the uncertainty of things now, she still tried to hold onto optimism.

Queen Emeline opened the door, revealing a room.

Lilith had never imagined how grand a room could appear with royal colors and pretty inventions. There was even a large mirror attached to a marble table and drawers beneath it. Lilith gawked at the design, then mentally reprimanded herself for thinking that she would be brought to a cell.

There was a bed three times bigger than what Lilith and Ruby were used to. Closets were full of clothes with materials they had never touched and accessories that shone under the touch of light. So, so, *so beautiful*, Lilith wondered, awestruck. It was a room fit for queens.

"Please, make yourselves at home," said Queen Emeline. The woman looked at Lilith and displayed no fear when she studied the demonic eyes of her daughter. "Bathe, and change. I will speak to your father and return in a moment."

A father? Lilith forgot that it was possible to have a father figure.

Queen Emeline stepped out of the room. Instantly, Lilith and Ruby turned to face one another with expressions that screamed, *What in Dicera is happening?*

"This is… insane!" Ruby exclaimed, covering her mouth with her hand. Insane was the understatement of the century. This was *impossible*, yet it was happening. "The royals are standing with us. Soldiers will join us in the upcoming battle," she said. "We have a chance, Lilith. We can achieve freedom by ridding the world of Morakques. We can win!"

Lilith did not bother to correct her friend. *You can win.* The amended words lingered in her mind. No matter the end, her story would cease, and Ruby's would continue. There was no way that Lilith could get her hands on an immortality vial in time.

Instead, to avoid saying the words that would destroy her lover, Lilith stepped towards Ruby and drew her closer.

Ruby's arms encircled Lilith's waist, and her laughter was the sweetest sound Lilith had ever heard. At that moment, Ruby seemed to embody Lilith's optimism while Lilith's own hope was waning. Ruby's joy was contagious, and for a second, nobody was on the brink of death.

Khaos danced around the room, celebrating as if they knew that Lilith's body was soon theirs to claim.

Lilith forgot why she was concerned about the future. All that mattered at the moment was Ruby.

They stood in a burning world, and they were immune to fire.

Lilith planted a kiss on her soulmate's forehead, then engulfed the girl in a homely embrace. That hug spluttered strings of messages with an impact that cracked her heart. *Take care, my love,* the words hung in the air like the structure with lanterns and its leaping tangerine-colored sparks outside. *I will not be here when you reign your monarchy.*

As the savior of witches and possibly more, Ruby was destined to be someone significant. As Lilith's partner, she might become a ruler of the kingdom.

Lillith glanced at her partner, whose eyes glowed the color of the finest red wine. There were so many unsaid words between them, but there was no need to voice them out. Lilith learned and experienced more than every witch alive in the Forest of Dahlia, and she decided that she was content.

It was Ruby who leaned in first, brushing her lips across Lilith's jaw. The darkness caved in around them as Lilith felt the grin against her skin, teasing and sly. She cast her gaze skyward, smiling. If only time could pause for death to slow its footsteps. Every gentle nip on her skin spoke a statement in the tension-filled room.

I will not allow you to break your promise.
We are fated to live. If we die, we leave together.
I love you.

Lilith lowered her head. In one swift, gentle movement, she caught Ruby's mouth in hers. It began like their touches—sober thoughts guiding every motion. It was gentle and slow, as if they had all the time in the world. With every second, with increasing desire and need to simply devour, the kiss became hungrier. Time was slipping, and their shield against the surrounding fire was vanishing, so they began to lose themselves in each other before surrendering to the burn.

Was it truly horrible that Lilith would do anything, *anything*, for her lover?

CHAPTER THIRTY-THREE

Comparing the Forest of Dahlia to Dicera's castle was like seeking the differences between a grotto and a cavern. Ruby discovered many things that she would not have imagined possible only a day ago.

Running water existed; clear water escaped from a faucet with a simple twist of a knob. Ruby thought everybody bathed in either a stream or pond, some cleaner than others.

"For Dahlia's sake," she muttered, mesmerized by the flowing water. The glistening and seemingly ceaseless stream of liquid did not fail to surprise her. If Queen Emeline were to stride into the bathroom, she would undoubtedly be incredibly amused. The two young witches stood abreast, knees bending and staring at the water that gushed from the mouth of the golden and curved tube.

The soap carrying the scent of lavender coated Lilith's skin with the same fragrance, entering Ruby's nose whenever she inhaled. It was intoxicating and distracting, and Ruby wondered if her lover found the smell of her skin just as addictive. She felt cleaner than ever.

Finally, it seemed, they had a change of garments. It thrilled them to no end. Lilith opted for a maroon-colored gown with golden laces that occasionally grazed the carpets. Cloaked in shadows, with her lengthy, black hair, claw-like nails and unsettling eyes, she looked every part a princess of the underworld. Ruby's pick was golden like the sun and Lilith's laugh, glittering and coupled with burgundy threads that formed shapes resembling vines of lilies.

"Are we dreaming?" Lilith muttered, the sound of sloshing drowning out her voice.

"We certainly are," Ruby replied, refusing to believe that she was truly in a castle. "Clearly, this cannot be real." She gestured to the running water, then gave another incredulous glance at the invention.

Lilith nodded, agreeing. "And there is no way I am the princess of the kingdom, the descendant of the strongest witch in history, and chosen by fate as the Queen of Darkness."

A laugh escaped Ruby's lips. Their discoveries were endless; it would probably take days to share and elaborate. "We were born to be leaders," Ruby said. The demon in her mind repeated the line thousands of times when she was younger, and she finally understood.

Lilith tore her eyes away from the running water. "I cannot wait to see how you fix this broken world."

"*We*," Ruby corrected, frowning. Emotions flared in her chest, and she dismissed the urge to remove them. "You are not going to die, Lilith. I will not allow it."

"You have power, plenty of it. But you do not have the power to control fate," Lilith said. The words slapped Ruby in the face, leaving a handprint and a lingering sharp sting.

Ruby opened her mouth to retort, but voices chased away the words she hoped to say. The demon spoke, the words replacing those that almost escaped her lips.

The forthcoming battle requires a sacrifice, Ruby, said the voices in a song of messy roars. *And she is right. You cannot control fate.*

Ruby bit back a sorrowful cry, although she knew that escaping from the truth was a waste of effort. She was born through a sacrifice; she should have been the first to know that it was necessary.

"So, this is it, then?" she asked, unconcerned about the crack in her voice. "You are just going to submit to death? You are so sure that there is not another option?" She bit her lips, furious that she felt so vulnerable. Her heart sank in her chest, every few pounds signifying another lost second with the girl she wanted to spend her life with. "Fate did not give you such extraordinary strength to simply *die*. Is there not an immortality vial? You do not have to end so tragically."

"I would not *simply die*," Lilith raised her chin. "I will be saving witches—generations of them. Our name will be recognized by the kingdom because our strength will change it for the better. That is my purpose." She tucked a strand of Ruby's loose hair behind her ear with a pointed nail. "You, however, will carry on with our story and *live*. Shine like the gem you were named after and rule like you were always meant to."

"I do not..." Ruby wanted to lift her head, look into Lilith's eyes with surety and state that they still had a chance to achieve a future together. But she could not. "I do not want to rule without you."

"You have to," Lilith whispered. Ruby could see herself through the reflection of darkness—red eyes glistening with the presence of building tears and face etched in an expression of sheer hopelessness. She would not cry. She *could* not. If she did, the uncertain liquid mold of her bleak future would solidify and become inevitable.

"Is Queen Lysandra reluctant to share the ingredients of an immortality vial?" Ruby asked.

"I doubt the price for that is worth the result."

"What in Dicera is more important than your life?"

"Many things," Lilith said. "Your life is one of them."

"Bullshit!"

Lilith blinked a few times at the language. Then, the side of her lips lifted to form a playful smile that carried an uncanny resemblance to the grin in Queen Lysandra's portrait. She snickered, then turned the knob to stop the fall of water.

"You shall not dare smile," Ruby sneered. "Can you not see? I *cannot* do this myself. It is not possible!" Lilith might have accepted the fact that she would not last long anymore, but Ruby certainly had not. It was utterly baffling how the Queen of Darkness did not recognize her self-worth and how much was on the line. Moreover, she was oblivious that Ruby could not survive building their empire on her own. She was born to demolish.

"Look where we are, Ruby," Lilith said. "Were we not just wondering how impossible it is to be here? Yet we stand in front of running water in a castle that we saw in a shared vision. Everything is possible."

Disbelief swept across Ruby's features, and fury raided her chest. This woman was unbelievable! Lilith was just contradicting herself at this point.

"You are impossible!" Ruby scowled. "You are not *blind*. Can you not see why I do not want you to die?" She raised her voice, rage fueling her words like wood to a bellowing inferno. "Can you really not tell that I am utterly and helplessly in love with you?!"

Silence.

Utmost silence.

For a moment, Ruby thought Lilith was speechless because she did not feel the same.

But before any sort of response could be provided, the sound of an opening door was heard. Simultaneously, they entered the bedroom, where Queen Emeline was present.

"Hello, children."

Typically, the demon in her mind would have something to say about the people they encountered. It expressed fondness for Lilith and was delighted when it first met Marco. However, when it came down to the Queen of Dicera, the demon conveyed a mixture of skepticism and gratitude. Ruby did not know what to make of it.

The Queen of Dicera was not afraid, or maybe she simply appeared that way. She could conceal her emotions very well.

"Mother," Lilith greeted.

How can I address the queen? Ruby asked the demon. It was instinctive to reach out to it.

I would call her my mother-in-law, but I do not think that is a bright idea. Just refer to her as the queen.

"Queen Emeline," Ruby said, then delivered a curtsey to be polite.

The queen nodded, looking too nonchalant for

someone who encountered her lost daughter. She set the books that the witches had handed to Des on the nightstand beside the grand bed before asking, "Will you answer a few of my questions?"

Ruby expected an order, not a request, but she brushed the thought away because she preferred the latter.

"Of course," Lilith replied.

"Why are you not in the forest?" she began, bewildering Ruby. It was startling that her first query was not an insult to their demon-like features.

Lilith began to explain, avoiding the nastier portions of the story. Ruby wondered if the ruler of Dicera genuinely cared about witches. Even though her kind was near extinction, she had never reached out to help.

"This darkness that resides in you… can you remove it?"

"Yes, but I doubt I will." Lilith's confidence in the subject was maddening.

"What can you do with this ability?"

Lilith contemplated for a moment before saying, "I can show you."

Ruby dropped her jaw but stayed silent. She disapproved of how little Lilith treasured her life, but she could do nothing when the Queen of Dicera tracked every discreet motion. Ruby wondered if the queen would execute her if she yelled at Lilith in foul language.

With darkness following her actions, Lilith traced out symbols and muttered an incantation. A swirling mist was summoned, and it gathered to form a marvelous show of spins and impressive leaps. It slowed as it began to huddle and create a ring of clouds that displayed a disorientated moving image.

Ruby recognized the setting of the image as the Forest of Dahlia. She was hit with the weight of how much she missed home—or, more precisely—her father. She remembered the last line he uttered before she left for a life-changing journey, *"Show the world what you can do and return to the forest with a crown."*

She would return with more than a crown. When she arrived back home, she would have the promise of freedom and safety and, hopefully, a lover. She glanced at Lilith, silently vowing that she would do anything in her power to save the woman from death.

Within the oval formed by darkness, a woman was… *crying*. Ruby bit back a gasp, realizing that the weeping woman was Lilith's grandmother. When she last saw the sorcerer, she was frail and abnormally thin, but that was nothing compared to how she appeared at the moment. She was like an empty shell—a body without a soul. It reminded Ruby of an ancient instrument she had read about. However, instead of producing immaculate-sounding music, it remained silent when played.

The grandmother looked broken. *Shattered*, even. The black circles under her eyes could be detected from a mile away. She looked so hollow that Ruby could imagine her lifeless.

It was made more disturbing because Ruby recognized what was transpiring. The knowledge she devoured about witches told her enough about how it looked to be deteriorating due to magic's consumption. It was her worst nightmare.

"What is happening?" muttered Lilith, fear shaping her features.

"Your grandmother," Ruby said quietly, "is dying."

"What?" Lilith drew back, lips parting and face engulfed by horror.

Ruby's eyes were fixed on the constantly changing picture, and they widened when it displayed the environment they were in. It was a place she despised to the very core: the forest's graveyard. A stone was extending from the soil, and Ruby squinted her eyes to read the name of the unfortunate soul engraved into the tomb.

She struggled, only able to make out a few letters. She pieced them together, wondering who exactly it could be.

Color drained from her face.

I am sorry, Ruby, whispered the voices. They filled her mind as music would in a silent room, stealing the glory of silence.

She knew that all mortals would die eventually, but fate seemed to find joy in robbing the world of the best people.

Delivered on a silver platter, as appealing as careful stitches on voiles, was death. It did not fail to unleash its vicious wrath, unexpected and tragically quick.

Out of everybody, it had to be the person she loved.

Ruby knew extraordinarily little about caring for somebody, for she spent too many years caged. Her mother was not tender and nowhere close to affectionate. Witches feared her for what she could do, and before Lilith, she never loved anyone besides her father.

The world must be conspiring against her because it was his name carved into the stone.

"Oh," she said, swallowing the panic and grief and agony building in her gut, pushing magic into her heart and soul.

She saw the way Lilith's shadows curled when their queen was experiencing waves of visions from loss of control. Ruby was told about the discomfort of burying magic when emotions were on the brink of bursting, but she had never experienced it before.

She felt it now, and she understood how painful it was. Usually, she would allow her magic to remove her overwhelming feelings. She would have already done it if not for the demon sharing her body.

Do not use your magic. Not now, it advised. It was peculiar to hear that phrase coming from its various voices. Instead of pressuring her to eradicate everything in her path and release her inner self, it instructed her to restrain the magic.

And she listened, although it was so unbelievably painful. How in Dicera was Lilith able to keep herself at bay?

Ruby's chest squeezed, and she tasted bitterness on her tongue. It felt as if poisoned talons had reached into her chest and sunk their pointed edges deep into her heart. A louder gasp escaped her lips, and she realized she was crying.

So much for wanting to save her tears just a moment ago.

She did not care that she was weeping in front of two queens (possibly three if Lysandra was in the room).

Ruby was skeptical about the truth, but she knew better than to doubt Lilith's power. The image showed what was happening in the present.

In it were half a dozen graves, but Ruby only recognized one name.

Lilith did not seem to recognize any, for her only reaction was a frown. Ruby could not see much of Lilith's expression because she was almost immediately embraced. It was yet another action with a message, "*It is okay. Breathe. I am sorry.*"

But it was not okay. *Nothing* was, and nothing would ever be. Ruby left the forest with a raised chin and wild determination for success because she yearned to make her father proud. But he would never again be able to see what she achieved.

No one left would be proud of her.

The image ceased, and darkness became nothing but wafting mist.

However, her emotions carried on building, forming a massive ball of fire that was more intense than anything she felt.

She could not take it. It was too much.

Wait, urged the whispers. *In a few seconds, we can use this strength to our advantage.*

I cannot. It is eating me alive. I can't, I can't, I can't, Ruby cried, in her mind or aloud, she could not be sure. Her vision switched between swirling oblivion and the castle.

Three more seconds.

Ruby bit her lips hard enough to cause bleeding. She could feel Lilith devouring her magic, but not quite fast enough. She was a living typhoon of elements.

Now.

The word echoed in her brain, and then a cacophony of screams and battle cries filled the air. It was muffled, coming from outside the castle.

Ruby swirled, hand in Lilith's, to gaze outside the window.

The bellowing came from an army of reckless and ferocious humans with a burning hatred to tear royalty and witches apart. The lush and enormous patch of land was no longer empty. The space was now utterly filled with attacking men and women carrying different looks. Some wore abhorrence as if it were a badge of honor, others determination, fear, brutality, excitement, and even lack of preparation.

Still, they marched onward as one.

"Morakques," Ruby managed to say. Her heart pounded, and she struggled to control herself.

Lilith squeezed her hand. "The battle is dawning."

CHAPTER THIRTY-FOUR

"Hide," Queen Emeline urged. The woman might have just watched her dying mother through a mirror of smoke a moment ago, but she looked prepared to go to war.

Perhaps the woman was remarkable in concealing her true countenance. Ruby did not know. What she *did* know, however, was the burn in her chest and the ache in her soul. It drove her to call upon the demon.

Bile rose to her throat.

"We began this war," Lilith said, her voice like a command. "We will finish it." If Ruby did not know any better, she would think that the woman holding her hand bore the highest status in the room. She wore her confidence like a jeweled crown of gold, stretching its points skyward as if inviting the world to view its glistening rubies. Her optimistic stance concerned Ruby extensively since Lilith made it very clear that she did not believe in surviving the battle.

Ruby had hoped for some time to convince the rulers of Dicera to provide a safe way home for witches and then achieve freedom with the help of royalty by annihilating Morakques. However, fate had other plans. Morakques were here, right now. Ruby was not yet prepared, for she did not expect the tragedy to arrive so soon. Something was lodged in her throat, and she realized that it was words.

"She is right," Ruby spoke. Her voice was stronger than she anticipated, and she hoped that Queen Emeline was not offended. She had read books about commoners receiving punishment for less. "We were tasked with seeking freedom for our kind. We will not back out when things are beginning."

She sounded so certain, but her heart begged to differ.

Suddenly, her thoughts halted. Why were they still speaking? An army was trudging forward, and they were likely to attack without care. They were threatening the crown, marching to destroy any obstacles in their path.

Ruby turned to look at her lover, whose pair of onyx eyes softened in a way that was reserved just for her. "Let us go," she said.

Ruby knew that both of them could not wait any longer. Emotions were bubbling and rising and creeping towards the line of explosion.

She nodded to the queen, then darted towards their enemy with a firm hand in hers.

One thought would allow her to peer into the future, yet she refused. Everything was unconfirmed, but one fact stood its ground—there was no happy ending.

The demon was roaring in her head, voices created by the desire to convey its thrill and fury. It was a sound that Ruby thought suited a trapped and abused wolf with the need to call its pack, then seek retribution. A million voices were articulated at once, shrieking the demon's opinions about their situation. It was chaos at its best, but nobody heard. Nobody but Ruby.

Then, there was one comprehensible and powerful

voice. It crossed Ruby's mind and disappeared within mere seconds, but it coiled in her thoughts even after any trace of it proved to exist.

The demon had said, *Sacrifice is a necessary factor to success, Ruby. Especially in a war.*

That was what this was—a war of many possibilities and a fight for freedom. There were two witches against… an army of Morakques. It could very well be beyond her calculated amount of ten thousand.

Ruby and Lilith stood still on a broad empty land of shamrock-colored grass, hands and souls connected as an army charged towards them. Their pretty gowns seemed silly now, like an attempt to roleplay princesses when graver things were at stake. They needed mobility, not beauty, and so Ruby set ablaze their dresses, leaving them charred with messy edges at knee-length. Lilith did not flinch.

The atmosphere was filled with the awaiting stench of death and the screams of a riot. Yet, a bizarre wave of serenity swallowed Ruby's chest. She was in excruciating anguish with the emotions and voices boiling within her. Still, the accompanying presence of peace instilled a sort of determination in her mind.

She closed her eyes, and a gust of powerful wind pushed her forth.

When she opened them again, she knew her red eyes glistened with the strength she was born with. It was two demons against the world who viewed them as such, and they were going to show just how they achieved the title.

Ruby slowly held up her palm, watching flames dance on her fingertips.

"Are you ready?" Lilith asked, although there was no other option.

Ruby allowed the fire to flare brighter. "The Battle for Ruth," she whispered. "What a suitable name."

Lilith nodded. "Indeed."

Pity sparkled in her eyes as Ruby gazed at the people charging towards them. There would be an inevitable and drastic number of lives pilfered. Soon, victims of the war would only exist as numbers in books and songs around a campfire.

How unfortunate, Ruby thought as flames soared from her palm. It felt like a hefty boulder was lifted from her chest, and the ropes that constricted her organs fell away, vanishing into a memory of agony. Relieved, she controlled the red mist that carried the heat of a thousand fires, forming creatures with gowns that billowed out around them. They scampered towards the Morakques as an exquisite and harmless work of art.

Little feet danced towards the Morakques, and the delightful creatures drew a cacophonous sound of terror from the crowd. That was all they were—pretty things with hideous intentions. Upon their touch, throaty and deafening screams erupted from their prey.

"DEMONS!" Morakques hollered. Many of them had faces painted with utmost fear, but there were handfuls who lived up to their title—courageous, determined, and *stupid*.

Skins prickled and ignited with flames, swallowing sons and daughters with a ravenous appetite. The power of such a simple attack startled Ruby, and she realized how effortless it would be to demolish. And, as horrible of a villain it made her, she pondered about doing it.

Destroy. Destroy. Destroy. The words were a ceaseless chant in Ruby's head, and she was unsure if it was the demon's voice or her own.

It did not matter.

The endless ripples of strength that coursed through her veins obstructed even the whispers and bellows that resounded in her head. Although her ears pounded with screams, she picked up the murmur of gushing water and the audible wicked crackle of flames. It spouted its sparks like a violent shake of a water-coated hand.

She was a well of infinite power, and Lilith was eagerly absorbing it just by touching Ruby's skin. They were so powerful that, for a moment, winning the war was believable.

Another wave of roaring arose before Lilith had a chance to strike. The witches turned, and their eyes widened. There, in the distance approaching them, were guards—*royal* guards, rushing into the battlefield with barbaric weapons of their own. On their shields was a symbol of rolling dice and swords.

It was not a fight that only involved two witches and thousands of Morakques. There were locals and nobles, formerly trapped witches and royal guards rushing into the lush greenery.

A laugh of disbelief escaped Ruby's lips, and she turned to Lilith to discover that the Queen of Darkness was already watching her.

"I am ready," Ruby said. Her eyes returned to the mass

of Morakques rushing towards them, approximately fifty yards away.

Lilith extended her hand, pointing at a sharpened nail to the sprinting figures. A sudden and rapid mist of darkness shot from her finger, reaching the group within seconds. It was frightening how its touch made people wither like a flower that lived too long. Petals caved in, shriveled, then fell. Their skins melted and *vanished*, becoming nothing but bones.

Pretty death, the demon commented. *Fallen flower. Falling Lily.*

Ruby yanked the strings attached to water, then imagined Morakques gurgling and spewing liquid from their mouths, choking on their fluids. Right in front of her eyes, it transpired. Power felt so fragile and addicting. So, she did it again and again until she became the type of monster she feared to become. Yet, she found that it was impossible to stop—

A vision blinded her, displaying an arrow and the stench of death she knew too well. Lilith seemed to have received the same warning, and they broke away in an instant. An arrow pierced the air where they were standing just a moment ago.

Archers.

They could not risk standing in one spot.

Ruby looked back, spotting Lilith in a graceful dance of darkness. Swirling shadows coated her like a blanket, witnessing and anticipating her every motion with glee.

They were separated, and the thought of living escaped

Ruby's mind like uncontrollable magic. She could not afford to *live*. She needed to survive.

She twisted her way through bodies and brutally stole lives with random flicks of her fingers. She wondered if this very moment would be captured in an artwork. Would she be painted as a monster or a savior? A villain or a hero?

She dove into a standing throng and left them dead in seconds.

She had never claimed so many lives, nor had she ever felt this powerful.

But power required a price.

She knew that she was unprepared to pay it the moment she spun to seek her lover again, only to see a figure entirely enveloped by darkness.

CHAPTER THIRTY-FIVE

Lilith tasted freedom, similar to one that belonged to leaves that soared in the wide azure yonder. She was a marvelous force of nature, spinning and following the directions of fate. Yet, unlike a bird possessing wings, she would eventually fall.

It was unavoidable, for she was in the midst of a war.

Lysandra left her side to perch on a branch half a mile away. Darkness bowed to the thousand-year-old witch as she watched a catastrophe embrace a kingdom she once ruled. It was baffling how peaceful she appeared. It was as if she watched a breathtaking scenery of futuristic megalithic structures. It was a stunning masterpiece—a serene figure with destruction in the background. Lilith found it strange, but she said nothing after Lysandra spoke her last words and left.

"No fight is without loss, descendant. You should do well to remember that."

Perhaps, this was the epilogue of her story and the beginning of the kingdom's tale.

She leapt like a leaf breaking away from its branch, then spun as darkness struck the hearts of Morakques and left them as gruesome corpses with eyes matching hers.

She had little time to do anything else but fight, and that was a blessing. She did not need to dwell in the guilt that followed the whisper of death that floated from her fingertips.

Grunts and screams filled the air, as prominent as the burning in her chest. It did not agonize her but instead empowered her. She felt like a blaze capable of ruining the entirety of the kingdom, a queen not to be messed with.

And she was.

She stretched her hands out and *ignited*.

She was a hurricane, a dancer who could not be kept up with, a wind without direction, a demon without a leash.

Lilith was not familiar with war, but she felt gifted when fighting.

The Morakques' voices blended into one while they chanted 'demon' as if it were an incantation for a spell to shatter her bones. She allowed the continual voices to feed her strength, to raise her above the clouds and beyond.

She was entrapped in eternity, where the battle was the present and future. Time stretched into a blur of seconds or minutes or hours, an unmeasured number of moments surrounded by the scent of violence and death. The taste of bloodlust lingered on the tip of her tongue like a tenacious desire motivated by an overwhelming load of encouragement.

Darkness swirled from her fingers like strings of gliding smoke, so much so that Lilith's hand was obscured. Khaos were supple shadows behind her. The power was almost too much to bear, yet she continued to delve into it.

She felt as if she were light enough to float atop a cloud. But in a spur of a moment, she forgot that all clouds would eventually dissipate. Lost in the image of shrieks and cries, falling had utterly slipped her mind. She was yanked back into reality by sudden impact.

Lilith gasped, eyes widening as control was hurled back into her body. She stumbled, then Khaos sprinted away in three different directions. First, an ache met her shoulder, then a severe burn began.

Confused, she glanced down to glimpse at the arrow that punctured that same spot.

She moved her feet and shifted before a spear whizzed the air where she stood a second ago. Panic seized her chest, tightening it mercilessly. Her wound burned with a constant pounding that nipped at her skin.

She had to move.

Khaos created a mountain of shadow, engulfing her in an attempt to conceal her. Darkness rose like a coat from the ground, offering Morakques an empty location to aim their arrows at while she sprinted away. Wind nudged her towards the giant rocks along the line of separation between the vast field and a forest.

She fell on her side, glancing at the arrow that protruded from her back. She felt her eyes burn and her nails sharpen when examining the injury.

She wanted to claw at herself, to bellow in rage and shriek in pain, yet she did nothing but allow her mind to race.

She shuddered at how she descended so far into darkness that she lost herself. Still, she had to admit that the power she felt was frighteningly pleasant.

Logic flowed back into her mind. She grunted, palming the shaft of the arrow before—

"Do that, and I'll puke all over you," a voice rang out. Lilith stopped, registering that boyish tone and familiar snarky remark. Joy flourished within her as she lifted her gaze of dissipating bloodlust.

"Hello again, Witch."

Lilith bit back from crying out of happiness, though her situation barely encouraged it. It was a relief to see a familiar face after being surrounded by cursing Morakques for the last few minutes.

"Marco," she said, an instinctive smile meeting her features. "What are you doing here?"

"Well, after you skipped off with the queen and abandoned little old me, I decided to eat a few more buns before coming. I've got honey from the witches you rescued, just in case something like this happens." He gestured to Lilith's shoulder and knelt beside her.

"I'm sorry for leaving without saying goodbye." Lilith winced.

"Ruby didn't, so it's fine. Besides, it's no wonder you forgot about poor me after seeing your mother," he said. "So what's it like, *princess?*"

Lilith scrunched up her face. "Does everyone know?"

"That piece of news spread like wildfire! Dicerians are so shocked after hearing about the lost princess and I had to hold back from boasting. After all, we are closer than siblings."

Lilith snickered. "Liar."

"It isn't a lie if nobody knows the truth." Marco shrugged. "Just like how a crime isn't a crime if you aren't caught. Anyway, that looks disgusting." His eyes fixed on Lilith's bleeding shoulder.

"Help me take it out, then," Lilith retorted.

Marco pulled out a blade from his pocket. Lilith swallowed the thick bile in her throat and braced herself for—

She gasped, then screamed, feeling as if she were turned inside out. The agonizing pain seemed accompanied by a hand sinking into her flesh and yanking out a piece of her soul. She attempted to douse the flame of destructive power in her chest, to calm herself before the entire kingdom was merely debris and ashes.

"For the sake of Dicera, stop moving," Marco gritted out. "Do not burn my perfect skin!"

Lilith bit her lips, then gritted her teeth. Another shock of searing pain traveled her veins, so much that it began to feel numb. Then, breathing ragged, she fluttered her eyes open and gazed at her wound.

Except, it was absent.

Marco pocketed his small bottle of honey. "You're lucky we're in the middle of a war. Or else, we'd already be caught."

Lilith scoffed. "Sure." She paused. "Thank you."

"Anything for my best friend." Marco flashed his teeth, then looked at the battle raging behind them. "You even got royal guards to fight on our side. Impressive."

"It is all luck," confessed Lilith.

"No, Lily. It is fate."

Fate. Nothing seemed so impossible now, and suddenly a reason was attached to every event that happened. If a rebellion could begin with one man's influence, then it took just one supporter to change the tide. The wind pushed her towards the Morakques, and her strength perked up from its place of temporary rest, engulfing her body once more.

"What in the world," uttered Marco from beside her. She swiveled her head sideways, peering at the area where his eyes were trained. "Looks like your parents joined the battle."

A breath was caught in Lilith's throat as she watched a man step from the shadows of the castle, fury painting the crooked lines on his face.

He bellowed, and for a time more insignificant than a second, the warriors grew silent. His words were heard by all.

Where her mother was petite and quiet like a blossomed and fragile flower, her father was powerful. He brimmed with wrath like a volcano ready to erupt, his eyes blazing with a fiery intensity. He ordered the Morakques to leave, reminding them that they stood on a territory that did not belong to them. But his demands and warnings were but an echo of what the Morakques already knew.

Lilith could not tell which side was emerging victorious, and that was far too dangerous. Then, randomly, she remembered something from the past, and the thought of Ruby lingered in her mind like a frantic and trapped bird. The red-eyed witch once told her that sometimes, the urge to win is stronger than any personal belief. "I am going back to fight," she told Marco, then smiled at him. He appeared so young and joyous, but the boy saw and lived through nightmares that scarred him.

"Go on," he urged. "Stay safe."

"Likewise." With that, Lilith rushed back into the face of death with nothing but the desire to survive. Darkness coated her like a gown of smoke, encouraging her.

She lost herself in the fighting again, but she ensured a steady link to reality. Her eyes scanned for Ruby, and her heart pounded with worry.

Yet, on the outside, she was a tyrant, the queen of war. Anyone who dared approach her was littered as bones with a mere look. Some fell unconscious before they could grasp the opportunity to think of who they might have been in the past. Perhaps, they repented their actions and wished for a second chance in life, where they would not have joined the Morakques and their cause.

The battlefield was no longer the breathtaking scenery it once was. Littered, not with rubbish but bones. Tainted, not with rainwater but with blood. Filled, not with silence but the cries of soldiers.

Lilith tried to seek Ruby but found nobody. She barely had the time to glance over the crowd before a spear struck the place where she formerly stood.

Then, a strange feeling seized her chest. She could still physically move and fight, but the world was melting away, and the burning void in her chest was transforming into a snarling force of pain. It began as a gentle caress, and then her heart started to ache as if her veins were snapping, one by one. No screams escaped her lips, though pleading for help seemed like the only thing she could do against such agony. It was so unbearable that it made thrusting an arrow out of her shoulder sound pleasurable. It felt like the beginning of losing control.

She stumbled frantically out of harm's way like a hound roped to a tree, hooked by its collar with limited directions to conceal itself. She shut her eyes, then allowed any image to form in her head.

She imagined a blanket of smoke plummeting on her attackers and eliminating them all. Her lips moved as her mind ran, chanting an incantation as her legs dug memorized symbols into the soil. Ruby would have chided her for being careless, for cherishing her life so little, and Lilith paused because she thought of her. Her chest was caving in on itself, but through the pain, she felt a slither of satisfaction because she had not yet lost herself in her magic.

When she peeled open her eyes, kneeling bodies encircled her. The eyes of their owners were as void as the gaping hole puncturing her organs. Lilith almost laughed at the irony of Morakques kneeling to a witch.

She panted, taking a moment to gather herself.

It was a mistake to believe that she had even a second to rest.

She did not register the attack in time to defend herself. Not when Wei—the leader of Morakques—came barrelling through the crowds of fighting bodies with a sword raised to strike. The weapon's deadly edge gleamed as sunlight touched it, highlighting the intricate etchings that adorned its surface.

Lilith was the Queen of Darkness, but even power could not save her this time. It was fated, she remembered, for her death to transpire. Perhaps, perishing earlier was a blessing because she would not turn into more of a monster.

She only wished for the pain to end. For the raging storm in her body to leave with the strength she was cursed with. Closing her eyes, she thought of the visions that never occurred, her grandmother and Ruby. Her greatest regret was not confessing to the woman she loved. Insignificant seconds had never felt more crucial, for it might have offered her the opportunity to utter three words to her lover.

"No, don't!" a voice cried, and Lilith thought it might be the sound of memory. Yet, she felt nothing, and she realized too late that it was not her voice but one that belonged to a boy.

Lilith opened her eyes, bewildered. She saw Marco, and she heard the terrible gurgle of his words as he spoke.

"Don't," he said, but the damage was done. The sword had plunged so deep into his stomach that the blade protruded from his back, leaving him gasping for breath as blood gushed from the wound.

The pain vanished, and finally, Lilith could breathe. She took those precious moments to bawl, gradually ripping the rope that tied her to sanity. She rushed towards the boy, wanting nothing more than to send his father to the underworld. Yet, Marco shook his head in a silent request. Skin met skin, and she could vaguely hear the grotesque sizzling from that mere touch.

"Oh, Marco," she wept, not daring to hold his hand. He was a friend who saved her life. Twice. Perhaps she could do something for him, too. Save his life, just like how he had done for both her and Ruby.

However, when her eyes landed on the dandelions that bloomed on the soil like delicate, human hands reaching out from a grave upon the taste of Marco's blood, she knew *this* was fated to happen. How many times had she received a vision about this moment? The dandelions and the grief clouding her chest, embracing her thoughts like a toxic partner. The boiling animosity in her system and the power surging her veins as if it were minutes from exploding.

Khaos hovered over her for a moment, then became smoke that covered her entire being. Every motion, every breath, they followed her.

Lilith still had so much fight left in her.

"Marco," Lilith murmured, wanting to avoid the truth for just seconds longer. But his eyes were drifting shut, and no amount of honey would help. Lilith loathed how she did not know the spell to heal but had memorized hundreds of symbols and incantations to kill instead.

She was a demon indeed.

His blood caused prepossessing flowers to rise. It was almost offensive for them to show in an environment that juxtaposed their beauty.

Lilith wanted to sob and release the emotions that resided in her chest. She wondered what it felt like to finally fill the burning void in her chest. Would it steal away her life by crushing it into smithereens?

"Lily," Marco muttered, then looked at Wei. "Dad."

In the haze of her grief, she saw the father drop to his knees. He scrambled to gather Marco's hands in his, frantic and agonized. The Morakque did not care that Lilith was defenseless in front of him.

He looked like a man on the verge of collapse. His usually neat hair had fallen out of his bun in a tangled mess, and he appeared more unkempt than Lilith had ever seen him. His armor plate was stained with blood, and his face bore scars that would have made him intimidating if not for the tears clouding his green eyes. At that moment, he appeared less like a seasoned hunter and more like a broken father. He reached out to cradle Marco in his chest, holding his son close to his chest and heaving desperate pleas.

"No, please, no," he heaved. "I've already lost your mother. I can't lose you too."

He rocked Marco gently, whispering to himself, apologizing and sniffling as he watched his son slip away.

Lilith's head spun. It was a tornado shredding her thoughts, making them clipped and ugly. She *despised* Morakques. She blamed them for everything and bothered little if they deserved it.

She seethed. Eyes blazed. Blood heated. Face wet. Thoughts screamed. Bones stiffened. Stomach flipped. Hands clenched.

She erupted.

Her magic was a phenomenon that turned the heads of hundreds. Shadows wrapped around her like engulfing fire, but they did not consume her skin. It made her more powerful, more out of control.

She felt a vague presence beside her, and she almost decided *not* to look. She needed no distraction and reason to quell her rage.

"Lilith."

That voice.

It was the only sound that could bring her back to reality, even if she were trapped in a different realm. That voice injected waves of reassurance into her, but it could not overshadow the strength that simmered in her guts. It did, however, call upon a few rational thoughts.

"My control," Lilith said, unable to hear herself, "is slipping."

"I know," Ruby said, her voice soft and overflowing with emotions. She helped Lilith up to her feet, frowning. Marco was *their* friend, a compassionate and lovely boy who deserved a life of adventures.

It was that day in Dakota again, where she watched the beheaded witch and the crowd that cheered.

Then, she was pained and disgusted and angered. She yearned to cry. Now, she was tired and sickened and furious. She yearned for revenge.

"I wish things ended differently," Lilith said, so empty and full at the same time. She was a taut string that was tearing apart despite its relentless effort to stay together.

Ruby rested her hand on Lilith's, and a silent message followed the touch. They were both balancing on the edge of a cliff, too many emotions blinding and leading them towards a direction where they could only plummet into nothingness.

The ground was littered with dandelions, and the wind carried their plumose hair to soar in the air.

"Me too," Ruby said, eyes glistening with the horrors of their surroundings.

Lilith's hammering heart was all the hint she needed to know that she had run out of time. Ruby must have felt it, too, for she seemed so detached that it was visibly evident that her senses were shutting down. Of course, her father's death would have played a role, just as Lilith's grandmother's current circumstance distressed her beyond belief.

Lilith sighed. The possibility of serenity was so far away yet close to the touch. With shadows cloaking the both of them and flames rising to form yet another layer to shield them from the war, she kissed her lover for what could be the last time.

Hunger mixed with sorrow, desperation in a heap of blinding emotions. It made their power flare brighter than moonlight. Lilith tasted fire on Ruby's lips—scorching and addicting in a way that watching blinking flames were. Their need was empowering, and it formed an anchor to the world. Their final promise to each other was to survive.

Then, they would be able to *live*.

The last thing she saw was Ruby closing her eyes. The last sound she heard was a roar.

The sky cracked with the unusual force of magic, and rain cascaded from the darkened canvas.

"I love you," Lilith said, then felt an invisible force steal away her control.

She knew that darkness was consuming her, and she would never come back from it.

CHAPTER THIRTY-SIX

Faye was uncertain if Ruby opened up to the demon on purpose or by accident.

It did not quite matter.

Faye knew that returning meant war—the battle that future generations would be aware of due to the destruction that rained on land. They would sing it around fireplaces, creative lyrics about how the Red Demon had possessed Ruby's body without consent. How their two queens adopted strength like never before, only to be sacrificed.

Ruby was born from a sacrifice. Was it fate that she would die from one too?

Faye could not tell if her death would happen just yet.

It decided to halt pondering and instead turn to the side where Khaos were.

Their eyes met. Red and black—a swirling mist of cruelty and beauty. They smiled, slowly, as if any sudden movement would cleave them apart again.

"Destroy," Faye whispered, the word echoing until it died out. "Destroy, destroy, destroy."

Khaos smiled, the curve twisting Lilith's feature into a promise of violence and nothing less. Only they were capable of that irresistible inhuman look.

The battlefield around them was chaos incarnate. The

clash of metal on metal echoed across the plain, punctuated by the screams of the wounded and the dying.

And yet, Faye and Khaos existed in a circle of calm in the midst of the cacophony of violence. The arrows that were aimed at them melted before they could even reach their targets. Not a single Morkaque dared to come close to them.

There were people watching with bated breath, their eyes transfixed on the display of power never once seen in history. Most of the Morakques and royal guards were still engaged in battle, but some had abandoned it in fear, tripping over themselves to flee. It was as if they knew that the witches did not intend to offer mercy.

The air around them hummed with power, its very presence commanding the battlefield.

"Will we perish tonight?" asked Khaos. It was a horrible question to ask amid war when the wall separating them and their enemies was moments from collapsing.

Faye knew the answer but did not speak it aloud. Instead, the Red Demon voiced out a thought Ruby had from what felt like hours ago. It was a shame that she missed the opportunity to tell Lilith. "It does not matter. If you leave, I will find you again. My soul and yours are one and only each other's to take."

Four different minds within two bodies. That was them—Ruby and Lilith, Faye and Khaos.

Flames crackled. The world tilted on its axis. Voices bellowed and cried and died out. Hunger flashed in the eyes of demons, and then the fiery mist encircling them ceased to exist. Faye clutched all of the strings in Ruby's heart, each connected to one of her abilities, then began to imagine.

Sometimes, the urge to win was stronger than any personal belief. Victory appeared in her mind's eye, and so did fire and water, wildlife and nature, blood and vengeance. She imagined power, so much of it, because it was finally time to use it. For years, Ruby's abilities were a whisper of power. Now, it was a holler of strength.

Power felt so, so sweet. But love was powerful, and it was sweeter.

Faye allowed its voices to stretch out as her abilities did the same, reaching outward like a force that needed no permission. If fate were present, it would have an expression of indifference because this moment was planned long before it transpired.

The world became an ashen face with blinded and white unseeing eyes. Furrowed eyebrows and puckered lips, frozen in a countenance of distress. As harm weaved through the land, decorating lushness with bloodied bodies, the ground became bleak and ruined, like a visage cracked and hideous and tragic.

Elemental magic blended with darkness, tasting overwhelmingly wicked. Rain pounded, but even the pleas of the sky were not enough to stop them.

The world shattered beneath their touch.

The gentle trace of their fingertips, like a wind's caress, was enough to shake the world.

Faye had known that disaster would rain on Dicera. It was shown in the form of a dream many times. But watching the madness paint reality was entirely different. It was frightening and surreal. The darkened fire roared upon the skins of Morakque, burning away their flesh.

At that moment, it felt like the war was between two of the strongest witches to exist and their enemies, who had hunted their kind for centuries.

Retribution was the blood that boiled in veins, choking and restricting the Morakques' breathing. It was the blazing heat that savagely consumed skins before they could blister, the darkness that turned bodies into gruesome pearl-white bones, the vines that reached out from the soil to wound ankles and disable hands, and the seemingly endless supply of magic before it dwindled and vanished, leaving the witches as empty husks with absent emotions. The grief that sobbed in their minds became a distant thing, something that did not belong to them.

Retribution was the death that surrounded them.

In the end, inventions and technology were useless against the power of fate and nature.

Faye felt satisfied and weary after magic had reached out to clutch those with darkened souls. It left those who could be swayed to believe in a future cause untouched—Morakques, royal guards, royalty, and witches.

Nobody attacked.

Khaos sighed, relieved. The ground was a river of scarlet, stark under the blazing orb of gold. The witches paid little attention to it because as peaceful as it was, it would not be for long. Darkness had stolen Lilith's mind, and the Red Demon now had control of Ruby's body. The latter, however, was temporary.

As if she had never existed, Lilith was gone. Dead, as one would say it.

Faye was watching it happen. Khaos was beginning to cease everything—the mind, the body, the heart. Lilith's eyes were drooping, and consciousness slipped away like liquid from a golden faucet.

Khaos was winning. Faye smiled, glad that power had reigned. The damage caused was worth her sacrifice. And yet, it felt like a hint of something else.

Sparking beside the demon's happiness was sorrow, piercing like poisoned arrows.

Sympathy blossomed. The demon frowned, listening to the audible murmur that belonged to a voice Ruby managed to possess. Her resistance was impressive, and her thoughts, though quiet, were an impactful scream of agony. *You will not succeed in stealing what is mine because my wrath is stronger than your determination*, she said, bitter and still fighting.

Faye knew that a fight required sacrifice. Marco was only one of many.

Footsteps sounded, and Queen Emeline rushed towards the witches with worry clouding eyes that might have once belonged to Lilith. When the Queen of Dicera approached her daughter with tears staining her face, Faye did not care to stop her from reaching out.

Her skin simmered, the sound sickening.

She pulled away instantly.

"Your daughter is no more," said Faye, voices echoing unnaturally. Lilith's nails were sharpened to a dagger's point, face still vicious and hair in a disheveled mess. The lily in her hair remained.

Liar, screeched a voice.

I am not.

Let me return.

I cannot.

Ruby was still battling, not in the war that raged but within their body. Unyielding, like a queen. *Lilith needs me.*

I am sorry, Ruby. I cannot.

Please. A pause. *Please, Faye.*

Faye paused, letting an emotion rise to the surface—shock. Throughout their lives, Ruby had never once addressed the demon by name.

It meant something significant.

Faye had always believed that hell would freeze over before Ruby shattered her pride.

It was a promise made long ago. One that Faye intended to keep.

If you call me by name, I will leave. I will return what belongs to you, and we will no longer share a body.

Faye smiled. Then, she decided to turn to fate again and return the body to a friend who deserved it more.

CHAPTER THIRTY-SEVEN

Ruby did not waste a second after returning to her body. Darting forward, she scooped Lilith up in her arms like she weighed nothing.

Ruby stepped over the bodies that littered every inch of the ground and followed the nudges of the wind. A swirling mist of black guided her further and further into a forest, away from acres of scarlet specks. She did not know where she was headed until a sudden vision of cobblestones and dim lights led her to the final location.

To the east of the battlefield, nestled amidst the lush greenery, was a cave.

Dheeksha Cave.

Its entrance was concealed by a thick curtain of vines, their tendrils snaking around the rocky exterior as if trying to claim it as their own.

Ruby raced towards it.

Inside it, the walls were jagged and uneven, with small crevices and alcoves jutting out from the stone. Moss and fungi clung to them.

Ruby dismissed any thoughts that begged for her attention. Her limbs ached, and her heart was lodged in her throat, as unmoving as Lilith. Flames flared on her fingertips instinctively, guiding her deeper into the darkness. She could almost hear the crawling of insects and the sound of spiders spinning their webs, but any fear she might have was irrelevant.

She laid Lilith down on a rock that extended upward from the rugged ground, decorated with unpredictable spikes and sprinkled stones. Ruby noticed how sharp Lilith's nails had become, coated in blood as if she had used it as a weapon to claw at Morakques.

One drop. The ground was painted black. Another, and another. The tap was running and losing its purpose with every second.

At such a crucial time, when the light of her life was dimming before her eyes, Ruby only knew to do one thing.

What can I do?

She reached out to the friend who shared her mind. The friend who gave up the opportunity to seize permanent control of her body.

She received no reply for a long moment.

Book, it whispered back without multiple voices to enunciate the word.

Ruby looked around, and there, to her side, was the transcription of The Forbidden Book of Lysandra. She let out a shaking breath and knew in her gut that Lysandra had helped to transport it.

Queen Lysandra, came the frail voice once again. Ruby barely recognized it.

She rushed to the book, flipping through worded pages as if she could perform any of the spells within. Unfortunately, the Book of Shadows was only for those blessed with the ability of darkness, and Ruby lacked that specific trait. The book's cursive letters blurred, and droplets of tears rained on the pages.

Glancing into the past and far into the future. Cursing dark souls to live as their ashes, bones, and shadows. Visiting those far away, close, and dead. Housing a lost soul within a jewel, ring and mirror. Calling upon a temporary slumber or a permanent sleep. Diving into minds, visions and hearts. Spells of all kinds flashed before her eyes, rapid and ceaseless. She did not know what she was searching for or if it would help in the slightest.

Her fingers worked like a skillful magician's, folding papers and vanishing them. She only stopped when they brushed the surface of the last page, words that possessed eyes and unspeakable intentions. It murmured a unique language that required a twist of the tongue, vicious and yet the only solution standing.

A golden vial of immortality.

Ruby had read about its existence and the failed replications after its ingredients were lost to time. Yet it looked unblinking at her, teasing her with a voice that could only be described as seductive.

How many times had she flipped through the book and missed the faint letters that mentioned the most important spell in the entirety of witchcraft? How many times had Lilith done the same?

Her breath hitched, and her heart stilled for what seemed like a moment stretched into hours.

Ingredients for a Golden Vial of Immortality:
A dark matter or a body of drained immortal blood

Nature's blood
A Soothsayer's promise
A lover's plea
An eternal oath
Five symbols of magic
A sacrifice.

They were strange ingredients that Ruby would not have understood if she were anyone else. She had spent years confined, trapped like a vulnerable creature and treated like a demon in the Forest of Dahlia. She took that time to devour information about the kingdom and learn all that was significant outside a home no one dared to leave.

A dark matter. That term was familiar, and it took Ruby minutes to realize that she had finally found a name to match that odd sensation radiated by Lilith's flower.

She skimmed the second line, analyzing and decoding. Lysandra had designed the spell, and there were no written sources that spoke of her destroying miles of land to have it 'bleed'. She could have wounded the kingdom or taken in molten heat of lava that symbolized blood, but such acts would have been recorded.

No, it must have been something close to her. Something simple, written in a complex phrase.

Dahlia. The senior was a nature witch. Ruby's head of sprinting ideas found another piece to the puzzle—the blood of a nature witch. The next line was something similar—Lysandra's blood. Fortunately, Ruby's blood ran with the power of all abilities.

A lover's plea. Lysandra originally created the

immortality spell for her lover, the king who ruled the Reign of Eara with her. History was repeating once again, but it involved two young witches who simply wished to continue living this time around.

An eternal oath. Ruby knew that the ingredient was more of a dedication than anything. To live forever would not always be pleasant, for everything would eventually come to an end. Immortality was often viewed as a curse, not a blessing.

But with the right person, any dreadful event could be pleasant. Ruby just needed more time, more lives to spend. She wanted to leave with content.

The second requirement from the bottom made her pause. There were no symbols scribbled anywhere like the other pages.

Time was running out, for every second meant another portion of Lilith was infiltrated and consumed by darkness. To seek five symbols alone was impossible. She needed a hint through a vision.

Faye? Ruby called. Before, she did not put much thought into the name since she never truly pondered about it. But it was a genuinely pretty name. *Faye?*

Faye had never been so silent, so absent. Ruby was so fueled with anxiousness and concern for Lilith to realize that something was horribly wrong.

Oh, Dahlia. Speak, Faye. What is wrong?

There was no response for a painful moment.

Have I not told you? she finally spoke. *Even before you were born, fate had planned this battle and its sacrifices. You can do anything but defy fate.*

What are you saying?

I am a sacrifice.

What?

I am a sacrifice.

Before Ruby could speak to refuse or even attempt to oppose, a vision flashed before her eyes. One that she saw before, a long time ago.

When she touched Lilith's skin for the first time, multiple powerful moving images had played. It spun a tale of the future, which was now the present. Dicera's crest and the swords within, she remembered. Symbols flared like a flame, but it was too unclear, like a haze of smoke.

It was enough of a message.

Ruby returned to reality. She instantly shut her eyes and pictured the presence of flames. It roared to life at her feet, then shot outwards like a thousand spiders released from the same spot. Marigold heat crawled like serpents darting forward for prey, leaving sparks that die off within seconds. The snakes illuminated the dungeon-like area as it climbed the walls and seethed with fury, displaying symbols concealed in darkness.

The crest of Dicera was carved into the walls. Rolling dice and twin blades with exactly five symbols on their handles—two on the left, three on the right.

Lysandra was the person who designed the royal crest.

A sound escaped Ruby's lips, and she could not recognize what she felt. Relief? Worry? Fear?

She got to work immediately, letting her hands guide her as if they had done the spell a thousand times. She guided a rock to split her palm open. A gaping wound stared back, and she could have sworn that the sight appeared once in a nightmare. Her fingers drew two symbols with the dark liquid on the left, and then she begrudgingly used Lilith's blood from a wound born from the war to sketch three symbols on the right.

She removed the lily from Lilith's hair, then gently placed it on the ground.

Almost immediately, the blood glowed faint golden and traveled towards the lily with an unknown force.

I do not know what to do next, Ruby said to her friend. She did not know if it was truly working.

The next step, replied Faye, sounding so inexplicably exhausted, *is me*.

The sacrifice? Ruby was clueless. Faye would never leave; it was impossible. So what exactly was the requirement of the last step?

She did not understand until she was yanked backwards. Darkness spilt from the flower, and then red mist began to fuse with it. The smoky scarlet came from her, she realized. It came from something *within* her. She felt something drain as she was jerked back once again.

Gods, she realized. Fear crept into her veins and froze her limbs. The world continued to progress, although she made a silent wish for it to stop.

Faye *was* leaving.

"No," Ruby whispered aloud. "No, do not leave."

Red eyes glistening, she could only watch as a faint and weary voice muttered goodbye.

She did not have the time to say it back.

Her breathing became rapid, and her eyes grew wider.

No more words left her lips, although a million hung in the air and the walls like invisible, shattered paintings.

Ruby failed to tell her friend, who was born into her mind, who was viewed as a demon with her, who made her childhood a little less lonely, that she was appreciative.

Like a sly, slithering snake, Faye slipped away.

CHAPTER THIRTY-EIGHT

Lilith thought she was dead.

Darkness lurked around her form, enveloping her like a jacket in the cold. She assumed that she had awoken in another realm where petals existed as eternally beaming blossoms and love existed without pain. Memories lingered at the edge of her mind like a sharpened claw, pouncing whenever she came too close to recalling.

She tried to open her eyes, but she was paralyzed. Nothing moved but her searing thoughts.

Ruby.

Her name was the sweetest poison.

"Wake up, Lilith." The voice was faint, like a gentle trace of wind. "You are all I have left."

Lies. How was it possible for Ruby to have lost everyone? They were queens with crowns of ruby and gold, finally accepted by the people who once loathed them for being who they were. Lilith lived within reality's imposter—a hallucination. The world was like a silk gown with royal embroidery and glittering jewels, blinding and distracting eyes that would have noticed its hideous tears and stains. She was happy in a place where everything was a dream—fake and brief.

"Come back." The words echoed in her land of breathtaking willows and lavenders, reminding her that she was the Queen of Darkness and the princess of a ruined kingdom. She had duties and affection in another world.

Lilith gazed at her glorious surroundings, closed her eyes, and imagined it in blackened flames.

She woke up with a jolt.

Before she could recall much of what transpired, arms were thrown around her. She felt strange. It was as if she had grown a few years but gained no additional memories. Her magic, once a scowling and struggling creature restrained by a rope in Lilith's enervated hands, now laid in her grasp without resistance of any sort.

It was as if her magic had finally accepted its owner. How odd, how impossible.

"Thank Dahlia," repeated a voice like a chant for a spell. "Finally, finally."

Confused, Lilith pulled back from the hug to meet glossy eyes that were the color of roses. The withering plants appeared sewn into her face, so deeply carved that it began to leak its fragrance and nectar of misery like a repaired tap.

"Ruby?" Recognition shone in Lilith's dark eyes. That name triggered a series of images to rush into her mind with a headache.

It felt so surreal.

Her powers should be drained and on the verge of consuming her whole, but it felt like just another day in a tranquil forest environment. She was not, however, in the Forest of Dahlia, surrounded by sorcerers who were losing the will to live. Instead, around her was a dungeon that looked exceedingly familiar. It was like entering the castle of aureate structures and scarlet streaks all over again.

"Where are we?"

"Dheeksha Cave."

The location's name triggered a memory of an ancient queen possessing multiple shadows, dressed in a grand, gloomy gown. A figure who was perched on a branch, observing, as the kingdom she ruled a millennium ago swam towards its impending doom.

Lilith glanced around and noticed something else. Usually, her shadows were silent. Now, they seemed absent.

Lilith thought that perhaps, her darkness had disappeared, but the thought dissipated when she glanced down at her demonic nails.

"How am I alive?" Lilith asked, patient, although her mind was flooded with questions.

Ruby was quiet. She was fatigued, Lilith realized. She appeared drained and on the verge of death, with glittering unshed tears clinging to her eyelids. At that moment, she looked so gripped by darkness despite lacking the exceptionally rare ability.

"You..." she hesitated. "You drank a vial of immortality."

What?

No.

Lilith could not believe her ears. Her face remained unfazed, but a bolt of bewilderment grasped her heart so quickly that she felt the need to fall back.

"What?" she choked out. "What about you?"

Often, someone wished to be immortal. How wondrous an eternal life would be, watching centuries pass like the flow of liquid, going on and on and on. But Lilith could only ponder about how lonely and dreadful that was. Immortality was a curse.

A ceaseless life was much worse than a short life.

Ruby explained the spell wearily, how she stumbled upon it and how Lilith was alive only because of it. She should be grateful, and she was, but she had so many questions. How did it work? What sacrifice did Ruby make? How did she decipher the ingredients?

Will she have to watch all of her loved ones die?

If Ruby was dying, their story would be ending, unlike her now-everlasting life.

"No." Lilith refused to believe that she would survive the war at such a great cost. "There must be another way. Another spell of some sort that gives *you* the vial, too."

"There is not."

"There will be!"

"Lilith!" Ruby said, her voice echoing in the cave like a taunt. "The person whom I grew up with, the voice and friend who taught me everything I know, was sacrificed. Marco was sacrificed. Many witches and Morakques were sacrificed. My father is dead, and you, the last person I have left, almost left me today. Please, Lilith. We have lost enough." Silence. Seconds ticked by. "Enough is enough."

Nobody was more vulnerable than the witch everyone feared at that moment. It was shown through her voice and the gleam in her eyes. It made Lilith fall silent because she, too, remembered the death that resulted from the war.

"Your friend?" Lilith inquired in a mumble. Ruby left out the information in her explanation.

Her lover looked away, eyes glassy and face twisted into

utmost sorrow. "I do not know how to go on without her. She was the sacrifice for your spell, a soul for another." She gazed into Lilith's empty black eyes, so full of emotions. "She wished for control most, yet when the chance came, she chose my needs over her own."

"Do you think we can bring her back?" Lilith asked.

"Magic requires more than you want to give," Ruby murmured. "Unless there is a miracle, I will not experiment with it any more than I already have."

Whereas Lilith felt like she had advanced in years, Ruby seemed to have truly aged.

"Would I be considered a miracle?" asked a voice. Another unsaid question was answered—the whereabouts of Lysandra.

Lilith turned and smiled. "Hello," she said aloud, looking into dark eyes that mirrored her own. Ruby looked in Lysandra's direction, seeing nothing but remaining quiet.

Despite feeling like her thoughts were not her own, muddled and blurred, Lilith knew one thing was certain— Lysandra, too, was leaving. Her memory served an image on a golden platter, reminding her that this was their final destination since the beginning. Dheeksha Cave was a symbol of loss and discovery.

Lysandra gazed at the wall, longing evident in her eyes. Fate had planned her arrival and departure, and unfortunately, the last chapters were dedicated to the latter.

"There is a kingdom waiting for you, my descendant," Lysandra said after a moment of pause. "It is in a terrible state that must be once again restored." The senior witch extended her arm, sleeves sliding towards her wrist with a gentle whisper, beckoning Lilith to step into a realm of mystery and viciousness. "Come."

Entranced yet lucid, Lilith rose to her feet unstably. She was frightened to face the consequences of destruction, but Lysandra did not intend to lead her outside the cave. Instead, she directed the young witch to a corner, then lowered herself before a decrepit rectangular stone coated with a thick layer of dust.

A stream of darkness flowed from her fingertips, utterly concealing the stone. Baffled, Lilith watched as Lysandra removed a lid to reveal a very ghoulish figure. She had never seen anyone so pale, nor did she think it was possible for someone to be the color of pearls. It was a body that should have been long decomposed.

Lilith bit back a gasp of horror, realizing that it was the king during the Reign of Eara in the coffin, still alive despite the impossibility of it. Beside him was a book titled 'The Reign of Eara'.

Lysandra, a sorcerer who saw centuries of life and death, gore and havoc, dropped to her knees before the casket.

"Oh," murmured Lysandra, removing her mask of confidence and nonchalance. At that moment, she looked more like a broken girl than a thousand-year-old sorcerer. "Oh, my Gods."

Lilith felt as if she had walked in on a forbidden scene, a private chapter of a book she should have never picked up. A queen on her knees was a sight that burnt her memories.

It made Lilith's heart plummet into her stomach. Lysandra looked at the lanky and ghastly mannequin with gutting bones the same way Ruby looked at her. Lysandra was in love, even a thousand years later.

She tore her eyes away from the king, gazing at the two younger witches. One immortal, one mortal.

"It has all been planned by fate, my descendant, and I believe it is time for me to play my part in your story," Lysandra said quietly. Her eyes sparkled in the dimness. "You have a missing ingredient to create another vial, and that is a dark matter. We do not have any more of that, but we *do* have him." She frowned at her husband.

Mouth dry and understanding very little in her muddled mind, Lilith stayed silent.

Lysandra twitched her fingers, and darkness found its way into the mouth of the man that looked more dead than alive. A string of instructions left the sorcerer's lips, and Lilith rushed to comply. Her heart was exploding. Thick hope, like overgrown trees, obstructed her perception of the world.

The man was immortal, and his blood could act as a substitute for the missing dark matter.

"For Dahlia's sake," gasped Ruby. "I must be dreaming."

A burst of joy sprouted in Lilith's throat, escaping her lips in quivering laughter. It was a blessing to have found peace in a time of chaos, a miracle in a time of war.

The stench of death and blood in the air intensified as the witches performed the spell. Lysandra's glorious gown pooled around her as she lowered herself to the ground, a corpse's head on her lap. She brushed a finger across his forehead, and a silent cry filled the air as she spoke the last syllable of the spell.

As if time stretched its flexible body, the moment lingered for a second too long. Then, the earth claimed what defied its laws—an immortal king and a summoned queen in a forbidden romance.

"Promise me something, my descendant," requested the queen in a whisper after becoming a flurry of gold. Particles soared in the air and painted the ground in the colors of Dicera. "Take care of our kingdom."

She could only muster a nod as the millennium-old queen vanished. Beside her, Ruby consumed the golden liquid within the vial.

The silence that followed was louder than any battle cry on a field peppered with death. The witches exchanged a glance that sobbed the words lingering in the air. They were drowning in agony greater than any, yet their magic was in control, suppressed by vials of immortality. Eternally powerful.

The weight in Lilith's chest held her down until she could barely breathe. Her legs gave away, and she settled down on the edge of the stone coffin. Ruby perched beside her, head as silent as it never was.

"We lived," Ruby stated, her voice a mixture of dawning realization and rising awe. She sounded brittle, and her red eyes were a pool of molten on the verge of overflowing. "Lilith, I am so, *so* tired."

The Queen of Darkness forced a smile for the woman who had performed an outlandish spell to save her life. It was genuine but difficult to muster. "Me too, but we have many things to do."

Ruby returned the smile. It was exhausting and required much effort, but it remained.

In a moment, she was attacked by gratitude so strong that her feet swayed. She tried piecing her feelings for Lilith into thoughts: The twenty-six letters of the alphabet and the flowery phrases they could form would never be worthy of measuring the love she had for her. The dictionary wept to have them. She was the letters that never existed and the phenomena that never occurred.

"I am so glad you are here," Ruby murmured. "I cannot wait for time to heal this wound of ours."

Lilith nodded, solemn but with hope. "We have an eternity."

The words seemed so strange, so *right*. It made the smile on both of their faces widen, and it fed Lilith with enough confidence to lean in. A gentle brush of the lips, a quiet part of the mouth, and they were a completed puzzle once again.

"I cannot wait to spend my life with you, Ruby," Lilith said, forehead pressed against her lover's.

The beautiful sound of soft laughter filled the air. "My soul shall take sanctuary in yours forevermore."

The two immortal witches left Dheeksha Cave and strode into the site of an unfinished battle.

The Kingdom of Dicera was in disorder.

Turmoil stirred in the atmosphere, and constant chants

poured from the mouths of Morakques and royal guards. "The king is dead!" they cried. "The king is *dead*!"

Bile rose in Lilith's throat. She was so tired. Tired of death and weeping and breaking. She could not recall her father, but the thought of the relationship they could have formed added to her misery.

Morakques were still alive, but they looked lost in a world of their own. Their leader was the reason for their distress. He was unblinking and depressed and resigned. Gone was the authoritative man who delivered speeches on a platform.

Two lost armies remained; the goal of the war long forgotten.

Everybody's face was wet with rain, but it had not stopped anyone from staring into the unfamiliar eyes of their enemies with abhorrence.

In the distance, a royal guard raised his sword to penetrate the back of an oblivious Morakque.

Lilith pointed to the scene, and darkness flung the sword away with enough force to stab a rock.

"Stop."

The word was a command that registered into the minds of royalty and guards, witches and Morakques. Nobody moved a muscle, not even Queen Emeline.

Ruby squeezed Lilith's hand, sending a streak of confidence amidst the sadness.

"I believe everyone knows about the Reign of Eara and Queen Lysandra—my ancestor and the first witch to exist alongside Dahlia. My bloodline carries her magic and the special ability of darkness. Beside me is Ruby, who possesses all abilities but mine. Together, we can ruin the world and heal it again." Her voice seemed to travel to all Dicerians, even those far away in the Forest of Dahlia. "Ask yourselves, why did this war begin? Was it the hatred between Morakques and witches? The long-standing feud between royalty and Morakques? What do we have to gain from a battle that will only result in casualties?"

The silence was a living thing, soaring the atmosphere and planting its seeds of realization. Lilith continued, "Dicera is broken. It has *been* broken because nobody cares to learn from history. Look around, and you will notice that there is no need to lose your life today."

No one spoke for a long moment. The truth was sinking into their skins, their chests, their guts. A witch had been ruling the kingdom, and the long-lost princess possessed the most dangerous ability. The discovery was shocking to many.

"I agree," rasped a man. It was the Morakque whose life was spared. Many glanced at his way as if urging him for an explanation, but the reasons were scattered throughout the battlefield.

It took a long moment before the next course of action was decided. Then, weapons were dropped to the ground. Metal fell and greeted the green-red ground. A look of defeat and comprehension coated the faces of enemies as they exchanged glances.

Words were not enough to sway them. It took war and death and sacrifice, but it did not have to be for nothing. At last, people realized that a victorious fight was one that never happened in the first place.

"What will you do about it?" someone said gruffly. "Are you going to fix this wretched place?"

Lilith raised her head, then looked at Ruby. "Yes. We will."

Ruby nodded. She gestured to a pool of blood on the ground, urging others to look as the earth drank the liquid and sprouted a field of dandelions. Life from death. Light in darkness. Love in despair.

Peace in war.

A rare, impossible sight summoned by Ruby. With every ceaseless patter of the rain, the flowers spread and spread until lifeless bodies were concealed by lively plants. Then, the girl once feared as the Red Demon raised her head. The clouds heeded her command and dissipated.

"We will restore this kingdom," Ruby said, more to herself and her lover than anybody. It was a promise, and they had no shortage of time.

The sight of the blossoms roused fascination and confidence, and soon, only a handful held onto their bloodied weapons. No one spoke for a long moment, but everyone understood.

"The king is dead," announced a final voice like a swooshing arrow in the silent air. It was stated by Queen Emeline, whose eyes were trained on her daughter. She took a deep breath before continuing, "I am not fit to rule. For years, I have been drowning in cowardice. I am ashamed to have done nothing for my kind in fear of cutting short my safe and blissful time as queen. I have been selfish, unlike Lilith, who was courageous enough to take on a quest to seek freedom for witches. It is with certainty that I declare that my crown be passed on"—all eyes landed on Lilith—"to the princess."

"What?" Lilith spluttered under her breath. She looked at her mother, confused. The queen approached her, sad and tired but confident under her royal mask.

"Am I not too young to be queen?" Lilith questioned. "I do not know how—"

"As long as you are willing to learn, you are never too young," said her mother, looking between her daughter and Ruby. "Besides, you have displayed enough to show that you are capable."

Then, the mother descended into a curtsey—one meant for a queen.

With her heart in her throat and a racing mind, Lilith watched as sorcerers, royalties, guards, villagers, and Morakques alike followed suit and dropped into a bow. Those who were uncertain conformed, and those who refused became uncertain. It would take effort and time to gain their trust, but the reign of Ruth was going to be successful.

The young witches would make sure of it.

Fate led them to the outside world, where witches were forbidden and killed. Yet, Ruby and Lilith returned as queens of the kingdom.

The former ruler, Emeline, smiled at how the future queens lifted their chins as they spoke, proud and unapologetic of who they were. She recognized the truth as she did her remorse: the girls were a gift to the kingdom—queens born to lead.

CHAPTER THIRTY-NINE

The familiar eternal plants stood with pride, their leaves stretched out as if welcoming them back, beaming with the sweet scent of home. Witches stood anxiously outside their houses, assuming the worst of the unknown visitors. They were living in everlasting fear of the outside world, Morakques and threats.

Fear that was no longer necessary.

Footsteps echoed through the forest. The atmosphere was brimming with clouds of terror before it was replaced with relief. They barely recognized the witches they sent on a suicide mission. They left in simple clothing but returned in gowns of gold and red.

Their eyes landed on the Red Demon, wearing a beautiful grin while her hand connected with a girl followed by shadows.

Gasps and chatter filled the area. Cheers rang out, followed by looks of disbelief and curiosity. They knew of the Queen of Darkness and the stories surrounding that title but never believed it to be true.

The two queens lowered themselves slightly in a greeting taught by Lysandra. The girl with onyx eyes smiled. She missed the Forest of Dahlia very much, for it was where she grew and learned and stayed. Khaos twirled and leaped as a single figure, then separated to become two crowns atop the heads of the young rulers.

"We have done it," Lilith announced, then searched the crowd for her grandmother. Far back, outside her house, frail and pale, Nana was supported by Aunt Lavern. The pride in their eyes squeezed Lilith's heart in a way that made her beam. She said, "The outside world is safe now. We achieved freedom and peace."

The incredulity of being able to claim such a thing made a joyous bubble of laughter escape her lips. She was weighed down by grief and sorrow but lifted by happiness and hope. With one of her hands grabbing her lover's and the other holding a book written by her ancestor, she felt like a true victor.

The elder approached them, followed by a woman. Respect and gratitude shone in their eyes as they exchanged a nod with the queens.

"Mother," Ruby greeted, red eyes fixated on the woman.

"Your father…" The lady started but stopped as if attempting to select the best words.

"I know," Ruby whispered. "Can I visit him?"

The tired mother managed a nod, and the queens sauntered down a path with jovial sorcerers applauding their arrival.

Ruby and Lilith entered the cemetery located within the Forest of Dahlia, and their moods immediately dimmed. They settled down beside a grave inscribed with a name, caring little about dirtying their dresses.

"I am so proud of you, Ruby," Lilith murmured.

A sad smile graced Ruby's mouth, curving it upwards ever so slightly. "If my father were here, he would be proud of me too. And I would tell him I was only able to achieve so much because of you."

"Oh? How cute."

"It is true!" she exclaimed. "You saved me more than you will ever know."

"How could I not? Fate practically pushed me towards the choice."

Ruby snorted, then grabbed the book from Lilith's hand. The title, 'The Reign of Eara', was written in cursive.

She flipped to the first page, then read aloud in the forest where they grew. Crowns of darkness hovered above their heads, glittering with spectacular sparks summoned by Ruby. Even the shadows were attentive. The wind whistled, nature danced, and it felt like even the sky eagerly listened.

"To my future descendant," Ruby read the dedication page. "Our kingdom is in your hands."

THE AFTERMATH

A long time ago, witches, Morakques and royals existed without peace. Morakques starved for fights and did not know why. They wanted to bloody the kingdom and give their lives to something supposedly useful. Yet, when the Battle of Ruth arrived, many realized how much they preferred to be a spectator instead.

I am a proud survivor of the war and was the leader of the Morakques.

I spent my entire life hating witches. Yet, my wife and son were both magic-wielders, and I love them unconditionally. Every waking hour, I grieve for them. I treasure my memories of them like a lost cause would a chance.

The tradition of witch hunting had run deep in my family, spanning generations through my father and grandfather and beyond. We led with stubborn passion, duty tainting our world so thoroughly that we saw and knew nothing but our rank.

We never understood the concept of peace, never thought it possible.

And yet, today, we see witches coexisting peacefully with humans. Sometimes, the sight of it still catches me off guard.

I remember harboring uncertainty towards the queens

at the beginning. I was mourning and pessimistic, but for the first time, I advocated for peace because I had no fight left in me. It was only when I encountered them at an event filled with lights and celebration that I decided to truly leave my hunting days behind. They danced and smiled and laughed as if they had forgotten their roles for a night, then offered families stories and food while making children squeal in excitement with their magic. They were so incredibly young, yet they had plans to develop the kingdom into such a beautiful place. They announced their policies and future actions, actively heeded suggestions from Dicerians, and assembled a royal council with great diversity.

I have a friend—also a former Morakque—who applied and was offered a position in the council. He now gladly serves the queens.

He told me many tales about them, but the one that captured my attention most was the story of Queen Ruby's crown. A jewel was said to be engraved into it, and he claims that it speaks with voices that echo.

—An excerpt from the leader Wei, a former Morakque, written during the reign of Ruth

END

Acknowledgements

This book has been in the works for years, and finally seeing it transform from idea to book is exhilarating. I have many to thank for it. First, to Craig Gibb, my publisher, for giving TROR a chance. Your faith in the book has set mine alight, and I am so grateful that you've been with me every step of the process.

To the Deep Hearts YA family for playing a tremendous part in breathing life into the book: John Robin, Alison Cybe, Francisco Feliciano, and Ave. Thank you so incredibly much for making this a dream come true!

To the several published authors and poets whom I connected with through workshops, I appreciate your critiques and comments. Thank you to Singaporean author Nuraliah Norasid, who provided me with some unforgettable and helpful tips.

Much appreciation for my parents, who allowed me to pave my own route from rubble, even though I often have no clue what I'm doing. To my sister, you know me best spiritually. I'm proud of you. To Eevee, for your continual support.

To my best friend Dheeksha Manavalan—we'll be together in spirit even if we are cleaved apart by our destinies. My gratitude for you is endless. I named a cave after you in the story and added an immortal human corpse inside you on purpose (to show my thanks). I love you, and you're welcome (for being included as a cave).

To my other BFF Natasha Lian, who has heard my truths and has never shied away from any of its ugliness. For you, I'll always be a loyal listener.

To Mak Kai Xin, for supporting me when I signed my first contract deal at twelve years old. Catherine Laos, for always being there for me, and Eliza, for supporting me while residing oceans away. I did promise you this book, so here you go.

Special thanks to Mr. Kenny, my literature teacher, who urged me consistently to strive for success.

To my extended family and friends, as well as the generous writing and reading community. Namely, Charlotte Ng, D.G. Marizztellah, Meredith Goh, Jovial Chng, Nathalia Lee, Carlene Toling, Kayden Ho, Allie, Freya, Allison, Akieo, and Pia.

During the writing process, I was heavily inspired by books such as *To Kill a Kingdom* by Alexandra Christo, *Serpent & Dove* trilogy by Shelby Mahurin, *The Young Elites* trilogy by Marie Lu and more. I have so much appreciation for these authors, and the Booktokers for carrying Tiktok's book community. You are the cause of my joining and staying.

Finally, thank you to you. For reading, for remembering, for living.

About Jazel L. Faith

Jazel L. Faith is a storyteller from Singapore who often introduces herself as Hazel with a J. When she's not writing, she's reading and if she's not reading, she's writing. At the age of thirteen, she published her debut book, "Fighting for Hope," as a stepping stone for her writing journey

Website: hazelwithaj.wordpress.com

**Deep Hearts YA publishes
LGBTQ+ young adult fiction.**

Please follow us on social media or
visit our website to find out more.

Instagram: instagram.com/DeepHeartsYA
Facebook: facebook.com/DeepHeartsYA
Website: deepheartsya.com